CHARLOTTE AND DAISY

AMANDA ROTACH HUNTLEY

Pikus helped.

This book is dedicated to my grandmother, Louise Rotach. You always wanted to see a book with my real name, Grandma. Here it is, I'm sorry that you won't get to see it in person.

For Charly

CHARLOTTE

AND DAISY

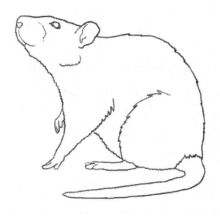

AMANDA ROTACH HUNTLEY

This book is a work of fiction. Names, characters, places, and incidents are the product of the
author's imagination or are used fictitiously. Any resemblance to actual events, locales, or persons, living or dead, is coincidental.

CHARLOTTE AND DAISY Copyright ©2015
Line By Lion Publications
4641 E. Mahalasville Rd.
Morgantown 46160
www.linebylion.com

ISBN: 978-1-940938-6-08
Library of Congress Control Number: 2015942663

INTRODUCTION

I crossed to the desk with a dozen eyes fixed on my back, or so it seemed. I am, at the best of times, certain that the word "crazy" is written in giant glowing letters across my back just as it is in the scars on my wrists or the faint burns on my temples. This was not the best of times. I gave my identification number to the receptionist, Cyber, I'm pretty sure, and found a seat at least one empty chair away from anyone else. My sleeves had worked their way up my arms. I pulled them down until the rough fabric brushed against my knuckles, and tried to take the deep, cleansing breaths that Doctor Alyce had said would help. They didn't.

The waiting room was pristine, immaculately decorated, so very different from East, from any of the state run and funded facilities to which I'd become accustomed. Those smell like piss and bleach and are decorated with flaking paint and whatever the last out of control patient had smeared all over the walls. Here everything was cool blues and off-white, with a SimWall depicting a beach or, at least, what a beach used to be. There is a beach down the road from my flat in Flower Town. It does not look like that. Still the crashing of the waves was nice. Soothing. In and out. Back and forth. In and out. I looked down, surprised to find I was scrubbing my wrists back and forth on my thighs, and rocking in time with the water. How long had I been doing that? Apparently a while. The skin was red and the other people waiting to be seen were pointedly not looking at me. *Fek.*

For some strange reason I thought of Tawny, her dark eyes wide in the dim light while angry footsteps pounded up and down the halls. "You picked a bad time to go loco, ese," she had said. She had been right. That time was bad, this one was worse.

I should just get out of here. They're not going to pick me anyway; I don't know why I'm even trying. As of right now I'd be out nothing but the hoverbus fare and maybe, just maybe, I could cling to whatever chip of dignity I had left. If there's any at this point. Sometimes I wonder. Of course, Dr. Alyce would be disappointed. I could just see the deepening of the lines across his forehead, his round face getting long. It's not like that's new. I've been disappointing Dr. Alyce for ten years or more, and he's just one on a long, long list, besides he gets paid to be disappointed anyway. My heart started thumping in my chest. I can't do this. I can't not do this. Stay and people will see. They will see what I am. And, worst of all, they will actually, and this is hilarious, decide that I'm not broken enough or too broken or who knows what. What if I actually fail at being sick? Go home though and there's no hope. None. Besides, they'll all be sitting here knowing I couldn't make it and laugh and talk amongst themselves about the stupid lazy wanna-be patient and how I was probably hung-over or strung out and couldn't find my way. I found my way fine, thank you. Better than they could if we took them out of their oh-so-pretty world. God, I'm just so damn tired. I looked again at the SimWall, where a brightly-colored bird was entering from one side. Okay, let the bird decide. If it flew through, just a tourist, so too would I be on my way. If it stayed, so would I. It soared across the blue sky, banking so that it looked like it was flying away, then curved and came closer, settling on the branch of the tree. All right. I folded my hands in my lap and gave what I hoped was a pleasant smile to the woman across the aisle, and did my best impression of someone who was actually sane.

"Charlotte," another woman identical to the receptionist was waiting at a door that I hadn't even noticed. So, there's one question answered, Cyber for sure. Her hair was blonde, long and silky, her eyes an unnatural blue. About as different from me as was possible. I ran my hand self-consciously over my springy hair. She guided me through a tangle of rooms and hallways, her high patent heels clicking on the tiles. One thing this place did have in common with East, it was a maze. She stopped, finally, and pushed a door open on silent hinges. "Thanks," I said, forgetting that you don't have to thank a Cyber. She gave me a programmed smile, flashing her flawless white teeth, and clicked back the way she had come. The office behind the door, like the rest of this place, was spotless, beautiful, with real wood furniture and soft fabrics. There were framed awards everywhere. It is obvious that they are used to people who educated, rich. People not like me. I'm surprised that they even let me in there, probably had a cleaning bot already programmed to sanitize the place after I left. I don't belong here. If they didn't need someone desperate to use as a guinea pig, a place like this wouldn't even answer my waves. Still, Dr. Alyce was waiting, along with two people I had never met. They were all looking at me. I wished that I had left when I had the chance.

Dr. Alyce stepped forward. "Charlotte," he said, clasping my hands in his, "I'm glad you could come, let me introduce you to our hosts." He turned, first, to the woman on his right, a dark skinned woman with God, she was terrifying. About six feet tall with a huge, square jaw and startling hazel eyes that just bore into me. She wore a lab coat so white it nearly glowed in the dim light. "This is Doctor Stevens," he said and, turning to his left his elbow brushed the elbow of the man next to him and passed right through, leaving a bluish glow behind. The other stranger must have holo'd in for the occasion. The kid, I swear he looked about a decade younger than me, was introduced as Cybernetic Specialist Nu. He wore a dark blue blazer embroidered with the stylized pigeon of the Tesla Academy. A scientist of some sort, then. That explained the holo. I'd heard that most scientists thought themselves hesitant to leave their labs, afraid that in the time it took for them to visit the latrines, someone would beat them to the next best thing. I'd seen the T.A. emblem before, of course. Once, on the leg of a drunk, homeless man that we were helping get cleaned up. Mostly, in the hospitals, though. The electroshock machine had T.A. engraved on it, in fact. I wasn't sure what to make of that. I bowed briefly to each, my right hand crossed across my chest, tapping my closed fist on my left shoulder in the true Benevolencia fashion. In other words, the fashion I hadn't used since we learned it in Primary.

"Thank you for considering me," I said.

They bowed in return, perfunctory flicks of the head, and the C.S. motioned to a seat. I sat, caught myself scrubbing at my thighs with my wrists and forced my hands to fold themselves once again. Dr. Stevens made a note in my chart. I felt my gorge start to rise and swallowed several times. Dr Alyce nodded encouragingly and launched into his prepared speech. We had gone over it together in his office so that I would know what to expect.

"Dr. Stevens, C.S. Nu, This is Patient 3245931B, Charlotte. I have had the pleasure of working with Charlotte for well over a decade. While her condition is indeed chronic, and I have reason to believe, progressive, I have found Charlotte to be a willing participant in her recovery. That last phrase I'd heard before, at least a hundred times. I had heard it at each of my Patient Release Meetings. There, it meant that I was going to make it to my appointments, take my meds, and at least try to not to kill myself. I heard it as a joke among the patients at East, our meager attempts at gallows humor. "Now, now, we'd say" when someone sat at the toilet, vomiting their way through the DTs, or the times that someone would descend for a moment into absolute insanity, turning over tables or screaming about spiders that weren't there, "is that a good way to participate in your recovery?" Once, I heard it from three male nurses as the reason that they beat the hell out of Denae, a schizophrenic drag queen and one of my best friends at East. I guess that sounded better than the truth, which is that they got mad when she refused to blow them in the iso room. Those nurses didn't last long, at least. Even the Doctors loved Denae.

I came back to now with a start and everyone was staring at me. I must have missed something. Fekegalo.

"I apologize," I said, "I believe I missed the question." Dr. Stevens scribbled again. A crease had appeared between her eyes. "I asked why you feel that you would be a good candidate for our trial." Ah. Dr. A had prepared me for this. I launched into our rehearsed speech.

"My disorder reduces my ability to live a normal life. I have a great desire to become a contributing member of society and feel that this procedure would grant me an opportunity to do so. If chosen I – The C.S. stifled a small cough. What did that mean? Was it some sort of code? It happened just as I said 'If chosen." I lost my place in the speech. Suddenly, the room no longer seemed to have enough air. Harsh, metallic sunbursts started to explode at the edge of my vision, leaving dark negatives in their wake. My field of vision was shrinking, and I could feel this straw that I'd been grasping so hard for so long start to slip out of my sweaty grasp.

"I just – "my voice quavered, "I just don't want to feel like this anymore. You don't understand it's," I tried to choke out the words, words that would explain the constant fear and perpetual loneliness, that could somehow show the pain of stitches and pumped stomachs, of failed relationships and lost jobs, and the constant exhaustion of clamoring and scrabbling at the edge of the pit only to have your fingernails tear off and dirt clods fall in your face but never, ever getting out. I couldn't. "Please," I said at last. "Please help me. I will do whatever you ask. I will follow any plan. I will work hard. Just please. I don't want to live like this anymore." Hot, thick tears built up and overflowed my lower lids. Dr. Stevens was scribbling furiously, though took a moment to wordlessly hand me the box of tissues. C.S. Nu looked studiously at his feet, obviously embarrassed, probably disgusted, at my outbreak.

"Thank you," Dr. Stevens said, "That will be all." The Cyber met me in the hallway, and I expected to be escorted out of the building. If I were lucky, they would have a cab that would take me home. Once there, what? I had been, I knew, at the top of a short list of candidates for this trial. If I had thrown this chance away, like I had so many others, what? I would have to figure out something, but first I thought I would sleep. I was, suddenly, unbearably exhausted. However, when we got to the lobby, the Cyber took me through a door on the other side. There was the feared cab, and in it Dr. Alyce, and together we went to the Facility where the surgery will be performed to give me a new brain and, if they are right, a new life.

SECTION 1

"The city is war-torn/And nearly impassable
I act the lovelorn/Dramatically laughable"

Unwoman "Heroine"

MARCH 31ST

My name is Charlotte Gordón. I am 27 years old. As of today I have been at the Facility for two weeks. As soon as I got here they took me to a room where I sat for hours just filling out forms. I hated it; it was like I had to put my whole disgusting life down on paper for people to see and judge. *Estes humiliĝo.* Education? No high school degree. Parent's current health? I don't know. Father's name? I don't know. Number of times hospitalized? Dozens. Reason. Suicide attempt. Suicide attempt. Histrionics. Suicide attempt. It's all in my record. Do you really need to make me go through it all over again? Are you trying to wear me down? To see if I'm serious about this? Or do you just want to laugh at the gutter trash from Flower town? They asked everything in about 20 different ways. I felt so stupid. "Do you understand? Do you understand?" Yes, yes, I understand! You're going to cut out my brain. I imagine there are dangers involved. I'm not like you, with your *franzia* degrees, your Center Circle accents, but I'm not stupid. Then people would walk in and it would start all over again, only they'd talk like I wasn't even there. "Does she understand? Does she consent to? Does she comprehend?"

By the time it was over I was a wreck, shaking all over, and my head was pounding so hard I couldn't even think. They took me to my room and gave me some lunch. I kept waiting for them to bring my meds, they were way overdue, but they never came. I started asking the nurses, but they wouldn't answer me. Like I was nothing. I wanted to scream just to make sure I hadn't gone mute. Finally, Dr. Stevens and C.S. Nu came in. That's when they told me that they'd be pulling me off of my meds. Cold turkey. You know, it's weird because I've sent my whole life with people telling me "take your meds," you can't just stop taking them," and that's exactly what they do. Dr. Stevens insists that that isn't true, that they had meds of their own that were able to combat the withdrawals. I think that's just something that she told me to make me go along with it, because it didn't feel like they were combating anything. I've been so miserable. Endless vomiting, headaches like someone was driving pneumospikes into my brain. Hallucinations. I was apparently convinced that one of the aides was my mother. They had to pull me off of her, or so I've been told. I don't really remember much. And through it all, endless tests. Vial after vial of blood, urine samples, CT scans, head measurements, more blood. I kept asking them to back off just a little. To let me have just a little dose of the meds. To just wait a little bit before poking me again. But, as C.S. Nu keeps insisting, we are on a time frame. The sponsors are ready to move on this, ready to see some results, and are running out of patience. This is, as far as I can see, another example of the people who have money making life harder for the rest of us. Still, I promised to be a model patient, and so that's what I'm trying to do.

The next step is to get a good "organic map." They need to learn about my personality, what I like and what I don't, how I move and how I think. I don't understand why I can't just tell them, but apparently that's not an option. "We want to make sure that you are still you," C.S. had said briskly. "Just a healthy version. We have no interest in building a robot." I'm not sure that I believe that, but okay. So, that's what I'll be doing the next couple of days, helping them map. All that they will tell me is that there will be "a series of tests." They won't tell me more, they tell me that they can't but I'm sure they just don't think I will comprehend anyway. So, I've been sitting here thinking of all of the things that they could be, and I'm scared. That's why I'm keying this journal entry. I have to write one every day from now on, two-thumbing it into a keypad that plugs into a special socket on the bed. I'll be doing this every day for the rest of my life. First to map, then to "track progress." They say that it will come naturally, but it feels really awkward. I'm used to guarding how I feel, not putting it out there for everyone to see. Survival, neh? Still, no matter what lies ahead, I have to believe that it will be easier than what lies behind.

APRIL 3

I'm tired. So, so *damne* exhausted. I keep trying to take a nap; that is not allowed. They need to "maximize mapping hours" which means that I have to keep these electrodes, there have to be hundreds of these sensors, glued to my head while we go through hour after hour of these really weird, I don't know, tests maybe? They're not like any test I've ever taken, though. In one of them I was in a stackflat like the ones down in flower Town. It could have been one of the ones that I've lived in, I don't know. They all look the same. But anyway, the flats were on fire. The smoke was billowing and I could hear the fire behind me and see the flames sometimes. There were people there, too. I couldn't see them but I could hear them yelling for help. I think that they were trying to see how fast I could get out of there, to see if I could even find my way. So, I just put my head down and ran. I got out pretty quick, so I think I did really well in that one, though I had to take some time after to calm down. I had just caught my breath from that when they took me back to my room. They hooked me up to a dozen or more different machines, these in addition to the hell glued to my scalp, and sat me in front of a computer. I don't know how long I was there, answering ridiculous questions, but by the time I was done my eyes were stinging.

That's when I asked, again, to lay down. They wouldn't let me. Instead they sent in this aide who started asking me all sorts of questions. What I liked to do in my spare time, my hobbies all that stuff. Here I am, sitting in the hospital in a gown and my underpants, my head shaved, shaking and trembling and exhausted and they send in her? She looks about twelve, like she's never had a care in the world. Her voice is like a bird chirping. I wonder how much they had to pay her to pretend to be my friend. I can just imagine what she's going to say to her real friends tonight, how she had to spend time with this disgusting freak. I hate what they've done to me here. It's like they took a magnifying glass and made all of my issues bigger, even more out there. I thought I was coming here to get better? So, I couldn't get her to understand that I don't have hobbies. I don't have things that interest me. One way or another I spend my time trying to survive. I work to try to have a place to live. I go to that place and sleep. If I can't fall asleep, if the worries and the memories and the nightmares get to be too much I find something to distract myself enough so that I don't end up in the hospital again. Do I read? Yes. Well, what? I don't know. The words are usually jumbled on the page and I'm too weary to try to figure them out. Do I watch television? Yes? What do I watch? Whatever is on. I forget what show I'm watching while I'm watching it. Do I go out with friends? Maybe. Sometimes. But it's never anything planned. We just hang out. After a while a nurse came in and told me I had to get dressed, that we were going to try something else. So they gave me some clothes and a wig to cover the electrodes, and put me in these special glasses that made me look even more ridiculous then they took me to one of the giant shopping malls over in the *luksa* part of town. I'd never been anywhere near there before. Obviously.

Seen from above, the city looks like a bull's-eye or a rock tossed in the water, with the Palace in the center and all the neighborhoods spreading out in rings. The best neighborhoods are in the center, all the way down to us in Flower Town on the harbor and the factories to the North. So, they dropped me off with the aide and told me to do whatever I wanted. What I wanted to do was sit by the fountain in the middle of the lobby, the one that shot all of these multicolored jets of water, and pretend that people weren't staring at me and maybe doze a little bit. People were staring, *infantoj* with their mouths hanging open. The adults weren't much better. Like they're so much better than me. Go ahead. Laugh. I am you, given the right circumstances. Every sin you have, every fear, I am that turned up. If you'd faced what I had, you'd be no better. So, mock away. *Iru inferen.* Mocking me mocks you.

I guess that wasn't the right answer because the aide started chirping at me about getting an "accurate map." I asked how it could be accurate if they had me doing things that I never did in real life. The aide walked off and soon Dr. Stevens was on the phone. She started talking about how she was concerned if I was really willing to put in the work necessary. I still didn't understand, I was there, wasn't I? I haven't walked yet, and believe me, I've thought about it often. Still, I got up and followed the aide around while she showed me all of the things that were for sale.

"Do you like these?" she asked, and pointed at these enormous wigs and dresses you could program to look like any fabric you could imagine. "How about these?" to a rack of helpbots, there was one that would cook you dinner, one that would paint you a picture. I shook my head. "Well, what kind of things do you like," she asked. I shrugged. My head was starting to hurt. We left shortly after that. I hope they learned something, because I'm exhausted. I asked if they could take just a few of the electrodes off, the ones just behind my ears itch like crazy, but apparently there's some pretty important parts of the brain just behind your ears. Or they just want to torture me. I keep telling myself that it's all going to be worth it, but I don't know anymore. It's starting to seem like some big joke, like this can't possibly work. Right now though, I'm most interested in sleep. They can map that, yeah? Still, they say I have a few more tests. So, I'm just going to hang on a little longer.

APRIL 4

I thought that sleep would help. I did. That was what kept me hanging on, the thought that at the end I could rest. Yes, ultimately this surgery, I'm still dedicated to that. As time passes, though, it seems hollow, less real. Sleep? Escape? That I can comprehend. That is *now*. *Diable*, I was wrong. They finally let me lay down after dinner, so long as I was willing to listen to a recording of the news until I fell asleep. That was fine. After a while I didn't even notice it. But then I couldn't get comfortable. The sensors were pulling on my scalp, which was itchy as hell anyway because my hair is starting to grow back in. I kept calling the nurses and asking for them to give me something, but they said I just had to try to deal with it. So I tossed and turned and eventually I fell asleep and then I had nightmares all night long. They were obviously from those stupid tests because I was back in the stackflats and there were on fire. This time, though, it was my mother and sister who were screaming for me. Which is weird because, except for that hallucination, I haven't thought of them for years. Not Mother, anyway. Daisy I think of sometimes, the girl that was, but I can't for too long because it hurts. It hurts in the way that lets me know that the trickle could become a wave and drown me. Instead of trying to get out of the flats I was trying to find them. Where there was one door, though, suddenly there were hundreds. I was opening them as fast as I could, one after another, but I couldn't find them. Finally, I would open the right door and there they would be, Mother with her long hair and Daisy, my sister, tiny and dark eyed and still six years old just like the last time I saw her. How long has it been? A decade? More? I would be trying to get to her and save her but Mother wouldn't let me. Her hands were on fire and she was hitting me with them telling me that the fire was my fault. I was to blame. I'd be fighting her still while the skin blackened and melted off of her bones, still fighting until the explosion brought me to shivering, gasping wakefulness. I must have watched them die a dozen times last night, woke up screaming each time, screaming and tearing at the sensors and begging for help that never came, and was still feeling shaky and raw when they led me through the corridors and stairways that made up this sterile maze. Up and down, left and right until finally we ended up in what they called the Nursery. As it turns out, my nurturing levels are very low. Like, almost non-existent, which I guess makes sense when you think about it. It has been more than I can handle just to take care of myself; I sure haven't spent much time worrying about taking care of anyone of anything else. Turns out, though, the ability to nurture is, how did C.S. Nu put it? "Necessary to optimal psychological well-being." So, I'm going to need to learn it. At first I freaked out a little. I thought they were going to make me, I don't know, be an aide here in the hospital or Godhelpme, have a kid of my own. I couldn't handle that. Thankfully, it's nothing like that. All it means is that I had to pick out a Cynimal. So, we opened the door and here were all of these animals crawling and flying around, screeching and barking and whatever. It was way too much for me and I had to leave. They found me in the wall, my eyes closed, trying to breathe. Why do they keep doing these things to me? Eventually, they found this little room for me and brought the Cynimals to me one at a time. I told them they could just pick out whatever one they wanted, it didn't really matter, but they wanted me to decide. So I played fetch with a dog for a while and fed fake crickets to a lizard, but I didn't like either of those. The dog was too jolly, brainless, and desperate to please. The lizard just was. The chimp creeped me out, it was just too much like a human and we had to stop for a bit while I got myself back under control. The miniature elephant weirded me out, too. Like, I know none of these are real, but that seemed too much like a toy. I kept picking it up and turning it upside down and eventually I guess I stressed it out because it just powered down. I asked for a cat, but I guess even programmed cats don't really make you nurture them, which is why I had asked in the first place. Finally, I decided on a rat, mostly because I was still thinking about all of my dreams from last night and the rat was tiny and dark and big-eyed and it reminded me of my sister. I even named the thing Daisy. So they're going to grow or build or hatch or whatever they do to *my* Daisy, and I guess she will be ready by the time I come out of recovery. It might be kind of cool, maybe. I never had a pet before.

APRIL 6

I knew today was going to be important when C.S. Nu came to see me in person, instead of holoing himself in. I don't think that he would ever leave his lab if he didn't have to. Even the nurses agree. I overheard two of them talking one day when they brought in the holo projection screen into my room.

"That man would holo himself to take a shit," one of them said, and they laughed. I laughed too, and it must have scared them. They don't really think I'm a person and it upsets them when I actually act like one. Just lay there; don't think. Don't ask questions. Just do what I tell you to do. They say they don't want a robot, but I think they do. Either that or they think I'm stupid, or not worth taking a minute of their time to actually treat me like a person. Maybe they're right. God knows I've thought the same thing before. Useless. Worthless. Waste of breath. Toxic. Poison. Still, it would be nice if they would, I don't know, actually acknowledge my presence. Anyhow I laughed and they got quiet. I think the C.S. Is probably a bit of a *kacisto* when he's not hungering for the opportunity to hack out your brain.

As it turns out I was right, about it being important, not necessarily about the C.S. being a *kacisto*. My procedure is scheduled for tomorrow. They figure that they will have all of the mapping done that they need to do by noon. My new brain has already been grown, they did that with all of the tissue and blood samples that they took, and now they just need to program it. They say that I should be able to have my sensors taken off after lunch, and then take a shower shortly after. They also told me to think about what I might want for dinner tonight. They said that I could pick anything that I wanted and they would bring it to me. Kind of a last supper, neh? At first, I couldn't think of anything special, and I was going to ask them just to bring me up whatever they were serving down in the cafeteria. Then I thought I might ask for something really *fantazio*, something I could never have any other time, like a real steak from a real cow, not SynSoy. Finally, though, I decided on some soup and a sandwich from Don's Cafe over in Flower Town. Partially because I thought it would be pretty funny, seeing someone from this place trying to walk down the streets of my home. Mostly thought because I had spent what was, looking back, the best two years of my life working there, and living in the extra rooms in the back. I started out with the most basic stuff, stocking the pastry case and pouring the ready-made soups into the pots to heat. Soon, though, Don promoted me to baker. I t was the first time I'd been promoted to anything. I loved it. The smells, the reliability of the recipes, the rhythm of kneading the dough. It was all very soothing to me, gave me a feeling of accomplishment. You do something right, it turns out good. The way life should be, but isn't. I let Tawny move in with me as well, she and Dmitri, her on again off again boyfriend. Dmitri worked long hours down by the harbor, and would come in smelling of oil and the sharpness of seawater. Tawny and I would hoot him down, laughing and taunting until he showered off the worst of it, then we'd settle in for the evening laughing, smoking, watching movies on the ancient flat screen that Dmitri had drug home proudly from the pawn shop one night. Even at our most flush we never had enough for a SimCenter. Sometimes, Dmitri would pull out his guitar and we'd sing along, but mostly we would just sit together dreaming our dreams. They were good days, the best, and while I never had anyone serious I even dated now and then. The nightmares stopped, my scabs healed, and thanks to then endless stream of breads and pastries I even grew a thin layer of flesh over my perpetually skeletal body.

But then it had to end and one night it did. It was fall, the period between the stinking heat of summer and the bitter cold of winter, when Flower Town is actually bearable. People had been throwing parties all up and down the streets for weeks. Finally, it was our turn. It seemed like the whole neighborhood showed up to dance and drink and eat the mountain of goodies that Tawny and I had baked. I'd gone off my meds the week before. I'd been doing so well and thought that, maybe, this time, it would be all right. Isn't that always how it goes? I'd also started drinking early, trying to combat the anxiety that came with the guests. By the time guests started to arrive, I had overdone it and was starting to feel a little on edge. I spent most of the night hiding in the corner, breathing deep and nursing a beer, smiling a little whenever anyone came close. Sometime around midnight Chandra, who makes a living busking on the street, telling fortunes, decided to start reading palms. It was pretty funny at first; she told Dmitri that he would end up married with three children. Dmitri yelled and gave her the evil eye. She told someone else, a guy whose name I can't remember only that he was a nephew twice or three times removed, and thus in the employ, of a local mobster that he'd someday be working in Capital City itself. Then it was my turn. I tried to refuse, but everyone chimed in, chanting my name and "oh come on" until finally I gave in.

Chandra took my hand, and her smile disappeared. His brows knit together. "Oh, Lotta," she said softly. "Death, death and destruction."
"For me?" I asked.

She nodded. For you, for everything you touch. You have the broken knot." She ran her long, psychedelic nail over a place in my palm where the creases came together for a brief moment before racing off in different directions. "What is broken cannot be saved."

The room started closing in then, and I heard a noise: a high piercing, endless howl that it took me a full minute to realize was coming from my own mouth. I started to claw at myself then, at least I've been told that I did, and managed to leave long deep scratches down both cheeks and one arm before they were able to stop me. It took three big guys to hold me down. They pinned me for hours, but every time they would let go I would start again. Once, I ran for the balcony. Another time I made it as far as the kitchen and the butcher knife we kept there. Finally, at dawn, not going what else to do the people who hadn't already freaked out and bailed loaded me up and dropped me, at Tawny's instructions, back at East. I was there that time for six months. Still, two years was a good run, the best that I've been able to expect really, and Don has been great since then about giving me a job at the Café when he thought that I could handle it and food when he didn't.

You know, they told me that I could have visitors tonight, but I couldn't think of anyone that I could ask. I wish I'd thought of Tawny and Dmitri. I'd like to see them one more time if. . just if. It's too late now, though. I don't even know where they live. Maybe I'll record them a letter though. One that Dr. Alyce can deliver if he needs to. In the meantime, though, soup and a sandwich. Roast beef SynSoy, extra Swiss, horseradish and cherry compote, maybe on that nice dark bread I used to make, the one with all of the seeds baked on top. That sandwich was my own creation, they called it Little Lotta. And whatever soup they have today. Yeah. That's what I want. That would be nice.

APRIL 7

As it turns out, the surgery is not going to be today. I'm not even sure right now, they aren't even sure, if there's going to be a surgery at all. I lost control last night, to the point that they had to sedate me. I just, I got to thinking, "what if this doesn't work?" I don't mean what if I died. The thought of death doesn't bother me, hell I've tried to get there on my own, would have if I actually had the courage. Turns out I'm even a failure at that. But what if it doesn't work and things stay exactly the same as they are right now? What if it's just like everything else that they said would work and that hasn't worked and then I'm right where I am now only then there's no hope. This is it. This is the bottom of the barrel. After this there is nothing and so if this doesn't work that means that I will stuck feeling like this for the rest of my life and I can't. I just, I can't bear the thought of that. So I was sitting here in the dark, by myself thinking of all those years with no hope and it just got to be too much. Eventually, they had to sedate me and I guess that they can't do the implant if I've had a sedative so we have to wait until it's out of my system before we can go on. Then there's Dr. Stevens. I don't think that she's ever liked me much and now she does not want to use me at all. I was only picked because Dr. Alyce and C.S. Nu thought that I was best. Dr.

Stevens had someone else in mind. Not that they told me that but, like I said, people talk.

But here's the thing, you pick someone for a surgery because they aren't well, because they can't cope with life like other people can, then you get upset when they can't cope. That doesn't make any sense. If I could deal with stuff I wouldn't be here in the first place, letting them cut out my brain. Would anybody do that if they thought they had any choice whatsoever? It doesn't mean I won't work hard. It doesn't mean that I won't try, that I can't be real, I can't be right. It just means that I need help. So why won't they help me? How can they get my hopes up and then just leave me out here alone? How could I possibly go home knowing I was this close to being normal, that I was this close to being okay, and then I just threw it all away? That they took it all away for me for having the sickness that brought me here? I can't. I can't do that. I just can't. Here they are now. I hope its good news. Please let it be good news.

APRIL ??

I don't know what day it is. I don't even know what time it is. In the Facility there are only two times: lights on and lights off. It is currently lights on. They just brought me back to my room from the ICU after I don't know how many days. Weeks, maybe? The nurses brought me the headset so that I could talktype this entry, to key takes way too much concentration right now. My eyes are still adjusting, and the amount of time it takes to make my thumbs move the way they should is endless and frustrating. Still, they want a record. So, I get to talktype for a few days. I should have asked them what date it was, but I didn't think to and they didn't offer. This room is much more spacious than my last; it's called a rehabilitation suite, so I guess I'm going to be here for a while. Not that I need much room yet. I haven't even gotten out of bed since the surgery, though I can sit up now which they say is about where I should be.

Dr. Stevens has been by several times to see me. She says that my healing is progressing well, that there are no signs of infection or rejection. She asked if I was in any pain, but I said "no." I don't know what meds they stock here but they are amazing. Worlds better than any they had at the state run facilities. If I start to get uncomfortable I simply hit the button for a nurse. One adjustment here, a click there, and could get up and dance, if I could get up, that is. I get tired easily, even more easily than before, but tired I can deal with. Mostly. What is the worst is the frustration. I'm frustrated at what I can't do. I didn't realize how much I would have to learn. I mean, they told me I would have to relearn most everything and I believed them. I guess I just didn't fully understand what everything meant. My new brain has been fully implanted and connected, but with so many pathways the signals could take, I guess it takes a while for the brain to learn what goes where. C.S. Nu says that I'm going to have to relearn how to use my body just like a baby. Though, of course, much faster. I hope so.

When I got to my room there were flowers on my bedside table. Actual, real flowers. They are about the most beautiful things that I have ever seen. There are little fuzzy white ones, and some with bright yellow petals and black centers. The red ones, I think, are roses. They look like pictures I've seen of roses, anyway, and they are velvety like the chairs in Dr. Stevens' office. There's a card tucked in with them, but I can't read it from here. I'll have to ask the nurse to hand it to me next time one of them comes in. I wonder who they are from.

No one has ever sent me flowers before. I'm going to nap now.

APRIL 14

Rage. Sorrow. Fear. Betrayal. I thought those days were behind me now that I've had the surgery. Apparently not. They lied to me. The doctors, the nurses, Dr. Alyce, they all lied to me just so they could use me. I was supposed to get better. They told me that after this, things would be better and I-I was stupid enough to actually believe them. How could I have been such a *stultaj*? I know better. I'm no *infano*, believing in Santa Claus or baking meals for my beloved dead. I know better. And still I believed. Still I trusted them. But now, now I know that it was just a – a cruel trick or some sort of hidden experiment or whatever. But not hope. I know now that there is no hope.

This morning, I don't know what time – early, it was still dark out anyway – two nurses came in to do rounds. I woke up when they came in, of course. For a place where people are constantly telling you to rest they sure don't give you much opportunity. Always poking, always prodding and questions, questions, endless *majstro* questions. I didn't want to deal with that, I was tired, so I kept my eyes shut and pretended to be asleep. I was hoping that if they thought I was asleep they would leave me alone and I could actually catch a few more hours of rest before my day began. No such luck.

They were quiet at least, scuffing around in their soft-soled shoes and using just the light from the bathroom. Soon, they began to talk to each other in low voices.

"Did you hear the story behind this one?" the first asked.

"Yeah," said the other, "can you believe it? I can't imagine asking for a whole new brain because, what, you are sad sometimes.'

"Depressed, but still. Okay. You're depressed. Get some meds. Get some therapy. For God's sake be strong and pull yourself together. Everyone's got issues, right? Everyone. But to have your brain cut out? There must be something else going on."

The second took over. "I don't know. Some people just don't want to deal with life. They want everything just handed to them and if life isn't just perfect," her voice climbed into a high wavering falsetto, "Oh I just can't take it. I have a disease." They laughed.

"Maybe it's the drugs," the first began again.

"Or the attention," said the second.

"Or the money."

They would have gone on longer, I'm sure, just like the pretty, flouncing girls in elementary school they never get bored when they have a victim that can't, or won't fight back. Then one of the machines that they have me hooked up to started letting out this high pitched beep and they started scrambling around pulling on tubes and pushing buttons. Finally, finally, they left and I could go ahead and cry. Is that really what people think of me? That I am some histrionic, desperate *ĉiesulino* ? Am I going to go through all of this just to have people continue to look down on me? Always the sneers. Or the pity. Always the afterthought. Never – NEVER having my thoughts or feelings paid any real attention to because, of course, that's just Charlotte and don't you know haven't you heard she's just a crazy *fiaĉulo* . Just because I am out of control sometimes, never given credit for the times that I'm not. And why do I feel this way? My heart is racing and I'm still sobbing. And I'm mad. Furious. I want to make them lose their jobs. I want to grab them and scream and rail, shake them claw them, tell them my story, until they understand. I want to hide, somewhere away from all of the eyes. Somewhere safe, if there is such a place. *Aktoj de la Akademio!* Wasn't that why I went through all of this? To not feel this way anymore?

APRIL 14 — LATER

It is amazing the difference a couple of hours can make When am I going to learn to slow down, to consider anything other than the seemingly obvious first thought that comes to mind? This morning I was so damned low, the whole future condemned by those *fiolino* nurses. I felt lost in a maze, not sure where to turn, surrounded by walls. *Malagaja*. I spent most of the morning staring at the clock, counting my breaths and promising myself that all I had to do was make it through another minute. Anyone could do a minute. After a while – one hour? Two? Of one minute chunks I was doing a little better. By lunchtime I had done my exercises, brushed my hair, and was trying desperately to lose myself in the SimCenter for a while. I was struggling, though, a wreck, still crying on and off. To make it worse the two nurses kept coming in and out, swishing around the floor and checking my numbers. Acting like nothing was wrong, smiling their fake *fikfek* smiles and touching me and taking my vitals as if they would care if I dropped over dead. Every time they came in it would start all over again. The sadness, the hurt, the anger. I'd just pull myself out of it and here they'd come again. By three I was destroyed. I had no appetite and so my lunch was still sitting on the bedside table. It had congealed into a single, putty-like mass. So, when the door opened my heart started to pound and I braced myself to start crying again. Instead a woman I had never seen before came in and flopped down on the foot of my bed. She flashed me a bright grin. "Hi Charlotte," she said, extending a hand with bright, clinking bracelets halfway up to her elbow, "I'm Basanti."

Basanti, I found out later, is my Rehabilitation Therapist. Of course, I didn't know that then. I thought that she was just another person come to look or poke or prod. So I sat, silently staring straight ahead, intentionally not noticing her. She just settled onto the edge of the bed, watching the SimCenter with me. For a while, I didn't mind. It was actually kind of nice to have someone there who wasn't asking anything of me, who was content just to let me be. After a while, her silence started to bother me, though. The way she just looked, waiting,. I sat up straighter, started to fidget.

"What do you want?" I asked. My tone was way harsher than I'd meant for it to be, but she didn't flinch, just turned to me and smiled. Her teeth looked very white against my dark skin.

She answered my question with one of her own. "Why are you so angry?" she asked. I told her. I still don't know why. Maybe because she hadn't pushed. Maybe because she seemed like she actually cared about the answer. Maybe, and I think this is probably it, she seemed like me somehow. I mean, she wasn't from Flower Town, or any of the other hovels on the Outer Edge but I get the impression that she's, oh, I don't know, seen more of Real Life than most of the pampered pets up here in the Ivory Tower. And so I told her, slowly at first, watching her face and gauging her reaction. Soon though it was pouring out. All of it. What the nurses had said, my feeling that Dr. Alyce had abandoned me, my fears about what others would see. Most of all, what my feelings meant. Was it really for nothing? By the end I was crying, snot bubbling out of my nose. Basanti waited until the flow of words and slowed and stopped.

Then she spoke quietly. "You are mad," she said, "and scared. And sad."

I nodded.

"Tell me," she said, "have you blacked out?"

I shook my head.

"Cut yourself? Tried to commit suicide?"

"No."

She didn't say anything, just looked at me with her head cocked to one side. And then it hit me.

"No!" I said again.

She smiled broadly. "See?" she said, "You are already making progress."

"But the rage, the fear-"

"-are all normal human reactions. You didn't think that the surgery would take away all pain, did you?"

I was quiet because, as ridiculous as it seems even now, that's exactly what I had thought.

"No, Charlotte, it won't do that," Basanti explained as if I'd answered. "And you wouldn't want it to. Pain is how we recognize danger. What this surgery did is give you the ability to deal with those emotions in a healthy fashion."

"But I still don't know how," I said.

"We will help you learn. Baby steps. Speaking of which, tomorrow I'll be bringing a walker. Be ready." She stood up, jingling quietly, and left.

Oh, and I found out that the flowers are from Dr. Alyce. Maybe he hasn't abandoned me after all.

APRIL 19

I was shuffling across the floor, my damp hair sticking up in tiny clumps, when there was a knock on the door. I don't know why they bother; the pattern is always the same. Quick, sharp, one two knocks that are immediately followed by the door opening, no matter what you say in response. I was just glad that they hadn't come five minutes earlier. I have no doubt that they would have just repeated the knock on the bathroom door and come traipsing in. My nakedness never seemed to faze them. I have to wonder if they would feel the same if the tables were turned. I tried to imagine Dr. Stevens performing surgery or giving a presentation naked, or C.S. Nu lording over the lab in only his pigeon blazer. I grinned. Sure enough, within seconds my room was packed. Nu was first, followed by Dr. Alyce, Basanti, and two TAs. People I didn't recognize. They looked so young, students I imagine. The first carried a closed plastic box, the second something covered in brightly colored cloth. They were smiling. Even the C.S. had the trace of a grin on his face.

Something about the scene struck me as funny.

"Me ne scias la cirko estis en urbeto" I said to Dr. Alyce, one eyebrow raised. I couldn't help it. It really did look like a circus parade. I half expected him to

reprimand me, but he must have noticed the resemblance too because he cocked his head and said

"*Vi vokas min klauno*?" "Are you calling me a clown?

"Not yet," I replied. Everyone laughed. "Seriously, though" I asked, "What's the occasion?"

The C.S. stepped to one side and nodded at the first student, the one with the brightly colored cloth. "Everyone loves a birth day," he said. Then I realized, Daisy must be ready. Suddenly, I was frightened. Excited too, though, much more than I thought I would be. My stomach was tingling.

"This is a rather special case," one of the students said, and I could see a slight flicker in his eyes as they focused on me. Cybernetic implants, then. I wondered what had happened to him.

"We've programmed therapy animals before of course, but Daisy is quite advanced." He

was about to continue, I could tell, but C.S. Nu held up one silencing hand. "We will spare you the details," he said. "Suffice it to say that everyone is very interested in the both of you." I bristled a little at that, being compared to a Cynimal, and Dr. Alyce could tell.

"Let's get started, yes?" he said quickly.

I decided to let it go. "Yes," I agreed. The drape was pulled from the cage and in the bottom I could see a round ball of white fur. " He placed the cage in my lap. Basanti stood close at my right, and put an encouraging hand on my shoulder. It's going to take me a while to get used to that, even though I knew her intentions are good.

"Remove her from the cage and hold her in the palm of your hand," Nu instructed. I did. Her fur was soft, but her eyes were closed, her body rigid.

"What's the matter with her," I asked.

"You have to wake her up" he replied. "Look." And he pointed to the back of her head. There was a small hairless square just behind one ear, and I could just barely see the shiny black surface of an identifier.

"You touch the identifier and say "wake up, Daisy," the cyber-eyed student explained.

Nu took over. "Yes. That's how you will reset her every morning as well.   "Reset?" I was perplexed.

"Don't forget, this is not just a pet. Resetting saves everything that was learned the day before and biocharges her battery. If you miss a day, she should be all right. Miss two in a row and she will become sluggish and lethargic. Miss more than that and she will power down."

"For how long," I asked.

He shrugged. "Permanently. The Cynimals may be grown in a lab, but the responsibility is very real.

A memory bubbled to the surface. Me at six years old, holding my newborn sister. I remember the holey afghan, my mother's perfume. Mama had on her heels and make up. She must have been going to work.

"She's your responsibility Lotta," Mama was saying. "Don't you let nothin' happen to her"

Then Basanti was squeezing my shoulder gently. "It's time, Charlotte," she was saying. "You can do this.

I placed my finger on the identifier. Daisy's' ear was small and velvety, I could feel the skin on the side of my finger. I paused. "What color will her eyes be?" I wanted them to be dark, like my Daisy's. "Black," the TA answered. I was glad. It made her seem. . more real, somehow. The red eyes would have been strange, creepy. I don't think that I could have dealt with that. My finger covered the square and I could feel a slight buzzing as she started to come to life.

"Wake up, Daisy," I said, and just like that she was alive, her eyes bright and her whiskers wiggling as she sniffed around. I held her up to my face to get a better look, and she touched her nose to mine. Then she was off, scurrying around the bed and onto the nightstand. I gasped and dove, grabbing frantically for her.

"Easy," said C.S. Nu. "It's okay. She is learning. When you want her to come back just say, 'Home,

Daisy.'" I relaxed a little, then, understood for the first time that this was not just a wild animal that I would have to train. This was a companion, a tiny friend if I wanted one. Something real. There was more talk after that, care and maintenance and everything. Mostly, though, I watched Daisy as she explored her new world, diving in and out, greeting the team one by one, and leaping seemingly impossible spans. I wish I had that kind of courage.

APRIL 20

Dr. Stevens came by for rounds and said that, physically, I am nearly ready to be released. Part of me is scared, all that I know of the "new" me is inside this little room. I don't know how I'll react to the real world. On the other hand, I know that there are people who actually find joy in normal day to day living. Who aren't afraid every minute of every day. I want to try that. I want to feel something other than scared all of the time, and angry, and tired. I want to have hobbies, and friends. I want to find out what I like to do when I'm not fighting just to survive. Yeah, I desperately want all of that. Like everything else, though, it's baby steps. They're not going to let me out into the world until they know that I have the best chance of success. And even though I know that it's my *franzio* new brain that they really care about, and not me, I'm going to appreciate it.

So, step one is to find a job. The Facility is paying me a monthly stipend, but having a job is still a *diablofar* requirement. They say that it's necessary to mental health, which really kind of makes me laugh. Most people that I know say that regular work is a detriment. We work because we need to, because we are hungry, or have run out of places to squat. We work for a case of beer to turn off the sights and sounds of the *fikfek* all around us. And when we work it's for those reasons, not for (devil-made) enrichment. Where is the enrichment in being up to your elbows in stinking, freezing fish guts? I told them this and they looked a little shocked. Then they said that first I need to figure out what I want to do. It's a strange concept, what I *want* to do. What I like to do. I don't know what I like to do. My entire life has been trying to figure out how to eat and where to sleep, how to dodge the dips and the hands and their bosses. All the while knowing that my brain is this giant time bomb, it's this bomb and any moment it's going to go off and if I'm lucky, if I'm very, very lucky, I'll only be stuck shivering and terrified in whatever I'm using for a bed, too scared to pull back the blankets. If I'm not lucky I come back to myself with cuts all up and down my arms and legs, scratches on my face. If I'm not lucky I lay there in bed until fear of starvation overcomes the guilt and the fear and the shame enough for me to stagger or crawl and hope for pity or mercy from a passerby. Let's see, for "reasons of mental health," I spent a couple of filthy months scrubbing blackened goo off of some conduits. There have been countless hours spend combing the streets and collecting anything that could be recycled for a handful of cents a pound, Once, I took tickets for the shows at the Geisha house, a two-hour stint that earned me another trip to East. I had thought, since it was a zero-nudity show, that I could handle it. I had been wrong. Something about the look in the patrons' eyes had reminded me too much of my mother's visitors. Those are some of the jobs that I've had. Not the best resume.

So, I've spend the last couple of days not just watching the SimCenter, but plugged into it as well, wearing the helmet and suit that allows me to try out different jobs. I spent several hours as a tour guide for an airship tour, lumbering around in one of the antiquated machines that are only used as tourist traps. Out of sheer curiosity, I tried being an aide in a hospital. I guess I wanted to see what it was like on the other side, what the patients were like. How they saw us. It was a lot harder than I had thought, it would be; I had no idea how much *fek*, both literal and figurative, aides took in any given day. I was doing all right, though, until I came across a patient who reminded me of Denae. Same plump body, same almond-shaped eyes. Except this version of Denae had been in a car accident and her face was torn and bloodied. I remembered how Denae had come in like that once, after one of her infrequent forays into the outside world. How she's seen me start to spiral out of control and had comforted me with lips that didn't move together anymore. "It's okay, baby" she's said. I ended the Sim quickly and went on to something else. Later, I painted make-up on Cybers' faces. I was terrible at it; they came out looking like clowns or the desperate pseudo-Geishas who tried to make money off of equally desperate men. It was fun, though; it reminded me of playing dolls with Daisy. The new Daisy, my Daisy was nearby through all of my experiments, sitting on my shoulder or watching from her cage. I tried a dozen jobs or more, but I didn't find anything that I liked nearly as much as the bakery. That's when it hit me. Why was I trying so hard to find a job I liked when I had one already, waiting for me. Excitedly I pushed the call button, told the hatchet-faced nurse to please call Basanti.

Basanti didn't share my excitement over the idea, though. "The point of the experiment was to elevate you," she said, "to take you to a higher level than you were before. What if you fall into the old bad habits?" The thing is, though, and I explained this, is that Don's Cafe was the place where I was healthiest, where I had the best habits. The bakery actually did "contribute to my mental health." She didn't believe me, I could tell, refused to believe it and I don't understand why. But I wouldn't back down and I think that surprised her. We went back and forth for a long time, and eventually Dr. Stevens was called in. She disagreed with me as well, but that was mostly because the harbor is a long way from the facility. I didn't imagine the look of surprise or disgust when I mentioned Flower Town, either. I don't think she likes her guinea pig that far out of reach. Still, they agreed to have a meeting tomorrow with the whole care team, to see what they thought. Hopefully, somebody would be on my side. Besides, Daisy loves bread.

APRIL 21

Danki Dion for Dr. Alyce. I mean, really, I would have given up years ago if not for him, I've known that. He was the closest thing to a friend I've ever had inside the system, even if it is a state-assigned and funded friend. And I've been wondering. You know? I've been wondering where he stood because he seemed so damned entrenched with Dr. Stevens and C.S. Nu, so different from the laid back, understanding guy he was at East. Like, you could almost believe that he was one of us. Not really, not all of the way, but almost. Then we get here and suddenly he is just another starched shirt. Never taking my side. Never caring about me. Always standing with them. Not today, though. Today he was the man I remember. The man I trusted when he said this would be good for me.   Dr.   Stevens   and Basanti arrived at the meeting with their minds already made up. I could tell by the set of their jaws, the rigid way they stood. C.S. Nu was there, holo'd in of course, but I didn't really expect him to have an opinion either way and sure enough he didn't. They can track and remote-download both Daisy and me (which I didn't know and kind of creeps me out. I keep forgetting that I am largely a computer nowadays) and so it doesn't matter to him where I live or what I do. The equipment is "biologically protected" which I guess means my skull. He explained that briskly and then excused himself. I pled my case to no avail. Basanti and Stevens didn't even flinch. So, it came down to Dr. Alyce. I was expected him to say "No" as well, follow the company line the way that he has so much lately, and was preparing myself for disappointment, but he shocked me by coming to my rescue. He explained what I had been trying to say all along, that Don's had always been a safe haven for me, a place where I had been allowed to flourish. He even suggested that Don filled a role in my life as a surrogate father. I don't know about all of that, but it sounded good so I nodded eagerly and smiled. We argued, all of us, for what seemed like forever and I was starting to feel my wrists start to tingle and my head ache until finally Dr. Sevens and Basanti relented with matching sighs and on the condition that I return to the Facility twice a week until they were sure that I had adapted. Originally I was just supposed to come one time. I can't help but think that that's going to be a pain in the *pugo* but at this point I don't really care. At this point I would have agreed to anything.

Then came the discussion as to where I would live. I think that everyone was surprised that I wanted to return to Flower Town; they assumed that I'd prefer to stay somewhere in the Center Circle. But I don't. I want to go back. Flower Town, as miserable as it can be, is home. It's all I know. Besides, it's where Don's is. I can't see how I can commit to my job, really give it my best, if I have to fly in and out every day. Not even Dr. Alyce, *la infero*, not even I thought that the stacks were a good idea, though. No one would pick those if given the choice. They are everything that's bad about the rim, everything that they push onto us to keep us poor, to keep us down. Neither of us could think of another valid option, though. I've never had the opportunity to really choose where I live, and Basanti has never even been there. Dr. Alyce, has, but he's not exactly been looking for real estate. Hospitals and half-way houses, those were his thing.

People were exhausted and irritable by that point, even Dr. Stevens looked tired, and so it was determined that if Basanti and I could find suitable house and if Don said yes, then I could go back. I could return to the closest thing to a home that I've ever had.

APRIL 24

Tre ekscitita. I spent most of my morning sitting by the window, taking in the sunlight. I still can't get over how clear the skies are here, away from the smoke and the soot of the harbor. That much at least I will miss, actually seeing the sun. I'm bored, though, bored out of my mind. I don't want to play on the SimCenter, don't want to watch more TV, and sure as hell don't want to do any more of my exercises. I've done them all a million times; if I'm not ready by now I never will be.

So, to pass the time, I was teaching Daisy how to tightrope walk. I'd gotten a piece of twine from one of the nurse and tied each end to my middle fingers. I put Daisy in one hand and a treat in the other. Then I wait, occasionally making kissy noises. At first she would only go a few inches before she would get nervous or lose her balance, but after a couple of hours I had my hands shoulder width apart. She seems to enjoy learning and I'm surprised at how much I like teaching her. I actually get excited when I see that she's making progress. We are learning together and it's nice to feel like I'm not alone.

I was so absorbed in what I was doing that I didn't notice when Basanti came in. When I turned around, there she was with a huge smile on her face. "She's doing so well," I said, nodding towards Daisy.

"No, *kara*, you are," Basanti replied. "I have good news." And she did, too. Don said yes. I was fairly sure that he would, but wasn't certain how he would take being approached by someone from the facility. We rim dwellers all have a bit of distaste for those in the center circle and I thought it would be best if I asked him. They aren't quite ready to let me out of their grip, though. They aren't going to let go of control until they absolutely have to. Or maybe they thought I'd lie about his answer. In any case I was kept out of the loop. I guess Basanti actually went to the cafe herself instead of calling, so I'm sure that helped. It seemed to have helped her, too. Flower Town may be a trash-covered hole, but Don's is a good place. It's got a good vibe, and I think even Basanti picked up on that. Even better, she was able to find an apartment for me, not in the stackflats, but in one of the old *bela* houses that, years ago, used to be vacation homes for people visiting the beach. The houses are run down now, like everything in Flower Town, but are still, I don't know, elegant maybe. Like an old woman who still hasn't forgotten what it was like to be young. They are a damn sight better than the stacks, that's for sure, and hard to get into. There's usually a waiting list of years and even if you manage to find a space usually only harbormasters and such can afford to live there. I guess not too hard when you have the power and resources they have here. Anyhow, three more days and I'll be moving in. Wow. Only three more days. . .

APRIL 26

I had another dream about Mother last night. In it I was a young girl. I don't know how old I was, but she seemed like a giant, looming over me, her eyes wild and frantic, and her body shaking. I cringed away from her, my eyes cast down, and my feet were clad in thin-soled Mary Janes, the shine and color rubbed off of the toes so that they were as gray as the sludge they so often carried me through. Four then? Five? I remember those shoes. I had loved them. I called them my Princess shoes and wore them until they fell apart on my feet. In the dream we were moving; Mother rushed around trailing smoke like a frantic train engine, grabbing hands-full of clothes and dishes and stuffing it all into plastic bags. This happened often enough in real life, I remember. We never stayed anywhere long and our moves always seemed to come as an emergency, or at the very least an unpleasant surprise. Every time I was left mourning something or another that was left behind. Somehow though every bottle of pills every tube of makeup or hair cream, every laddered stocking made it into the bags. Somehow. Suddenly, mother came stomping up to me, furious. Her hands, she often didn't have enough to feed me, but her nails were always immaculate, were hooked into claws and her teeth were clenched.

"Aren't you ready yet?' she shrieked. "I told you to be packed."

"Yes Mama," I answered. My voice was very small. "Really?" she said," picking up a dirty stuffed animal, a rat, I could tell by the long tail. "How about this?" she threw it and it struck my shoulder. I picked it up and hugged it to me and it turned into Daisy, my Daisy. Soon the air was full of projectiles as she grabbed anything she could reach and threw it at me. "And this?" she said as a dish broke above my head. "And this" a high heel bounced off my hip. I just crouched there, trying to protect Daisy, taking the hits until finally something, it looked like the vase that held my post-surgery flowers, cracked against my head and I woke up.

I told Dr. Alyce about the dream when he stopped by. He says that the meaning is fairly obvious, that the dream showed just how nervous I felt about leaving. How unprepared. He's right. Of course he's right. How could I not be scared? On some level I know that it's not the place that's different, it's me. Still, though, I can't help but think that out there life was incomprehensibly, inescapably horrible. In here, it's been okay. Better than okay at times. Dr. Alyce pointed out that for my first three weeks life in here was hell too, how I fought them every stop of the way and hated them for the help they were trying to offer. I don't remember much of that, and what I do remember isn't anger so much as fear. Was a really so ungrateful, uncooperative? Or where they as unreasonable as I see through the haze? Have I always been like that? Time will tell, I guess. Maybe that's one more thing I will have to pack someday. In the meantime, I have eight hours until the hovercab will take me to my new place. Eight hours to meditate, to pray, to run some more Social Simulation exercises. To play with Daisy. Eight hours to get packed.

MAY 1

I stepped out of the hospital and into a whirlwind and have been riding the currents ever since. I've never been so busy in my life, and certainly never been so eager or able to take in all that life was bringing. It is incredible to be free, free finally of that paralyzing terror that change of any kind always brought. Don't get me wrong, I'm still scared often, *terurita* sometimes, but even in that I can actually move, can think and react. It's amazing. I feel as though I've been granted parole, that the electrocuffs have been removed, and I'm out of jail and into the light.

The hovercab took me to and my two meager boxes of belongings to my new apartment which was, as promised, in one of the old vacation homes. I even have my own bathroom, something I never expected and that I never had in the stacks. I hadn't realized before now how nice it was to take a shower without fear of someone barging in. Hell, even in the hospital I didn't have that. I think I've taken six showers in the past couple days, scrubbing and twirling and just letting the water sheet down my face until the hot water ran out. The apartment is largely empty, the SimCenter that the Facility sent rises from the middle of the floor like an enormous island. All that I own, except for a few battered bags, came from the Facility, I wouldn't even know how to begin looking for the few things I left behind when I was whisked away to East what seems like a lifetime ago, and so I find myself embarrassingly without furniture, or even a can opener. I discovered this the first time I tried to make myself some dinner, and found out that I couldn't actually get into any of the foods I'd bought myself. I was really upset for several hours, angry, pacing. I mean, it's not like I haven't skipped a meal before but I was really hungry and I felt incredibly stupid. Mostly it was the stupid that bothered me. Then I realized that I could just go and get some more food and felt stupid all over again. I'm not used to having extra money, to being able to buy at my leisure. Still, this seemed like a good opportunity, so I did, I walked down the street until I found a vendor, an old withered man who had an ancient and rusty cyduck sitting on his cart. The duck quacked loudly at Daisy. I placed my order and an egg rolled out from under the duck on a small ramp that the man had obviously built for her. The man cracked it into a wad of slightly gray dough, synflour, I knew that from my time at the bakery, and fried it in a kettle of ancient grease. The grease snapped and popped and I noticed that the skin of his hands and arms was shiny from scars. He must have been doing this for years. I ate my dinner on the way home, then stretched out on the floor and slept. I have no furniture. I need to fix this. I don't need much, but the floor is exceptionally hard after the recent months in the *franzia* airbeds of the hospital, but I haven't had the time as of yet. Truth be told, I wouldn't know where to go to find things like that even if I could find the time; the stacks generally came with someone's old couch or beds that they couldn't or didn't take with them when they left and that the land lord was too lazy to lug to the curb. After a while, you learned to ignore the stains and stale smells of secondhand mattresses, and became adept at maneuvering couches up and through the narrow stairwells. Still, with the exception of a sore neck in the morning, the emptiness doesn't bother me. It doesn't seem to bother Daisy, either; we've been too busy exploring together, sticking our noses into the cabinets and closets, getting used to the sounds of both the neighborhood and the old house itself. The first two nights I woke up every two hours, ready to be poked and prodded. I actually got a little lonely when nobody came, as much as I grew weary of the constant human contact it's what I've become accustomed to. With the loneliness and the night comes the anxiety. It doesn't attack, and I'm so grateful for that, but it cruises by just within sight, just like the giant sharks we see sometimes at the harbor, all silent, watching malice. I've spent a lot of time breathing deeply, practicing the exercises that Basanti and Dr. Alyce taught me and, occasionally, talking to Daisy. As crazy as it seems, they must have programmed her with some rudimentary emotions, because I would swear that she understand me and, more than that, empathizes. She sits daintily on her back legs while I talk, her tail wrapped around my feet, her head cocked to one side, and sometimes she runs up my arm to snuggle in the hollow of my neck. I've started teaching her more words and she learns quickly and easily. She likes to turn the water on and off when I brush my teeth, and I've kept some of the wrappers from my food to teach her colors. Meanwhile, I have a lot to learn as well; I just hope that I can be as good of a student as Daisy is. I had better be, because tomorrow is another test. Tomorrow I start work.

MAY 2

There are so many words, so many terms, concepts, that have become commonplace for me since the day that I walked into the cool chrome waiting room in Center Circle. Cyber-Bio Compatibility. Intracranial transplant. Bineurology. I've spent the last few months in a bubble in which these terms are tossed around as easily as profanity at the docks. Medical professionals, and certainly scientists, seem to look upon it is some sort of self-degradation to talk in anything other than terminology, so by necessity all of this worked its' way into my vocabulary just as the electrosynapses wormed their way into my nerves. Naturally, thoroughly, inseparably. And so I forget that a season ago they were just as foreign , perhaps even more so, than any of the dozen or so languages spoken here in Flower Town.

Today, though, I was reminded. If I'd caught on to what was happened any more slowly, I think I would have lost a lifetime friend, our friendship would have rotted slowly from the inside out, killed by frightened glances and awkward silence, and so I'm so thankful that I realized what was happening as soon as I did. Poor Don.

I was so excited to go to work, to see Don, to meet whatever lost soul like me had found refuge in his place.

As soon as I arrived, though, I could tell that something was wrong. My hair has started to grow back since the surgery, but right now it's this wild untamed mass of tiny corkscrews pointing this way and that, that , at least in my mind, draws attention to rather than kids the scar that spans my head from ear to ear. So, I decided to wrap my head in a colorful scarf, the same one that covered Daisy's' cage when the techs first brought her to me. Don was friendly enough when I came in, I suppose, but I could tell that something was wrong. There was ho hug, customary after what he called "my little vacations." There was no humming as he kneaded the dough with his gnarled hands. There was nothing. Just silence, and distance and the nervous glances that he kept shooting my way when he thought that I wasn't looking. I chalked it up to time; it has been a while since I'd been in, or maybe he was irritated by being pressed by the Facility into rehiring me. I'm sure that they are paying my salary, but still Don shares the outer rim's inherent disdain for anyone Circle Center, which may or may not include me. I decided not to address it, just went about my day, doing all of the tasks I used to do. The way I saw it, he would talk about it, or not, when he was ready.

By the time lunch came, though, I was feeling the strain. My shoulders were locked into tension knots and

I was beginning to wonder if Dr. Stevens and Basanti have been right about this being a mistake. It was becoming hard to breathe. My friend, my old friend hated me, or was afraid of me, or I'd done something wrong and I had no idea what it was. My heart was pounding and I broke out in goose bumps. I knew that soon I'd have to leave and if I did what would happen to me? We made it through the rush and flopped down in the old mismatched chairs back in the break room. I took Daisy out of the cage that I'd gotten to keep her in while I was at work, and let her run around for a little bit on the faded no-color Formica while Don scratched away at one of his endless books filled with crossword puzzles, muttering to himself as he worked out the answers. I'd been sweating; the kitchen of the cafe was hot even in the winter, one of the reasons that I loved it, and this late in spring it was sweltering. My head itched under the scarf and so I reached up and unwound it slowly, bunching it into a ball that I then threw on the table with a sigh. It took me a few seconds to realize that the muttering and scratching had stopped. I raised my eyes to find Don staring fixedly at me, his eyes and mouth wide.

"I'll be damned," he said, "It's really you under there."

We were both silent for a second, and let out matching guffaws, the sounds echoing off of the cinder block walls and just like that Don's was familiar, home again.

"*Fekegalo*, Don" I exclaimed. "What did you expect?"

That's when he told me that he'd had no idea what to expect. Basanti had showed up one day, jingling and beautiful, and had starting spouting off all of those words those words I've recently come to know, and had left him thinking that I'd be I know don't what – a robot. Some freak with wires or even a whole brain hanging out of my head. I think I realized then that I have become a part of that other world, to some extent. Will I ever be able to fit in here again? Is dual citizenship simply too much to ask? I haven't heard from any of the old friends yet. I don't know how they would handle me even if I did ferret them out. How they would react. Would they be happy for me now that I can really be happy too? Or would the distrust of anything Center Circle, a deep seeded distrust built of hears of hunger and filth, extend to me now, too? I don't know. It broke my heart to see how Don had shied away from me, that's for certain. Still, though, he let me come back. Even believing that I was some fiber-optic Medusa, he made a place for me here. I have to remember that if things get tough. Even with all of that, he let me come back.

MAY 13

Today Daisy and I returned to the Facility for another of our bi-weekly gauntlets that we are expected to run. I saw Dr. Stevens first, a brief, perfunctory visit. Blood pressure, heart rate, a couple of minutes in their modified CT scanner. Next, I visited the C.S. Lab. Dr. Nu already had, he said all of the data that he required, but I spent a couple of minutes showing the students the tricks that Daisy has learned since we've left. I felt like a proud parent whose baby had learned to walk. The students seemed genuinely impressed, though, and taught me some exercises that I could try when we get home to help her learn even more. Next was Dr. Alyce. This was the first time our schedules had allowed us more than the briefest of meetings since I'd left, and we talked easily for well over an hour. I told him about everything that had happened since I had left. The joys, the anxieties, the fears. He seemed pleased, said that overall I am "reacclimatizing very well." I left his office, my feet moving soundlessly on the thick carpet- how different this was from his office in East – and was surprised to find Basanti in the waiting room smiling her broad smile.

"So," she said, "What do we want to work on today?"

I was confused at first, didn't understand what she was asking. Before now our meetings had been scheduled almost to the minute, and Basanti was armed with a list of objectives that she consulted often on her microcomp. As it turns out, all of that changed now that I'm living independently. Now, part of my job is to help decide in what areas I'm struggling and we go from there. It's kind of a daunting prospect; I've never been trustworthy enough or, to be honest, interested enough to know what I needed. That may be a problem in itself someday. Today though, it wasn't . Today I knew exactly what I wanted to do.

"Basanti" I said, "I need you to take me shopping." She burst out in laughter then, loud long trills that sounded like tinkling bells. I smiled uncertainly at first, not sure what she had found so funny. Then, I started to get irritated. I thought she was laughing at me.

"Do you mind sharing the joke" I snapped.

"Oh 'Lotta" she replied, "Don't you remember?"

I didn't, had no idea what she was talking about and told her so.

"Charlotte," she said, taking my hands, "We've been shopping together before. "

I was completely and totally lost then. I know that there was a period where everything was hazy, but that? I think I'd remember that. What on earth was she talking about? Then I remembered the ridiculous test that I had don't before the surgery, and the vapid, childish "aide" who had accompanied me. How I hated her! I tried to conjure up her face in my mind, but all that I could imagine was a caricature, a gum popping, blank eyes spoiled *franzia*.

"That wasn't you!" I exclaimed.

"It was," she replied.

"But I hated you" I said.

"You hated most everyone, Charlotte," she said. My face flamed red and I hung my head.

"Don't be embarrassed," Basanti replied, putting her warm hands on my arms. "It was how you survived. Still, you'll understand why, when you didn't recognize me, I didn't bother to correct you. I thought it best if we 'met' for the first time then."

Betrayal rose in my throat like vomit. To think that my Basanti, my friend, and that vapid spoiled child were ne and the same. But then, I hadn't noticed, so what did that say about me, my perception? I watched Daisy as she leapt back and forth from one hand to another as I struggled with the emotions flooding me. Finally, I smiled a little.

"Well," I said, "We don't have to go back to that mall, do we?"

"*La infierno neniuj,*" she exclaimed. This time, we laughed together.

Basanti hailed a hovercab and together we went, not to a mall or a plex but to a series of small shops tucked in along a tree-lined street. As we entered the first a small metal bell rang above our heads. The door shut behind us, leaving us in a dimly lit room with soft music. My eyes adjusted and I gasped involuntarily. It was like nothing I'd ever seen. Everything was old, from before the Unification and there was not a single piece of plastic or ply or metal to be seen. Instead the furniture was low and round, overstuffed and covered in soft fabrics. I wandered back and forth through the overcrowded aisles, running my fingers across this and that, delighting in the feel of things. Finally I came across a set, a giant chair and matching sofa the soft green of sea grass at the end of the summer. I sat on it and let out a small yelp as I sank in several inches. Basanti looked up from the small pottery candle holders she was handling and smiled.

"So these are the ones?" she asked. I nodded, grinning. We made a few stops after that, and Basanti taught me how to barter and arranged to have the items delivered to my apartment. I had yet to check the balance in my bank account, didn't even know how, and so she showed me how to do that as well, keying in the information and scanning my thumb over coffee. I've never had a bank account, not one that I used anyway, and so we made a plan to go over it in more detail the next time we saw each other. I was dumbfounded at how much money I had. It seemed to me an astronomical amount, though Basanti explained that it would get me through barely a month in one of the center circles. It was all too much all of a sudden, and I found myself exhausted. When I asked to go home, Basanti didn't argue.

I arrived at my house just before the deliverymen and soon the apartment was full of activity. I unpacked my purchases, and took the boxes into the spare room where I made a giant maze for Daisy. I ended up not even using anything that I had bought, instead spent the evening playing hide and seek. The sun had set before I raised my head and realized that I was both tired and hungry, and so I put Daisy on my shoulder and padded to the kitchen. There I made my first dinner in my new home, served on my new plates. It was simple, a SynSoy micro-meal that I bloomed with hot water. Still though, it was mine. I earned it. I picked it out. I made it. And I loved every bite.

MAY 21

It was late when I prepared to leave the cafe tonight. Don hasn't been feeling well; the dampness has been playing hell on his hips and hands, so he had gone home early to rest, leaving me to close the shop. He has never done that before, not even in the two years when I was at work nearly every day, and it made me feel good that he trusted me that much, you know? It made me feel good that I could be trusted that much. That, more than any test, more than any graph, more than any stupid Sim, shows me how much I've grown. I was nearly strutting around, taking special joy in all of the closing tasks because I wasn't just doing something for Don, but I was doing something because it thought it was important. He must think a lot of me.

It was a slow night anyway. Fridays always were once the weather got warm. I could hear, even above the chugging of the dishwasher and the music we kept playing throughout the day, one of the first of the block parties and the faint rumble of thunder from one of our frequent summer storms. They came nearly every night in the spring and again in the high summer, fierce storms that came wooshing in and out in nearly the same instant. The thunder grew louder as I wiped down the old stainless appliances. I gave them an extra shine with the bottle of vinegar water that we kept on hand. Daisy watched from the chest pocket of my apron, her long nose quivering with curiosity. Animals, even Cynimals, were banned from restaurants, but Daisy had thoroughly charmed Don and so he was more than willing to look the other way as long as she stayed as inconspicuous as possible. Daisy loved it. A nearly unending stream of new people and tasty pastries, it was a little Cyrat paradise. I moved quickly, one eye fixed on the large plate glass window at the front of the store. I detested getting wet, even though I took showers all of the time, and even though I knew the thought was ridiculous, there was a part of me that was afraid that a rainstorm would somehow lead to a short. I had visions, often, of me laying in a puddle, jumping and quivering, cartoon jolts of electricity jumping from my head. I told one of my nurses that once and she actually laughed out loud. I laughed with her, maybe so she wouldn't know how serious I was, but still I thought about it every time it stormed.

In any case, I wanted to be safely home before the rain hit in earnest. Basanti has started encouraging me to go out and make friends, and I had intended to do so tonight. To try anyway, tough admittedly I'm at a bit of a loss as to how to do so. I'm not going to school, and the people here at work have never moved past just casual acquaintances. I have no interest in going to bars. The rest of the tenants in my house are way older than me, and our hours are so different we rarely cross paths. I don't know where any of the old crew has gone. I thankfully, blessedly, don't have the forced intimacy of East to contend with. It kind of limits my options. I know there has to be a way – people meet and make friends all of the time, but I just don't know how. I've never tried to make friends before, they've always just kind of happened. In any case, it was going to have to wait until another night. I was just finishing up and was reaching for the light switch when I was startled by a pounding on the door. This happened fairly often; it was common knowledge that Don would give away any leftover bread or soup at the end of the day. He, like most of us on the rim, knew what it was like to be poor and hungry and was generous almost to a fault. I'd seen him take a loaf fresh out of the oven and give it away, claiming that it was day old even as the steam rose off of it. Quickly I tossed some sweet rolls and a loaf of bread, crusty and topped with cheese and herbs, into a bag and went to answer the door. I pulled it open and gasped; a millisecond later I was lifted off of my feet and wrapped in a pair of heavily muscled and tattooed arms.

It was Dmitri, as stocky and sardonic as he'd always been. Still reeking of fish as he always had as well. I was pleasantly surprised at how delighted I was to see him. I mean, I'd thought of him, time and again, and Tawny even more. Still, they'd been wrapped up with the pain and humiliation that was that time, and locked in a strongbox like so many of the others I contained. Kept behind barbed wire and covered with the warning signs that marked the conduits that ran through town. I squealed and punched his shoulders in mock outrage.

"Put me down you *fek*" I cried, "You reek."

He laughed and returned me to my feet. "We thought you were dead *kara*" he said, "no one had heard from you." I laughingly assured him that I was alive, even did a little dance to prove it, and we sat down at one of the scratched and faded tables. We stayed there, washed in the dim yellow light and nostalgia, until well after midnight. God, I'd forgotten how good it felt to be among friends, among those who knew how broken, how screwed up you were and didn't try to fix you they didn't judge you, they just let you be. They could accept anything. It's this amazing feeling of being on the inside for once, instead of just looking inside. Of being an "us" and not a "them." *Those* people. *Those* freaks. No, it was us. We freaks and *fek' al vi* if you don't like it.

I was so engrossed that I forgot all about the storm that had broken and was raging outside. Finally, the sandpapery feeling of my eyes and Dmitri's yawning forced us outside. We parted ways under the awning and he promised to bring Tawny back soon. I made sure that he keyed my address into his microcomp as well, and invited them to come and see my house anytime. I saw his eyes widen at the street name, but he didn't ask any questions. I was glad. I want to tell them everything and I will, eventually. Tonight, though, I was happy to talk about the little, insignificant things, about the old days. I know this wasn't what Basanti meant when she told me to make friends, She, like the others, is still hesitant regarding anything from my life before. She isn't likely to understand that, even when my life was *merd'*, there were good things. There were joys and people who cared about me and for me the best that they can. That my life was a mess in spite of them, not because of them. I've never forgotten how they drove me to the hospital that night. They must have been as scared as I was and they could have just left, or shut me in a room to do whatever it was that I wanted to do to myself, but they didn't . They took care of me. That's just how they are. Yeah, Basanti may not see that, but I do, and I'm thrilled that he came to the door.

MAY 23

I was right; Basanti wasn't thrilled, and we actually quarreled a bit about it. No, those were her words, "Charlotte, we don't have to quarrel." Let me use my words. I was happy about something. I was really happy and she refused to understand.

"It's like you want me to give up my whole life – who I am."

"Wasn't that the point? To start new?" she said.

"Yes, but you're trying to turn me into some *aroganta* Center Circle Cyber." She disagreed of course, told me that she was just worried that I would fall into bad habits.

"But that's just it," I retorted. I don't have the capability for bad habits anymore. I don't cut or scream or black out when I get hurt. I don't hide for days when I get scared. That's all gone now." She didn't say anything, just watched me with her huge, dark eyes. *Diable ĝi!* Why doesn't she ever seem to have to blink? The seconds ticked away, and I realized that I was chewing on my nails, had gnawed two of them down to nubs. Basanti continued to say nothing, but one eyebrow rose slightly. That just irritated me more. "That's not the same and you know it." I countered.

"Isn't it? What if the bad habits of which I speak are more in the line of nail biting and less related to your blackouts and avoidance?" She sighed. "It's not just that Charlotte. I worry about you. Emotionally you are still very young, you are still learning. I am concerned that those friends of yours are not what you think they are."

"Because poor people can't be good people, right? Everyone outside of circle five must be *forĵetaĵo*." And you know what? I really think that's what it comes down to. Because I see it everywhere. It's in the eyes of the people in the waiting room every time I come in here. It's the upturned noses of the waitresses when I pronounce something on the menu wrong. To them, I will never be enough. That's why I want to be with my friends. To them, I always was enough. Just me.

Basanti held her hands up in surrender. "All right, *amiko* all right. I will trust you. I will try to trust them. Just promise me you will watch out for yourself. Outside of here" she gestured to the multi-tiered walls surrounding the courtyard and soaring into the sky, "our ability to protect you is limited."

I saw the genuine worry in her face then and touched her hand. "You don't need to protect me from them, Basanti." I said.

She smiled "I hope that you're right."

We left then, and I trailed behind her to my next appointment. There, everyone was in uncommonly good spirits, pumping one another's hands and chattering excitedly. C.S. Nu was there in the flesh, and even Dr. Stevens was grinning broadly from ear to ear.

"There she is,' Dr. Alyce exclaimed " Our shining star!" I was utterly taken aback. I would , I think, consider Dr. Alyce to be a friend. Basanti too, my irritation with her notwithstanding. Still, their shining star? I was certain I'd never before been referred to as anything resembling that. I knew that something big must have happened, and sure enough it had. Dr. Stevens and the rest of the experimental team have been invited to share their process and the results at an upcoming annual conference. The conference is in a little more than one month's time and is apparently an incredibly big deal. I won't pretend that I understand even half of it. I'm just relieved, no beyond relieved,, I'm ecstatic that they –we– are going. Not because I care so much about the frou frou, the celebrity, or even the shuttle hop. I mean, I'm excited, sure. Every girl wants to be a princess at least once in her life and I want to pretend that I don't, but if I take a minute to be honest I have to admit that it would be nice. I want to put on a pretty dress and drink champagne and be part of a party that is, kinda, being held for me. I've never had that before. Sure, once a month in East they would buy a cake, one big cake, and they would write the names of everyone who was having a birthday in that month on it, but does that really count? A birthday party when you could be sure that someone was going to slam the cake on the wall and other people wouldn't even chew if you didn't remind them? But this? We are going to celebrate the new me and yeah sure I want that, but it's way more than that. It's because they wouldn't be willing to go public, wouldn't open themselves to potential embarrassment, unless they were sure that the experiment was a success. This conference means a lot of things to a lot of people. To Dr. Stevens it's the fruits of two decades of surgeries. To C.S. Nu it's validation of his cybernetic programmable tissues. To Dr. Alyce it is finally seeing one of his patients cured. But, to me, it is confirmation that the surgery – that I- have succeeded. That I am finally well. And that I'm going to stay that way.

MAY 30

It is late. So late that I've gone past exhaustion into that state where you are wide awake again. I mean, granted, it's a kind of brittle wakefulness when my laughter seems to shrill to my own ears and my limbs are buzzing. If I look outside I can see the eerie sapphire blue that arrives just before dawn. I've seen that before. Lots of times. Some of them have been good. Some of them have been shivering with cold and just trying to hang on in the hopes that the sun will bring some warmth. Some of them have been me just counting my breaths, trying to convince myself I can survive through taking one more. That the fear may take me but that it was *not* going to take me in the space of the next breath. This time, though? This is one of the good ones. One of the very good ones.

I'm keying this report from the small hand-held unit in my bedroom and trying to be as quiet as I can. Daisy gave up on us hours ago, and is sleeping in the comical and charming way that she does, with her head bent all the way around so that her ears lay flat against the bottom of the cage and her nose is pointed back between her hind legs. Rat ball. Cyrat ball. I have to fight the urge to stroke her back. I know that if I did she would be up, awake and eager, in an instant. They don't really need sleep after all, it's just programmed into them to want it, but still it seems cruel somehow. In the living room, Dmitri and Tawny are asleep as well. For a week or more I had been home every night, waiting, looking out the window every time I heard someone on the sidewalk. I practiced what I would say. The things I would say to make them laugh. How just at the right time I would apologize. I would tell them what happened and how they could trust me now. I had brought home extra food from the cafe, just to have on hand in case they were hungry when they came. I even remembered their favorites, or at least what used to be their favorites. But they kept not coming. I thought they wouldn't and then I thought they might and I tried to tell myself that it was okay but it wasn't. By last night I had given up on them even coming by, had figured that the memories that they held of me were too horrible, too much for them. I couldn't blame them. The memories I have of myself back then are too much for me sometimes, too. But I was starting to feel pathetic just sitting there waiting. Starting to hear some of the old voices again, the ones that tell me that I'm workless. Unloved. Unwanted. So I finally decided to take Basanti's advice and try going somewhere new.

Down the street from my house is a nightclub. Akaifūsha. I pass by it every night when I walk home, and have a couple of times found myself lingering on the sidewalk outside, swaying to the heavy beat, watching the laughing couples and groups as they came and went. Never singles, though, and I knew I'd feel ridiculous walking in by myself. Still, to lose myself in the music and the flashing lights, that has always been one of my favorite things to do. The bouncer knows me by sight, though not by name of course, and he's taken to yelling a greeting whenever I pass by. Tonight, when he did, I walked over.

"Finally coming in, *Belega*?" he said. "I knew we'd get ya," and pushed open the door. I walked in and was immediately engulfed by the sheer, utter chaos. The lights. The laughter. The colors, God the colors. The walls were smothered in nothing but graffiti, Bright, loud, childish colors that somehow came together to form something beautiful, something greater than the sum of the parts. I saw most of the local tags, the names and siguls that marked everything in Flower Town from billboards to conduits, and they greeted me like old friends. I knew them, the signs and sometimes even the people behind them. I had the mark of one tagger on me; he'd tried to convince me to take of my shirt so that he could draw it on my back. I wouldn't. He knew I wouldn't, that's why he'd tried. So we'd compromised on the top of my foot and then someone else, I don't even know his name, just that he'd brought his sticks and inks along with him, had gone over it and made it permanent. I looked for his tag on the walls and didn't see it. He's probably moved on, one way or another. That night was a long time ago. Still though, the place was damn near magical. And the music. Oh the music. I'd forgotten how much I had loved music once. The way that the beat thumps and worms its way inside your blood until your heart is beating in time. The way that you can lose yourself, just forget as your body takes over. The way the world dissolves behind the melody. You can get outside your head for once. Just finally break free of all of the "what ifs" and the "what now's" and the million things that wrap around you until you can barely *fekanta'* breathe. And you can get loose of all of that. I didn't interact with anyone. Didn't say anything outside of the occasional "thank you" or apology, but even so I felt nothing short of amazing. I left grinning.

"That's right" the Bouncer said, and for one crazy second I actually thought about hugging the man. The salt-scented breeze off of the ocean dried my sweat-slicked skin. My joints felt loose, oiled. I walked home bathed in something like euphoria, every sense heightened but my mind blessedly at rest. I kicked off my shoes, placed Daisy in her cage, and was asleep before my head hit the pillow. Seconds later, or so it seemed, I was yanked back to wakefulness by a banging on my door. I thought that I had imagined it at first, but as it went on I ignored it, certain that someone had gotten confused after a night of revelry. It didn't stop though, just went on and on and finally I padded across the floor, rubbing at my sandpapery eyes, and cautiously pulled open the door. There they were, leaning on one another and peering at me with identical drunken grins.

"Hey Charlotte," Tawny slurred as if no time at all had passed, as though we'd seen each other only yesterday.

"Hey Tawny," I replied, a smile stretching across my face, "you wanna come in?" And as easy as that we were all together again. We talked about the old days, who we know and where they are. We talked about all of the trouble we got into with and for each other. I'd forgotten about some of it, probably for good reason. After a while, I opened a bottle of wine and we talked our way through that, too. I finally got up the courage to tell them about my operation. All of the carefully scripted words I'd thought up were gone by that time, though, and I stuttered and stammered my way through it, terrified of what they would think. I told them all of it, the Cybers in the waiting room and where I had been right before that and the deal I'd worked out with the facility to let me stay here. And when I was done I just waited. I didn't know for what.

'Well?" I said finally, when the silence had spun out for so long that I couldn't stand it.

"Well what?" Tawny said, "I'd heard something had happened. Hand me the bottle." And so I did. They're going to stay for a while. They're having a hard time and it's the least I can do. They didn't want to, I know they didn't . Dmitri said he had it worked out and I'm sure he did. Dmitri is good at nothing if not working things out, but I begged them. It's the least I can do. As exhausted as I am, I can barely sleep, I'm so excited for them to wake.

JUNE 7

I came home from work today, again, to friends it my house. It's nice. I was surprised to see Dmitri there; usually harbor work lasts until late, but it seems like this is their slow season. They don't have work for him every day. It's kind of strange, I didn't know there was a slow season on the docks. I mean, there's always fish in the sea, yeah? Still, though, I'm aware that I don't know much about that kind of work. I told him about a couple of other places that I know always need help, and he says that he's going to check them out, go down and see what he can do. In the meantime, I'm just glad that I can be a help. And I really do enjoy their company. They had the SimCenter on when I came home, were still in their pajamas, and so I threw on something not covered in flour and joined them. The air conditioning was kicked on high, I'm still amazed at how steady the electricity is in this particular part of town, but Tawny threw back the blanket and I joined them, sitting together on the couch. After a while, Dmitri rolled a cigarette. Daisy sniffed at the smoke for a while and sneezed. I thought about asking him to go outside; I don't really want my place smelling like smoke, but we were comfortable and laughing and so I decided that it didn't really matter. We must have sat like that for two hours, watching the

SimCenter and laughing about the things that happened in the course of the day. They were still awake by the time that I had to go to sleep, and I could hardly drag myself away. They kept joking around, telling me that I should just call in sick. "You'll get paid anyway, *kara*," Tawny said. I'm not going to lie, between trips to and from Center Circle and the job I wouldn't mind an extra day off. Still, eventually I did wander back to my room though, with Daisy riding on my shoulder. We played with the tightrope for a couple of minutes, and now I'm getting ready to turn on some music and go to sleep. I'd forgotten how much I missed having people around.

JUNE 20

Tension is continuing to build between me and the experimental group. It has been, slowly, ever since I left, but since Tawny and Dmitri moved it in has snowballed. It's terrible, so stressful that I almost skipped my appointment today. I couldn't deal with another round of them not understanding me, of telling me what to do. I am a grown woman. They trusted me enough to decide I wanted this surgery, but then they second guess everything I've said since then. It doesn't make sense. Still, at the last possible minute I waved a hovercab and came rushing in, ashamed and apologizing and ten minutes late. Of course, that didn't improve my reception. The thing is, I can't seem to curb my resentment. I just cannot stand their unending *fikfek* arrogance. It's like today, we were arguing, again about Dmitri and Tawny living with me. This has become a consistent part of not just my visits but of every day. I get messages at my SimCenter, calls at the bakery, and I'm just tired of it. After somewhere between fifteen minutes and an eternity of listening to them go on and on I finally snapped.

"Fine" I said, "I'll pay extra for their rent, will that solve it?" That wasn't enough.

C.S. Nu looked at me for a long time before he responded. "You must understand, Charlotte, that you represent a serious investment of both time and resources."

"That doesn't give you the right to tell me how to life in real life, outside of here!"

"On the contrary, that's precisely the rights we have, the rights you agreed to, especially if your behavior is unsafe," said Dr. Stevens. I was dumbfounded, frustrated and nearly in tears. Wordlessly, she handed me the contract that I had signed prior to my surgery. She pointed with one perfectly manicured nail to section 11A: Patient agrees to conduct personal affairs in a manner so as to, to the best of her ability, protect the installed equipment and provide for the most positive experimental results. Failure to do so can result in a relinquishment of adjudication.

I didn't even know what half of those words meant. I tossed the papers on the floor and ran out of the room. Eventually, Basanti and Dr. Alyce tracked me down where I had hidden in the Cynimal lab. I loved it there, and the students treated me like a peer. No, more than that, almost like a mentor. They admired me, listened to me, they had ever since I'd shown them all that I had taught Daisy. We always had a good time sharing stories and tips.

"What is this?" I asked when they came through the door. "Good cop, bad cop?"

"Do you really feel this level of hostility is warranted? How about productive?" Dr. Alyce asked.

"I don't know anymore," I said, "and to be honest I'm not sure I care. If being productive means being a lapdog, jumping when you say jump, rolling over, I don't know if I want to be productive. All that I know is that I feel like I constantly have to defend myself, defend the decisions that I've made." I looked down at the Cynimal in my hands; it looked like a primitive metallic millipede, its multiple legs rippling as it twined itself around and around my wrist.

"You don't look at me like a person. None of you do. At least, not an adult."

"Well in many ways you aren't," Dr. Alyce said, "You are making decisions, in a way, for the first time in your life. We want to protect you."

"No," I laughed humorlessly, it stuck in my throat and hissed through my teeth. "You want to protect your investment. Why did you even let me out of my cage?" I glared at them for a long time, but neither answered. Suddenly, I couldn't stand to be there anymore either. I lay the millipede back in its container and slammed through the door, ran down the sterile halls and outside. My hovercab wasn't there yet, so I climbed into another one that sat idling, water dripping from its' tailpipe.

"Where to, Miss," the driver asked in a bored voice.

"Flower Town," I replied. He looked at me, one eyebrow raised, taking in my tear-mottled make-up and splotchy cheeks.

"You okay, Miss?" he asked.

"I have the fare," I replied.

"That's not what I meant."

I met his eyes in the mirror. "Yes it was," I said. We pulled away from the curb.

JUNE 27

I had the strangest dream last night. I was on the edge of one of the old minefields that still dot the landscape even now after the Great War of Unification is long over. They can't, I'm told, even with all of the technology and know-how easily at hand, ever be sure that they have detonated all of the explosives, or even discern what kind of explosives may be lurking under the ground. I'm not sure that I believe that. I mean, it could be that destroying the fields is too risky, too difficult, but I get the impression sometimes that they like leaving them there. They're reminders of how bad it can get, reminders to all of us to, literally, watch where we step. Anyhow, in my dream I was standing at the edge of one of these massive fields and I was trying to find my way across. I thought I had it sorted, too, but all of a sudden people starting shouting directions from the other side. Basanti was there smiling encouragingly, but I could see the fear in her eyes. Come to think of it, the entire Facility staff was there; Dr. Stevens was scribbling furiously in a notebook, and C.S. Nu's holo'd image wavered in the smoke. Tawny and Dmitri lay together off to one side, naked, their limbs entwined. Mother stood at the wood line, a toddler version of Daisy clinging to her legs and peering out with enormous saucer-like eyes. They were all yelling. "Two steps forward!" "

Go right!"

"No, Left!"

"Stay there, you'll never make it!"

"Hop!"

"Run!"

"Crawl!"

It was a horrible cacophony, confusing. My eyes were watering and my temples throbbed. I was certain, absolutely certain, that if they would just leave me alone I could discern the path. I was almost there, but they wouldn't stop. I was begging and pleading and still they just wouldn't stop. Finally, in desperation I took a step. That's when I exploded.

I burst out of bed, was on my feet before I was fully conscious, my chest heaving, dripping sweat under my layers of nightclothes.

I crossed to the window and flung it open, feeling the rancid but somehow comforting smell of the harbor brush against my face. After a few moments my heartbeat slowed a little. I closed the window and pulled Daisy out of her cage. She woke at once, lively and inquisitive, and I took her back to bed with my. For a while I just lay there, gently stroking the soft silky fur between her eyes with my index finger and feeling her small warm weight on my stomach. After a bit I fed her a treat from the small box that I kept on my nightstand. She sat back. On her haunches and held the treat in her oddly dainty, human-like hands. When she finished she cleaned herself fastidiously from nose to tail and then settled in once more. My eyelids were growing heavy at last, and so I moved her to my pillow.

"Stay Daisy," I yawned. As I slipped from consciousness a memory rose like a bubble from somewhere in the depths of me. I was 15 and in the middle of one of my stays at East. One day they admitted another girl my age. I can't remember her name, but I can see her face as clearly as if she had just left the room. She looked like a porcelain doll, her skin was so fair that it was nearly transparent and white-blonde hair curled at her cheeks and around her eyes, giving her a vaguely rabbit-like appearance. The orderlies and nurses, even Dr. Alyce, encouraged me to befriend the strange pale girl, there were very few of us so young roaming the mildewed halls. She seemed to want my friendship as well, spent her days wafting after me like a tiny ghost, a negative shadow. I, however, was having none of it, something about her pulled like a fishhook in my brain, made my eyeballs itch. When they made her my bunkmate I became hysterical, screaming and clawing, banging my head against the metal bars of the bed until a syringe of clear liquid forced me into dreamless submission. I was fiercely reprimanded that time, lectured and scolded by everyone from the *tre grasa* floor nurse who was hugging the ghost girl to her massive breasts all the way to Dr. Alyce.

"Positive social interactions are important Charlotte," he'd said mildly, "and I know that you know that." I'd refused to answer nor capitulate and was sent to solitary then, confined to the small windowless room with only my thoughts for company. So it was that I wasn't there when it happened that night. When the girl, having apparently stolen a knife from the kitchen, went on a wordless, wild-eyed rampage, starting with the nurse who had comforted her. She cut some six people that night, to the tune of over 300 stitches, before they were able to stop her. We found out later that this wasn't even the first time she'd committed such an act, in fact her tenure on the street began when, as a pampered Center Circle girl of no more than eleven she'd stabbed her new baby brother to death and fled. Still, everyone seemed to either blame me for her sudden violence or forget that they'd chastised me at all. Everyone except Denae.Denae sat behind me later that week, patiently pulling the mats from my curly hair. "She had everyone fooled, Baby" Denae murmured, "everyone except you. You knew what she was. You got good instincts," she'd finished, "You just keep trusting those instincts."

I lay for a moment, eyes closed, on the verge of sleep, wondering why I had conjured up those apparitions after all this time. Then it struck me. "You got good instincts, girl" she had said. Trust. I need to trust myself. At last I know what I had to do. I closed my eyes and slept until morning.

JUNE 29

It took a couple of days to process, but I think that I know what I need to do. I am terrified, anxious, my hands start to tremble every time I start to mentally rehearse my speech. I don't want to do this; I don't want to take this chance. Still, there's a certain level of peace. No matter what happens, after today something will change. If I am, as the voices whisper every now and again, overestimating my value to the experimental team, my life could change for the worse. I could leave the Facility today homeless, jobless, without a penny to my name. Or worse, find myself unable to leave at all, pound in their panic and locked in the white walled prison that is the hospital. *Ho bone.* It wouldn't be the first time for either, and the simple fact is that I can't go on like this anymore. I feel like I'm being ripped in two, torn between trying to determine for the first time, who I really am. I need to determine who Charlotte is under the sickness, and living up to the unfairly biased expectations of the Facility team is hampering that. It's ridiculous. *They* are ones not being productive, and one way or another it has to stop.

That's what all those dreams, all those memories have been trying to tell me, I'm sure of it. Today at the facility I'm going to tell them that I can't live under their thumbs, under fear of disappointment or threat of punishment any longer. They have to trust me; they have to let me learn to trust myself. I can't key in another journal entry terrified that it's going to lead to more conflict. I can't choose my friends or my job or my house to please the snobs at the facility. Especially since the simple fact is that they cannot, up there in their cosseted pampered arch, possibly know what it is like for us. You know? To constantly feel like the square peg in the round hole, to actually be able to feel the waves of condescension washing over you all of the time, and then to find the comfort of community, even if it's just one or two others. To know that they really accept you, as broken and screwed up as you may be. They can take joy in your joys and lesson your sorrows. How, I imagine, they feel all of the time. Dr. Alyce used to understand, kind of; after decades of working part time at East he sees us as people at least, but even he is starting to wear on my nerves. The others? They don't see me as a personal at all, except for where I serve one of their purposes. So, they trust me. . or they let me go. From now on they can step on only when I'm nor following through on my end, or I'm in real, imminent danger. Short of that, they need to stay out of my life. The other option is that I take myself out of this experiment completely. As completely as I can, anyway.

I can't give the brain back but I swear to God the only information they will get will be what they can download. If they want more they can come and get it and I guarantee you I can find my way through the alleys and side rooms of Flower Town better than they. One way or another they will treat me like a real person. One way or another I'm breaking free today.

JULY 4

What a morning! I left this morning terrified, paralyzed,
I came home from the Facility feeling like a 200 kg
weight had been lifted from my shoulders. Relieved.
Elated. I couldn't stop grinning. I got back shortly after
lunch and burst through the door. Tawny and Dmitri
were still asleep or maybe sleeping again. I don't know
which but either way I roused them. They came to
slowly, blearily, Dmitri reached for his pants, filthy and
disreputable and laying in a crumpled heap on the floor,
and pulled an equally battered pack of cigarettes from
the front pocket. He tapped three cigarettes from the
pack and looked at me, one eyebrow raised. I shook my
head and he slid one gently back into the pack. The other
two he lit at one time, blowing twin plumes of smoke
from his nose and handing the other to Tawny. She
inhaled, still shielding her eyes with her bangs. After a
few drags she looked at me. He voice was scratchy with
sleep.

"Que pasa, Ese," she said.

"Get your *azeninoj* out of bed," I grinned, "We are
having a party."

"Whose birthday?" Dmitri asked, looking at me
with hooded eyes.

"Mine." I said.

We left Dmitri in charge of finding guests; as much of an *ektiroas* as he could be he was equally charismatic. There was no one who didn't know him and most smiled, some angrily and some wryly, but smiles all the same, whenever his name was mentioned. Meanwhile, Tawny got dressed and she and I headed down to the open air market down by the harbor. It is still such a strange luxury to be able to buy, well, perhaps not everything I want, but absolutely everything I need and some of my desires. The Facility has been generous, a fact of which I was reminded several times during the course of our talk today, and that I've never denied. Still, I earned it, and they can't forget that either. Anyway, by combining that stipend with my pay from Mr. Don I was able to shop freely for little treats and delicacies that would make the party special in more ways than one. Real strawberries, grown on a rooftop garden; a huge basket of gray, wriggling prawns; flour and sugar that were, I was certain, at least 50% the real thing, not the cheap created replacements that always left a vague oily aftertaste. We brought our spoils home grinning like some sort of culinary pirates, and spent the afternoon working side by side in companionable speechlessness, surrounded by the thumping beat of the music.

Dmitri didn't let us down; I was sliding a shimmery gloss over my lips when the first guests arrived. They came in a trickle and then a flood, smiling, laughing, and carrying bottles and drums, the occasional guitar. I was kept busy running back and forth from the kitchen to the living room, chatting, mingling, making sure the trays of food were full. I turned laughingly from a group that Dmitri was holding in thrall with one of his hilarious and off-color tales and nearly walked right into him. He was new. A stranger. Most people were, of course, to some degree or another, but I'd never even seen his face in passing. With skin so pale I could see the faint tracery of blue where his veins criss-crossed and his shock of bright orange hair, I'd have recognized him if I had. Everything about him from his face, to the intricate cuff he wore on one wrist, to his air of nonchalance was utterly unfamiliar and utterly beautiful. He was tall; so tall that even with his slouch and my heels he had to bend over to be heard over the cacophony that surrounded us.

"Rumor has it that you are the lady of the house," He said. His voice was almost music, tinged heavily with some sort of accent that was as foreign as his face.

"I am," my eyebrows furrowed a bit questioningly, but I found myself smiling as well. He stared at me for a minute with eyes the clear, pale green of the ocean when even the whitecaps and spray had frozen. He seemed to be waiting for me to say something more, but my mind had gone suddenly and damnably blank and so I just stood there smiling like a fool.

"Do you have a name or shall I simply call you 'Lady," he said at last.

"Charlotte."

"Well then, Charlotte," he replied, "this is for you." He reached into the pocket of his shirt and pulled out a palm frond, bent and braided to look like a rose. It was a cheesy gesture, just boyish and silly and sweet enough to be charming and I surprised myself by allowing him to tuck the blossom behind my ear.

"Lady," he said one more time, and bowed slightly before turning on his heel and walking away. We didn't talk for the rest of the night, but I found myself scanning the rooms and the crowd looking for him, and more than once I looked up to find his eyes on me. Finally the last of the partygoers left, and I clutched Tawny by her arms.

"Who was that," I demanded, sure that she had noticed him just as I had.

"Who?" Her eyes were glassy.

"The *belega* with the red hair"
She looked puzzled, "I have no idea, Lotta," she said. Dmitri was lost as well.

I was surprised to find myself on the verge of tears, unreasonable sad, as I went to the kitchen to load the dishes. I was gathering glasses from the sink to put in the washall when I saw it witting on the windowsill, a sleek chrome micronote, its message light blinking steadily. I picked it up, cool in my hand, and pressed the tiny black button on the side. Slowly, his face appeared on the screen. Grinning lopsidedly at the camera, one eyebrow cocked slightly. I pressed the button again, "Aidian," it read, and a number flashed across the screen. I felt my stomach do a somersault and I started to beam. I wrapped my arms around myself and did a silly little dance there in the middle of my devastated and filthy kitchen. It wasn't just him, maybe wasn't even mostly him. It was the feelings that he caused. Giddy. Girlish. Flirty. I had thought that those feelings, even the capability for them had been stolen from me along with so much else back when I was just a girl. I am so *malbenita* surprised, so grateful to discover that they haven't.

I remember, back in primary, we spent a little bit of time learning about Indpendence Day. Apparently it used to be celebrated here, on the anniversary of when the United States that was separated themselves from what was then England. The teacher told us about what an act of savagery, of backwards thinking that was, and I agreed. It's unification that we should strive towards, history has shown us that. Today, though, I stepped away. I fought for my independence, my freedom, and it was amazing. Today I understood those savages a little bit. Today was my Independence Day.

JULY 11

I haven't called him. I haven't called him, but I have dialed his number enough that I now have it memorized. I don't think that I have memorized a number, except for maybe Dr. Alyce's, in my entire life. Every time, though, I shake the call before it rings. Tawny calls me *patosa* and she's probably right, but I can't stop thinking about him, wondering what he's like, replaying our brief conversation over and over again. I know that nothing will come of it; that he was probably just being friendly, or maybe he's some sort of self-styled Tonyboy, charming the women with his smile and his accent just for the game of it, just because he can. Still though. Still, maybe I will flash him tonight. See if I can actually hang on until he answers. But no, what would I even say? What do you say to someone whom you know nothing about? I haven't the first clue.

"Hi, I'm Charlotte. . .no I never finished school. . . no you wouldn't have seen me there. .. or there. . Why? Oh, well, when I'm not throwing house parties I've been generally too petrified to leave my bed, let alone my house and most of the time I'm vacationing in exotic East Circle Psychiatric Center." Exotic. Yeah, that's a word. "Hobbies? Oh you know, I like playing with my Cyrat. Family? Somewhere. .. maybe." Besides, it's not like I have time to date right now anyway, even if by some miracle he decided he wanted me. The conference is in a month, and Mr. Don is still not feeling well. I'm beginning to worry that there is something *terura* going on that he's just not telling me. I've pushed him as hard as I think is wise, harder even, time and again but he refuses to answer, just waves his gnarled hands at me and tells me to get to work. It's that damned rim pride again. Pride and stubbornness , I think it seeps in from the smog. Every last one of us has it. He is, at least, letting me take over more at the cafe. He still opens, he says that after this long he can't sleep past 2 or 3 am anyway, but he's started going home after the lunch rush and clean-up. So, I've been in charge at nights. We hired a temp until after the conference, a new girl who can work the register and take over some of the cleaning and side work that was mine so that I can focus on baking, chatting with the customers, that sort of things. I'm thinking about changing a few other things as well. Just little changes that I think will make a huge difference, bring in a bigger crowd. I haven't gotten up the courage to talk to Mr. Don about them yet; I'm not sure how he will take it. Besides, all of that is going to have to wait until after the conference anyway. For the next four weeks every bit of energy and focus I have has to go to that; I owe them that at least. And Aidian. Maybe a little can go to him.

JULY 14

I don't need a hovercab tonight. I may not ever need one again. Right now I'd swear that my feet don't touch the ground. Why do people do drops? Why do they get drunk? Or fade? This is better than any high I've ever had; better than anything.

I came home from work tonight and found Aidian sitting on my steps. He was slouched over, his elbows on his knees and a cigarette three-quarters gone dangling from his lips. It looked like he'd been sitting there for hours, and when I saw him goose bumps broke out over my arms. *Fek,* but he's beautiful.

"Been waiting long" I asked stupidly.

He startled, his eyes refocusing. "Not nearly as long as I would have," he said.

He got to his feet, his long, lanky arms and legs unfolding like a ladder. He bent down and picked up the long, brightly wrapped package that lay at his feet.

"Here," he said, handing it to me.

"You brought me a present?" As soon as I said it I felt *ridindaj* . Obviously he had. I blushed furiously.

"Actually no," He replied. "I brought it for your furry little accomplice there," and he nodded to Daisy who was peeking, nose twitching, from my shoulder. He held out his hand and she stepped daintily into it. He stroked her gently between her ears with one large, square-tipped finger. I removed the metallic paper and revealed a white board. Black pieces of ply ran across it , breaking it into several small squares.

"What is it?" I asked.

"A lightboard," he said, "You can teach her all sorts of things with it. Pattern recognition," his teeth flashed in the dark "all the latest dance moves."

"Thank you," I said, my voice cracking slightly. We stood there for a while, just looking at each other. At first I couldn't think of anything to say, was struck dumb the same as I had been at my party. As the minutes spun out I felt ridiculous, nervous, and anything I tried to say couldn't find its way around the lump in my throat. I swallowed two, three, times and could feel the tears start to well in my eyes.

"Would you go for a walk with me?" he asked, just as I was turning to flee inside. I nodded and ran to my room where I deposited my things, including Daisy and her new gift, onto my bed. "Stay Daisy," I said, knowing that she would curl up and sleep until I returned. I stopped for a second in front of the mirror, fluffing my hair and sliding a little bit of polish on my lips. My color was high, pink touching my cheeks, my almond eyes glittering. Worried that I'd already taken too much time, that he'd have changed his mind, I rushed back out to where he was waiting.

"Ready" he asked, and offered me his elbow like we were characters in a movie from a century or more ago. I slipped my arm in his; it was warm, and I could feel the slight bulge of his bicep on my arm, and off we went.

We wandered around Flower Town for hours, with no real destination in mind. Every now and then his shoulder or hip would bump against mine, and every time it did I got chills. He smelled delicious. It was a weird combination of cigarette smoke and aftershave and some kind of dark-smelling oil that should have been repulsive but somehow was not. I should have been frightened or at least anxious as well, after all I know better than most what happened in Flower Town after midnight. It was all still going on, all around us, the rat-faced men with their knowing leers, the runners with their fast feet and even faster hands, the screams of love, or rage, or pain, there were all still there, all around us, as much of a part of the town as the sea air, the graffiti, the Japanese characters left over from when this was a cherished and coveted vacation spot. Somehow, though, with him, it didn't matter. I should've gotten tired, too, or felt embarrassed, or run out of things to say but I didn't do any of that either. I didn't! I'm not tired still.

We talked about everything, I mean about absolutely everything under the sun; I told him things that I've never told anyone before, and he told me a lot too. I couldn't hear enough. Of course, listening to his voice he could read the Unification Scroll and I would be mesmerized. This was even better. As it turns out he's not from Flower Town. He's not even from the Rim. He live about three circles in, which shows how much he really wanted to see me because trips from there to here don't come cheap. The powers that be don't much care for us to mingle, I don't think. He's a Maker. He builds these amazing sculptures out of everything from industrial equipment to circuits to bits of torn down buildings, He's amazing. At least, I imagine that he is. He told me about his work and it sounds absolutely stunning. That's how he thought to make me the palm frond rose. That's just the kind of thing he does, ken? He doesn't make much off of his art yet, though, and so he also works as a hacker, all very secretive and under the table sorts of assignments. Finding out about that was the only uncomfortable part of the whole evening. As soon as he told me I felt cold all over, like someone had dumped a pitcher of November seawater over me. I yanked my arm out of his and folded it with the other protectively over my chest. I picked up my pace so that I was walking a few steps ahead of him.

"Charlotte," he called, and even then I couldn't help but smile a little at the way my name sounded coming out of his mouth. "May I speak with you?" I slowed, the clopping of my heels softening and then stopping altogether, and waited until he was in front of me.

"A hacker" I spat, looking at his knees so he wouldn't see me cry. "Really? A hacker."

"What's the problem?" he said, "are you opposed to. .. slightly criminal activity?"

"No, I was just stupid enough to think you were interested in me, not just my brain."

"Lady," he said, and lifted my chin so that I was looking into his eyes. "I won't lie, that's what brought me to your party. I'd been hearing whispers about you for a while, rumors. I wanted to see this wonder with my own two eyes, and when I heard that *trompi* talking at the Harbor about your party, well, I couldn't resist. That's why I came to the party, but these," and he touched my eyebrows, "and this," he rubbed his thumb lightly against my lip until I smiled, "that smile, that glorious, life-affirming smile of yours, that's why I came back." He bent over and kissed me then, slowly at first. His lips were warm and slightly rough and they opened only slightly, questioningly. One hand was still on my face, the other he wrapped around my wait and rested his fingers on the small of my back and suddenly I pushed myself up to my tiptoes, throwing my body against his. Our teeth clicked quietly, but I didn't care. We kissed until I was lightheaded with the need to breathe.

"Bloody hell, Bird," he whispered when we finally parted.

Bloody hell. Bloody hell is right.

JULY 24

Perfect. Aidian. He is absolutely perfect. He came into the café tonight, just to see me. He was such a gentleman about it, too. I was busy when he first came in and so he just sat at a table waiting until I was done with the customers. I could see him looking at me, though, sneaking glances out of the corners of his eyes, and it made me flush enough that one of the customers asked if I was all right. When, finally, they were gone, he stood up and I came around the corner. He gave me a quick hug even though I was covered in flour and soup and who knows what else, and a kiss on the cheek. I could feel the stubble of his beard even though it is so pale that I can't see it at all. Don liked him, I could tell. He came shuffling over and asked if I was going to introduce him to my boyfriend. I waited for Aidian to correct him, to tell him that we were "just friends" or "hanging out," but he didn't. He just grinned down at me and so I introduced them and Aidian shook his hand and soon they were chatting like they'd known each other forever. Aidian was so polite and asking Don all sorts of questions about him and the café. I learned a lot of things that I hadn't known just by listening to them. When it was time to go back to work, Aidian sat there and worked on some of his art. He takes apart broken comps and uses gears and bits of conduit and makes these amazing sculptures and jewelry out of them. He's incredibly talented. The sculptures are gorgeous, and I could watch him using his big, square-fingered hands making these tiny pieces forever. Finally, Don let me go home and Aidian reached down and took my hand. He tucked my arm around his and held my hand that way, and even though my legs are shorter than his, it seemed like we were even walking in step. We talked for hours, strolling around Flower Town, and even when we were in the rougher spots I felt safe, just being with him. He does that, just gives off this aura of "safe," and that's just amazing for me. I've so rarely felt safe about anything. And he knows so much about everything, art, and music and science. After a while it got late, so he walked me home. When we got to the door I turned to give him a kiss goodbye. I planned on stopping at one, I did, but somehow I just couldn't let go. I couldn't stop. I didn't want to. It feels so good to have his arms around me, his hands at my waist, and his mouth against mine. So, we stood on the porch, until my lips were slightly swollen, and the mosquitoes drove me inside. "See you tomorrow," he said, as he turned away. Tomorrow!

JULY 30

There are certain things, certain concepts, that you give up on when you've had a life like mine. Eventually you reach a point when you realize that there are experiences and feelings that are simply out of your grasp. You don't notice their absence, really. After all, they were never there. For me, romance was pretty high on that list. Romance requires dating, first of all, and I've never really dated. Not beyond the most casual of relationships. And even if I had it seems like most of the men that I've met aren't interested real intimacy. Sex? Absolutely. But intimacy? Actually connecting with someone, caring about their wants and needs and interests? Neh. Which makes what happened this morning so much incredible. Aidian showed up just before sunrise, which really pissed Tawny and Dmitri off. They didn't say much, but I could see it in Tawny's eyes when she came pounding on my door to let me know that he was there. He waited on the porch, smoking, until I'd washed my face and snapped on a clean shirt.

"This is a nice surprise," I murmured, after we'd kissed hello. I could feel his stubble, still invisible in its blondeness, scratching lightly at my chin.

"It's about to get nicer," he replied. He stood, and picked up this rucksack, giant and battered, a leftover from the Unification war. It was bulging. He took my hand and we walked down to the old amusement park. The light was gorgeous. That blue that washes everything right before the sun starts to break, and the breeze coming in over the water was cool and crisp. When we got down to the sand, black and stained but still sand, he reached into the bag and spread out an old, worn blanket. It had been washed so many times the fabric had little nubs, and it smelled like him. I buried my face in it and inhaled. He hit a few buttons on his microcomp, and soft music flowed out. Then he stretched out and pulled me down beside him, both of us looking out over the ocean. I could feel his body pressed against mine and God I'm always so aware of him. My body, starved for any kind of affection, soaks up his touch like a sponge, and I can feel his touch coming while his hand is still inches away. His head was propped on one hand, and the other was wrapped around my stomach. Occasionally, he would pull me even closer, pressing my tightly against him. We couldn't get close enough. We can't ever. Sometimes I just want to crawl inside him, ken? It sounds strange, I know, but I want to get rid of any space, any distance, and just feel him all around me. I could feel him run his lips across the back of my neck from time to time and after a while I started to turn towards him, sometimes the need to kiss him is as present as another person. It grows in my mind and clouds it until there is nothing else. Just then the sun crested the water, spilling this perfect golden trail all the way to where we were lying. It was incredible, and romantic, and I can see us being just like this for always. In fact, I can't imagine us being any different.

AUGUST 1

The conference, the conference, the *stulta*, *fekantá*, conference! I would be incredibly happy if I never again heard about that event. I wish now that I had never agreed to go. I did, though, and I've regretted it ever since. Never more, though, than since I've been wait Aidian. I don't want to leave him, not for that long, especially to go and parade around, talking to a bunch of *enuigaj geniuloj*. It's not that I don't think that it's important; I know that it is, but I have been waiting my whole life to be able to go out and actually live and that's what I want to do. I want to bake cookies, and play with Daisy, and party with my friends, and be with my boyfriend and just be left alone. I'm happy. That's what matters more than anything. I don't see how they can claim that they are oh-so-invested in my happiness, but they want me to give up what I'm doing that actually brings me joy in order to go and give a bunch of presentations that are causing me a lot of stress and anxiety and tears. I've cried so many times the last couple of days. Don is pretty upset as well. He's gotten used to having me around, I think, and the idea of a temp doesn't appeal to any of us. I tried to use that at the Facility today, hoping to appeal to their senses of duty and obligation, but no dice. To them, my primary duty and obligation is to the Facility and to others who may someday benefit from the surgery that I underwent. I tried a lot of different approaches, actually. I talked about the detrimental effect that the conference was having on my emotional wellbeing. I talked about the costs associated, about Tawny and Dmitri. Aidian. None of it worked, and at the end Basanti of all people snapped at me.

"Stop, Charlotte," she cried. "Just stop. So little is being asked of you anymore. You must give us this thing. Do not try to manipulate me!"

"Manipulate *you*" I yelled. "Maybe you should stop manipulating me. I don't want to do this."

She was so patronizing. She said that doing things that we don't want to do was part of being an adult; that we must understand that we our wants must be balanced with our obligations. As if I didn't already know that, hadn't known that for years. We went back and forth, a conversation that left us both red-faced by the end.

Today was supposed to be the last big meeting before the conference, and Basanti and I spent most of the time arguing. She phoned ahead to the rest of the team and asked for more time, which they granted, begrudgingly I have no doubt. Once we'd taken a few minutes to calm down, she brought out a microcomp, bigger than the palm of her hand, and tried to go over the itinerary with me; where I'd be going when, what I was expected to do, what the trip there and back would be like. I couldn't focus though, didn't really want to. If I'm really as obligated, as trapped, as she says, does it really matter what they have planned for me? I'll just have to deal with it, whatever it is. So I tuned her out, thought about Aidian and the dinner party we will be having at my place later this week, tried to nod in all of the right places. I must not have done too *spektakloriča* of a job, though, because I could see the color rising in her face before too long. "I need you to listen," she snapped. "I am," I barked back. I wasn't, but I wasn't about to tell her that. Eventually, she just beamed the information to my microcomp and I promised her that I would read it when I had the time, when I was in a better mind frame. She sighed, but agreed. After that, she walked me down to Dr. Alyce. I was on edge, frightened of another confrontation, but more than ready to engage in one, as angry as I was. Surprisingly, though, the meeting wasn't really much of anything. He told me about patient-client privilege, and how in this circumstance it would have to be waived, in order to create the most relevant presentation. He told me that he'd be sharing things from our sessions. I wasn't too sure what to think of that; there are things that I have told him that I don't necessarily want public knowledge, ken? And so we talked for a while, and he let me set the parameters of what he would reveal. I told him that he could hint at my trauma, could speak vaguely, but could not go into detail about what happened to me when I was living with Mother. He agreed. I also said that I didn't want him disparaging Flower Town. That's when the meeting became difficult; what I view as him degrading my home he views as "providing context," and so we split hairs and negotiated until we could agree on a, how did he put it, "agreeable verbiage." I spent the whole time, though, feeling like I was being manipulated, but I couldn't quite put my finger on why. He was giving me, ultimately, exactly what I wanted. Still, my stomach was tied up in knots and I was incredibly angry with him by the time I signed the forms releasing my information. I was, for the first time ever, actually kind of excited to go and see Dr. Stevens. At least with her I could count on her being rude and perfunctory, and I wasn't let down. Cybers came in first, and went through the preliminaries, testing my heart rate, reflexes, and blood pressure and chirping as the data was uploaded directly into the records system. Dr. Stevens came in just for a quick moment and explained that I would be expected to sit in on four of her panels, before having me sign some medical release forms and ordering some CT scans and X-Rays. That was it for her. C.S. Nu was last, and I spent more time with his aides than I did the man himself, helping them to prepare for their presentation with Daisy. That part was actually kind of fun; I guess when you're on the bottom of the totem pole you still remember how to talk to real people. I like those kids a lot, even though they don't realize how very lucky they are to even have this opportunity, and when they get to squabbling about how this professor mistreats them, or how long the hours are, there is this little, vindictive part of me that just wants to punch me in the face.

Finally, I was done. I had told Mr. Don that I would go in for a while and help to train the temp help who will be taking my place while I am gone. So, I did, but I didn't stay very long. I want to help Don, I do, but I'd had a really, really long day and I just didn't feel like I could do much for anyone else. And the girl is really not my kind of person. She strikes me as too hard, hard enough to not be strong anymore, but brittle. Not in the vulnerable sort of way, though, the opposite. She strikes me as the kind that would try to take someone down with her. After I tried to explain the register to her three times and she just would not listen, I could feel myself losing my patience. I was taking my time to help her; the least she could do was listen to me a little bit, that was why she was there after all. So, I told Don that I had a headache, it wasn't a lie precisely, and went home. I don't think that I imagined the look of disappointment in his eyes, but I couldn't do anything about it; the girl wasn't going to learn anything, and I'd given all that I could for the day. I got home to a bit of a mess; nothing huge, but after years of squalor I like to keep my place clean. I tried to talk to Tawny about it, but she said that she and Dmitri weren't feeling well, that they must have gotten some sort of virus, so I just went to my room and shut the door and that's where I've been, playing with Daisy, trying desperately to pretend that this conference doesn't exist.

AUGUST 6

Aidian and I went out again last night, after I got off of work. I knew that I shouldn't- that I'd be tired today, and I am, but somehow it's not as bad as I thought it would be. It's odd. I don't seem to need sleep like I usually do – or food either. I'll stay awake until 2 or 3 in the morning, chatting on our comps about anything and everything, look around at 8pm to realize that I haven't eaten yet. The only thing that I can't seem to get enough of is him. I hang up the phone with difficulty, and have to fight the urge to pick it back up, to call him again, get a few minutes more. We get together and I can't stop touching him. I want to soak him up through my hands. So, I said yes, of course, when he asked, and after I closed the café we climbed into a cab and soon we were soaring west.

I could see the lights long before we arrived, blue and green and pink and yellow, swirling and dipping and flashing. "A carnival" I cried, clutching at his arm, "Oh, Aidian it's a carnival." I hadn't been to a carnival since I was a girl, before everything started to really fall apart. Aidian grinned and pulled me close, kissing my temple. "I love to see you happy," he said. And I was trying to do everything at the same time, see the lights and kiss him back and keep my balance as the cab banked to land and so I missed and our foreheads bumped. We were still laughing as we stepped out of the cab. It was magnificent, just *imponega*.

At first it was a little intimidating, the crowds, all of the barkers shouting at me. It made me feel too prominent, too visible. Aidian was unfazed though, even shouted back a couple of times, playing around. At one booth, he let himself be goaded into playing a game. I tried to talk him out of it, those games a rigged, a waste of money, everyone knows this. "I gotta impress my girl," Aidian shouted at the heavily tattooed man running the game. "Don't worry I know the trick," he whispered in my ear. He walked up to the table. A few feet away, some holographic cats flickered and buzzed Aidian pressed his thumb against the payment pad and the man handed him a ball. "Though guy!" the barker crowed. "We got ourselves a tough guy. What' ya say, lad, you tough enough to take out a little alley cat?" Aidian flexed pulled the ball back to his ear. I could see the bulge of his bicep and felt a shiver run up and down my spine. He threw, aiming not for the hologram, but at the table just beneath it. The rickety structure shook and the projector toppled over, winking the cat out of existence. The barker was mad at the loss, I could tell, but he took it well, handing over a stuffed animal nearly as tall as I was. The new creature in tow, we walked on.

We stopped at a few of the food booths next, and Daisy ran out of my pocket to sample some of the goodies, great handfuls of pocky, heavily seasoned meat on a stick, it was all amazing.

Eventually we came around a corner to an area that was almost deserted. "Kid's Kingdom" the flashing lights displayed. There weren't many kids about, not that time of night, and so we almost walked past. Then I saw the sign for the potting zoo. "Real animals," it exclaimed. I tried to hide my excitement, it seemed juvenile, but Aidian saw it anyway. "Do you want to go?" he asked. I stammered, not wanting to look foolish, but I hadn't seen a real live animal in so long. "Let's go," he said. And so I went in there and there was a cow! It was a real, live cow, almost extinct after the battle of Unification. It was small, just a little more than a baby and it was so sweet! It came right up to the fence and stuck its muzzle out and it was so, so soft, like velvet. Its eyes were huge, limpid, and I sat for a full ten minutes, nose to nose, just scratching it's jaw. "It was a cow" I must have told

Aidian a hundred times after we left. "A real cow."

By that time it was late, so late that my eyes were starting to droop, and so we headed out. Before we left, though, we stopped at the statue booth. It was tiny, so small that we had to squish in together, and just before it scanned us Aidian turned my face towards his and kissed me. A couple of flashes of blue light and by the time we had disentangled ourselves our stature hand been printed. I stared at it for a minute, stroking the ridges and curves gently before storing it in my bag. I started to doze on the cab, my head resting on Aidian's shoulder. "Aidian," I asked sleepily, "why do you like me so much?" I could feel as smile against my face. "Because you are beautiful, and brave, and secretly joyful and that joy is contagious. It makes me want to be around you just to get more of it, to help create more of it. You are strong and vulnerable all at the same time, and that's a incredibly combination. I want to go on this journey with you. See who you become." Soon, I could feel the descent of the cab, and I reached up and kissed him, a long soft kiss just on the edge of his lips. "Thank you," I whispered. "Anytime."

AUGUST 11

Well, tonight was awkward. It was awkward and little bit horrible and I still don't exactly understand what happened. All that I know is that I don't understand how these people, people who I care about a lot, could have done this to me. They understand that I can't have awkward right now, not with the conference in a matter of days. At this moment, I need all of the joy and relaxation that I can get because the simple fact is that I'm terrified. That's why I had planned this stulta party to begin with, to have something light and joyful and instead it all just fell apart.

I had brought the idea up to Aidian about a week ago; that I thought maybe it was time that he met Tawny and Dmitri and they got to know him. They are all huge parts of my life, ken? I thought that it would be nice if they could be friends with each other. And so I had built it all up in my mind. I used money that I probably shouldn't have spared to bring in some sushi from one of the few places on the rim that I think might actually be serving fish, and untainted fish at that. I pictured us sitting around the table, sharing spicy rolls and maybe some drinks, and laughing together. I figured that Dmitri and Aidian would play some music and maybe sing together, and Daisy would run around all of us, taking joy how she does at our happiness. That's not what happened, not at all.

Aidian showed up on time, so freshly showered that his hair still curled, a little damp, around his corner, and carrying a six-pack of beer in one hand and some flowers – I'm getting used to receiving flowers by now and have to admit that I don't love it any less than I did the first time, in the other. I hugged him for a long time, trying to memorize like I always do the way that it feels with his arm around me, and kissed him right at the edge of his mouth, the spot where only the very corners of our lips touched. He tried to kiss me again, deeper that time, but I pulled away after just a minute, sure that Dmitri and Tawny would be arriving any second, and I didn't want them to feel uncomfortable. They didn't show. They didn't show and didn't show and Aidian and I just sat at the dinner table in the kitchen, making stilted small talk, while the sushi got gradually warm. Eventually I got up and put it in the refrigerator, knowing that it wouldn't really stop it from wilting, but feeling like I had to do something. They finally came in, an hour late or more, and I could tell as soon as they walked through the door that they were on Drops. Their eyes were dilated and they, Tawny especially, couldn't stop giggling. They sat down at the table after staggering and wandering about for a little while, bumping into one another, but once they were there they wouldn't eat. Drops are like that, they get rid of your appetite, but still I couldn't believe it.

Aidian tried, as he and I plowed our way through what was suddenly far too many sushi rolls, he tried to make small talk. It was no use, though. When Tawny did answer, she was sullen, snarky, answering in sarcastic one and two-word bursts. She kept cutting her eyes at me, making these little comments that were supposed to be funny about how no one had been able to get me into bed, how he was navigating "Uncharted territory," and just started calling him Sailor. I hated it. She knows. She knows how private I am about the fact that I don't' get intimate with anyone, and why. Then she started talking about him being Inner Circle, and having as many siblings as he has, kept making references to Papo plianto, and no matter how loudly she laughed and punches his shoulder, I didn't really believe that she was joking, not really. Dmitri didn't speak at all until dinner was over, just sat there staring through the cigarette smoke that he kept blowing towards the ceiling. After dinner, though, once we had retired to the couches, he suddenly came to life in the worst possible way. I could see it happen. He looked at Aidian, his eyes narrowed, as if he were noticing him for the first time, for all I know he was. "So, what's your intention with our little Charlotte, *suviče riča knabo?*" he asked. "'Cause I'm a little protective, you know, Lotta and I go way back," and he sauntered over and kissed me, far too long and far too wet, on my jaw line, staring at Aidian the whole time. Aidian didn't answer, and I begged him with my eyes to just not do anything. Dmitri didn't get like this, not often anyway, but when he is as far gone as he was tonight, its best just not to mess with him. He can get mean, has put a couple of people in the hospital, and I could tell by the way that his eyes flashed and his knuckles were white that he'd had way too much to be trifled with. Aidian, finally, had had enough. "Right now, I intend to take her for a walk," he said, and he untangled me from Dmitri's grasp. I could hear their laughter follow us as we headed down the street.

Aidian was upset, I could tell. His strides were longer than usual and his jaw was set, even while he rolled and smoked his cigarette. I could feel the panic start to rise in my chest, tightening around my heart. "Please don't be mad at me," I said in a small voice. He stopped, and I could see the muscles in his cheek tightening and releasing. I could feel the tears start to rise and burn in my eyes.

"I'm not mad at you, Bird," he said at last. "I'm mad for you. I'm angry that your friends would treat you like that."

I don't know why, but suddenly I had to defend them, had to convince him that these people, my best friends, weren't what they'd presented them to be.

"They're not usually like that," I said. They don't usually do things like that. Really, they're nice, and fun and-"

"They're common." He said shortly. "And they embarrassed you."

"They were just nervous." I replied.

Aidian was quiet for a long time. All I could hear was the blood rushing in my ears.

"You're better than that, Love." He said. I didn't know what to say. Part of me wanted to just take the compliment. The other part of me couldn't wonder, if they were low and common like he said, what did that make me? After all, I was the messed up one in the group. I was the one who had to have my *fikfek* brain replaced. They just. .. like to have fun every now and then.

Aidian exhaled heavily and pulled me close. I could feel his breath tickling my neck as he ran his lips lightly against the tender skin behind my ear. "I wish you could see yourself," he murmured into my hair. "I wish you could see how amazing you are."

"So you're not mad?" I asked.

He kissed me between my eyes. "No," he said, "not mad."

"And you'll give them another chance?" I asked. I could feel the muscles in his back tense when I asked it.

"One thing at a time, Bird," he said. "Let's get through the conference, first, then we will work on them."

"Okay," I said, lacing my fingers through his. We walked along in silence. We stayed out a lot longer than I had planned, hoping that by the time we got home they would have crashed. It worked. I came home to a silent house, but now, while I'm lying here in bed, I wish there was something to distract me from my thoughts. I just. .. I thought it would be so nice.

AUGUST 15

I'm not ready. It's tomorrow morning, and I'm not ready. I must have packed and unpacked my suitcase at least ten times, and with the exception of Daisy, who I know that I have to bring, I have no idea if any of it is right. I don't have anything nice. All that I have are Utiliclothes, and I honestly didn't think about it until tonight. They said at the Facility that they would provide me with clothing for the dinner parties and whatnot, but does that mean that they will provide me what the other clothes as well, or is that on me? The Utiliclothes are me, that's for sure, they've been my unofficial uniform for over a decade, still I don't know what or not that 's the image that they want me to portray. Should I have prepared speeches. There I things I want to say, ken? Concepts that I want people to understand, and suddenly I don't know if I have the words to get them across. I should have prepared something. Don isn't happy with the temp. I'm not either, but I don't know what can be done about it at this point. I told Tawny to check in on him and she has promised that she will, but still I'm nervous. I don't even know where exactly we are going. I was going to read the handouts, I kept meaning to, but it was all so big and scary and I thought I'd have more time. Suddenly, though, I'm out. If Aidian weren't coming tonight, I think that I might just go to bed, just go to sleep and turn the volume down on the world until it is morning and there's nothing that I can do except go and get in the cab. He is, though, and that's my saving grace. He will be here in an hour and when he asked me how long it had been since I'd had anything to eat I wasn't paying enough attention to lie and so I told him. He said that I need to be ready to go out for dinner, because I have to eat. He's right. I know that he's right, but I don't want to. Going out among a bunch of people is nearly the last thing that I want to do. The only thing that appeals less, other than going to the conference, is to have to putter around the kitchen, flashing meals or cleaning up after. Tawny and Dmitri will be there, of course, where else would they be? They're having a hard time right now; with both of them being out of work I know they're always a little scared about how they're going to make ends meet. Somehow, me leaving makes them even more nervous and so I have them a hundred dollars to help get them through the next week. It seemed to make Tawny uncomfortable; I know she doesn't want to take things from me. Or at least I knew that. I don't think that I imagined the shine in her eyes as she grabbed the units out of my hand. It made me wonder. A lot of things are making me wonder lately, but I'm trying hard just to trust. After all, she's like me. She was born and raised like me and has known me forever. We are an us, and if I can't trust her, who can I trust. So I will, but sometimes it's hard. Of course, right now, everything is hard, so I'll just chalk it up to that. I'm even a little stressed about Aidian coming over tonight. He will be staying over so that he can see me off in the morning and I don't know that I'm ready. Even though I'm the one who asked him, I just don't know. I want to take him into my room, just so he doesn't have to deal with Tawny and Dmitri, but I don't' want to give him the wrong idea. Sure, it's possible just to cuddle in someone's bed, I've done it plenty, but there are certain connotations, and even if he's not expecting sex, lying in bed can give such intimacy. I love him. I do, which is terrifying enough in itself, but I don't' know that I'm ready for intimacy, ken? I guess I can just add that to the list of things I'm not ready for. Here's the thing, though, you can say that you can't handle something. You can scream it from the top of the stackflats. But whether or not you're ready, whether or not you feel like you can handle it, life goes forward. You don't' get a break just by saying that you need one. Besides, I've spent too much time running. I will walk into my future, step by step, even if my legs shake.

AUGUST 16

He loves me! I'm in the hovercab flying to the hop pad and I know that somewhere inside I'm terrified, but right now I can't feel it. Which is weird, because right now I can feel everything else. I can feel the rushing of my blood as it buzzes through my fingertips, making them tingle. I can feel the stupid grin that keeps crossing my face. I can feel the laughter bubbling up inside my chest, and the feel of his lips on mine the last time that he kissed me and the voice that keeps chanting in my head, the voice that tells me that I can rest now. I can rest and be happy and feel safe because he loves me and so I am home. I have found sanctuary at last. It's restful, but exhilarating at the same time. How could it not be, when I can still remember his lips on my neck, his breath on my back. I want to laugh and cry and scream and nap all at the same time. I've been in love with him for a while. I think the first time it crossed my mind was the night he sat talking with Don, though there was this whisper that's been there since the moment that we met. I tried to ignore it; I didn't feel like it could bring me anything but harm, but ever since he handed me that silly rose there was this voice inside me saying "I know you. I may not know you, but I KNOW you." What I didn't know was whether or not he felt it too. Part of me thought that it couldn't be possible. That I was this charity case, or that he felt somehow obligated because I cared about him, or that it was all just in my head. But now I know that it's real. It's real because he loves me too. We woke up this morning after only the third alarm, and he started the coffee while I took a quick shower. He met me at the bathroom door with a steaming cup and a kiss and we stood there, just holding each other, until my microcomp blared again, shrilling the alarm I set to remind me to go outside. "I don't want to go," I said. He kissed the tip of my nose. "I don't' want you to," he said, "but you're doing a good thing, Charlotte. You'll do great." He walked me outside to where a cab was already waiting, and while the driver loaded my bags I turned around for one more hug. That's when I saw it. He was holding out a bracelet. It was the most amazing thing that I had ever seen. Chunks of green motherboard, faceted, and bent to look like gems, sparkled up and down the length of it. In between the gems were tiny bits of conduit, bent and soldered into filigree,. And it was all held together with these tiny bolts. It was stunning, incredible, and he took my hand and laid it on his chest. I could feel his heartbeat as he fastened the bracelet into place. "To remember me by," he said and his accent was thick with the morning and. . something else? Could it be that he was nervous too? Intimidated? By me? I don't know. I can't believe that, but whatever it was, he got over because he drew me close and kissed me one last time and that's when he said it. That he loved me. And suddenly it was as thought the sun came out from behind a cloud. There wasn't time to savor it, not properly, because I had to go, but I'll be savoring it until we are together again. Somehow the next five days feel like they could be five years. I wanted him to go. I wanted him to be with me so badly. I've gotten used to having him around, and am not sure what I would do without him, but there was no room for him on the hop. "authorized personnel only" they said. So, five days it is. I'll be counting the minutes. . .

AUGUST 16 (LATER)

I've not even been here 12 hours and I'm already a disappointment. I don't' know why I'm surprised. I'm sure Dr. Stevens isn't; I could see it in her eyes. I'm supposed to be at the Official Opening Tapas and Wine, as it says on the schedule. I was, for a little while, not doing incredibly well, but at least holding it together, especially considering how the day began.

I climbed into the shuttle at the hop, and almost before I could sit down the aerial assistant was upon me. She pulled thick straps, lined with some sort of soft synthetic, right around my wrists and ankles, and I could feel my heart start to pound, my body grow cold. It was when she held out this mouth guard, a small piece of fitted black rubber, that I started to protest. At first I just nodded, pulling away, but the Cyber didn't seem to understand. Instead she just brought the bit closer to my mouth. I shook my head more violently. "No," I choked, "No, please." The Cyber didn't relent, just started to chant a preprogrammed mantra. "You must put in your oral protections," she chirruped. "You must put in your oral protection." "It's okay, Charlotte," Basanti said beside me, patting my leg. But it wasn't. "I won't," I said. The Cyber didn't change expression. She just turned away, striding up the short, narrow hallway of the shuttle, and disappeared behind a door. Soon, another woman appeared, this one real. "Can you tell me what the problem is," she asked. I could tell that she was real, because I could hear the irritation in her voice. We were supposed to have left one minute before. "I don't' want to wear that<" I answered, nodding at the mouthpiece that the cyber, no having miraculously reappeared, still carried in her hand. "You have to, it's regulations. You agreed to it when you bought your ticket." I was aghast. "No, " I exclaimed. "No I did not!" The official looked at Basanti who nodded at me. "It was in the packet that I beamed to you," she said softly. "The one you insisted on signing." "Well, I've changed my mind" I said. The muscles in his jaw hardened. "If you we do not leave in the next three minutes, we have lost our window," she said. "You won't make it to the conference any other way," Dr. Stevens said. Dr. Alyce and C.S. Nu exchanged places, and my old friend put his hand reassuringly on the arm that Basanti wasn't patting. "We will get you through this," He said. Basanti nodded. I cried, could feel my whole body shaking, but still I opened my mouth. The Cyber darted forward and suddenly the guard was in place. I tried to spit it out, but it was too late, tried to scream, and my words only bubbled against it. Then, I took a breath. And I could smell it. I could smell that rancid black rubber and I started to shriek because suddenly I was back in there, in the ECT therapy room at East and the shuddering of the shuttle became the shuddering of my body and as we took off I was slammed against the seat. But I wasn't there anymore. I was bracing myself for the shock to wrack my body as we tried in vain to remove the memories, to train my brain and body how to cope with life, knowing that any jolt could be the jolt from which I would never come back. I tried to pull my arms and legs out, to get out of the seat, to get off of that table, to get anywhere, to do anything, but I couldn't move them. I was trapped, pinned, against my will. They wouldn't let me go. I was powerless. And with that knowledge the scenery changed. I wasn't in the ECT therapy room anymore. Suddenly I was in my mother's stack that very first time. The rubber guard became a man's shirt, stinking with his sweat, shoved in my mouth after mother yelled from her bedroom, "shut that bitch up." My hands were pinned down by my sides, my whole tiny body pressed into the couch and I couldn't breathe. I was dying, I was sure and my eyes were closed but still it was there. And then, in what seemed like an instant, I could hear the voices all around me.

"Come back, Charlotte. Come back to us." Not him then, but Dr. Alyce.

"She's coming around," Dr. Stevens with a hypodermic in my arm.

I realized then that I wasn't restrained. Hadn't been, it seemed for a while. Still, I was gripping the armrests so hard that I couldn't let go. My hands were frozen.

"Help me," I said softly. "Please."

Gently, oh so gently, Dr. Alyce pulled me away from the seat, carried me in his arms. "Are we still on the ground?" I murmured, blinking as the stacks gave way to a spaceport, covered in sleek black cabs.

"We are there, Charlotte," he said. "We landed almost an hour ago."

"And we are very late," C.S. Nu said from behind me. Someone shushed him. They took me straight to my room, moving in a circle around me to attempt to hide me from the photographers who appeared, seemingly, out of nowhere.

"No pictures, please, no photographs," Basanti called out, trying to make her voice sound stern. Once we were in the room, Dr. Stevens pulled out her full kit. I felt three different injections before I could think clearly, became aware of the clammy sweat that covered my body. Basanti stayed with me for the opening ceremonies, and Dr. Alyce came and went, both doing their best to soothe me and, slowly but surely, I came back into now. Eventually, I convinced them that I could attend the dinner. Basanti pointed to a dress already hanging in the closet and disappeared. By the time that she came back I was sitting in the bed where I had been, staring at the cloth in dismay.

"Charlotte," she said, "Are you not coming?"

I looked at her, tears sliding down my face. I have never felt so out of place, so ignorant in all of my life. *Stulta. Ača.* I nodded towards the dress where it lay on the bed. It was, essentially, just one long piece of fabric, alternating between opaque and sheer. "I don't know how to put it on," I said. Basanti picked up the fabric and with a few wraps and tucks it was snugged into place. "Better?" she asked. I nodded. There wasn't time for more, because just then there was a knock on the door and we had to run down to the reception. And I was doing fine. I was. Shaken, exhausted, but I was doing all right and would have been fine except for that woman. All of them, really, looking at me with judgment in their eyes, looking for me to make a mistake, but her most of all. I'd rehearsed answers, practiced for weeks how I should respond to all of the things that people might ask. What I didn't prepare for, though, was people ignoring me altogether. They had questions for Dr. Stevens, sure, and Nu, even Dr. Alyce, but they talked about me like I wasn't even there; like I was some sort of inanimate object to be stared at, manipulated, but a real person? *Neh.* Not one. As the night went on it got worse. I could feel the room start to close in and my vision narrow until I knew without looking that my pupils were the size of dimes. Still, I held fast. I kept it together. Then she came up, clicking daintily over to us in her giant heels, and her hawk like nose and God she looked just like Mother. Like Mother would if she had been some rich, inner circle inaĉo anyway. And she looked at me like I was nothing. No, like I was worse than nothing. She looked at me like I was some beggar on the street, covered in filth and asking her for money. Her lip raised in a sneer. The sedatives had worn off, and I could feel my blood start to buzz in my wrists. I sipped a bit of wine and swallowed hard. "Can she communicate?" she asked Dr. Stevens, looking right past me. Dr. Stevens' eyes widened.

"Of course she can, Moriah," Dr. Stevens replied, her lips pressed into a tight line. "Her damage was emotional, not intellectual, as well you know." The two women hated each other; it was as purely of a chemical thing as I had seen, but somehow I knew they couldn't- or wouldn't- take their hatred out on one another. No, if there was going to be bloodshed, it would be mine. I didn't have long to wait;.

"Indeed," the woman said, "You've done good work, but I have to admit that I was surprised that you didn't pick a more. . .appealing candidate."

Suddenly, I couldn't take anymore. After everything that had happened today something in my just snapped. I watched as the woman melted into my mother, her nose thickened slightly, her chin became more pointed. It was more than a resemblance, they had become one.

"Talk to ME," I yelled, louder than I had intended. The chatter around me quieted. Even the airharpist stopped for a moment. I tried to stem the flow but I couldn't. It was too much. Just. .. too much. The whole day had been more than I could bear. "Talk to ME," and my chest started to buck and dance with sobs. I tried to stop them, I tried but I couldn't. Basanti materialized out of nowhere and took my arm to lead me out of the room, but I couldn't stop. "Please, "I begged, "just talk to me." It was like I was watching a movie, I could see my face, see Basanti with her hand on my arm even as I heard this childish voice starting to wail, "please Mama, just talk to me."

Minutes later, or was it hours, I was back in my room, another dose of sedative softening the edges of the furniture, creating halos around the lights. I could hear Basanti chatting quietly on her microcomp, could see the concern and not a little bit of disappointment in her face as she looked at me, the downturn of her mouth and corners of her eyes. All at once, though, I was too tired to care. She put down the comp and came over to the bed,

"I'll do better tomorrow," I mumbled. "I promise."

She didn't say anything, but I could see her twisting her rings around and around her fingers. I'd let her down, too.

"I will." I insisted. "I just need a rest."

"Do you think you could sleep?" she asked.

I nodded. After a while, she left, but not before setting up some sort of camera, to keep an eye on me, I guess.

"It's just a precaution," she said, even though I didn't even ask.

"Get some rest," she said as she left. And I will. I'm going to flash Aidian then I'm going to sleep. It can't come soon enough. And tomorrow will be better. It has to be.

AUGUST 18

The mono is hurtling me, finally, blessedly, away from that *fekanta'*, *monstrajô* of a conference and all of the *kadukaj malnovaj bastardoj* who make it up. We are going fast, so fast that if I listen closely I can actually hear the wheels screaming against the rails. So fast that the Circles come and go in nothing more than concentric rings of light. Still it isn't fast enough. It could never be fast enough. I'm trying to outrun all of it; the Facility, the *oficiales*, the hatred and resentment and shame and there's not mono that can do that. There's no machine that can take me out of where they have put me. Still, at least I'm not there anymore. I'm supposed to be; the conference still has another full day, but I couldn't stay another minute. There would be nothing left of me if I had. They've already made me so small in the time that they had. Just diminished and small and insignificant and I couldn't let them take anymore. So, I waited for a time when the whole team was busy with presentations; it wasn't hard, they usually had four or five going on at any minute, all over the center, then I excused myself saying I had to go to the bathroom. But I didn't. Instead, I went back to my room just long enough to grab Daisy and my micro and then I ran. I didn't even change my clothes. I just ran as fast as I could and used my thumb to charge a mono ticket back home. I don't even know what I was thinking; I don't think I was. It was just survival. They were going to kill me. Even if my body survived, they were going to kill everything that I've worked so hard to become and I don't' think I have it in me to rebuild again. I know I don't. I have rebuilt so many times in my life and I just couldn't. So I left before they could kill whatever is left in me. There will be consequences. I don't know what they will be, but I know there will be some and I'll just have to deal with them as they come because they can't destroy me again.

I went to this conference thinking that I would help people; that this would be my debut into the world as a real, whole person. Instead, I was treated as less than human. They wouldn't let me speak, just talked about me and around me and left me sitting there feeling like a fool. No, not a fool, a *prostituitino* dressed up nice and pulled out for them to use my body for their purposes but with no interest in me. I half-expected it out of Stevens and Nu, not to this extent, that's for sure, but to a certain level they've never seen me as real. Dr. Alyce, though? He should have known better. I thought he was more than that. But he was the worst. That was the one that sent me over the edge; he gave this presentation and he showed videos of me from our treatments together. There I was in front of everyone. The times that I was sitting in the room, staring, drooling a little. The times that I was rocking and sobbing uncontrollably. The times that he found me sleeping in the street. There they were on this giant fikfek screen and I was expected to sit in front of it, listening. I'll never forget what he said, what this man who I thought was my friend said about me. It's burned into my brain and it echoes there over and over again until I think that I'm going to go insane. He just sat there, looking smug, while the videos played. God. Recordings of our sessions together even, all of my secrets there for this group of robots, they're the robots not me, they can't even *fikfek* feel, I'm sure of it, and they're sitting there staring back and forth from me to the screen, looking at me with their hungry eyes. Like the eyes of the men that used to come by the house. Not Alyce though, he was proud, kept smiling at me as if I should be proud, too. How could he do that? Then at the end he stood. "As you have seen, Charlotte was emotionally and practically debilitated. She could not participate in her own self-care or contribute to society in any way. Now, though, she has been created. She has been made into a complete person, and participating member of society." Doesn't he see? Doesn't he see that I was always a person? I'm not a person because he made me one; I always was. Broken, sure. Terrified and tired and broken, ken? But always real. Always a person. And

I always contributed as much as I could. Of all people, he should know that, but neh. He's bought into the Facility and their bottomless *merdanta* egos; disregarding all of the work that I've done, disregarding ME. That was when I knew that I couldn't do it anymore. I couldn't stay. He has flashed me over and over, Basanti has as well, but I'm not answering. If I'm not real, if I'm only a creation of theirs, they can just imagine what I'd say. They can make me, in their minds, everything they want me to be. But I will make them see me. They will have to see me now. They won't have a choice.

Daisy is sleeping in a small ball under the seatbelt, cuddled close. She's been so patient with me, from bouncing around while I ran tripping down the hallway to cuddling under my chin while I sobbed, she has been there. She'd wake up in again if I asked her, but I don't need her just now. Right now I'm numb. Shut down myself and staring out of the window, trying to will us closer to Flower Town. I've flashed Aidian and he will be waiting. I think that's the only thing that's keeping me sane. I feel like I can hear his heartbeat from here, steady and strong and connected to my own. With every beat it draws us closer. He will understand. He will keep me safe. He will keep me real. He has to. Almost there, now. Almost to my home, my sanctuary, my love. If I can just hold on a little longer I will be safe.

of achievement. To make demands like I
ething?"

said quietly, "you kind of do."

me like an explosion. I rocked back in my
r the blood rushing in my ear.

I growled. "Take me home."

Bird, I only meant-" hearing his voice
eous.

shrieked, and my voice was deafening
cab. "You're supposed to be on my side."

t's just-"

ing." I spat. I wanted to hit him. Hurt him
me. "Take me home." I snatched Daisy off
er and held her on my lap. He signed and
le it worse. I'm making him weary, yeah?
didn't say anything else. I don't think that
taken it, and shifted the car into gear. We
in silence. When we got there, he actually
with me. I sent him away. I sent him away
ore than I could imagine but after how he's
once I discovered who he is I didn't want
another minute. "I'll see you tomorrow,
as he turned back towards the cab. Weak
y didn't I see that before? How could I ha
someone that weak could ever protect n

AUGUST 19

It never ends, neh? No matter how perfect, how amazing everything seems to be, no matter how well you think you know someone , it's only a matter of time until everything, every *fekanta* aspect of your life falls complete and totally to *merd*. It's like some giant cosmic joke, ken? You're staggering though this tunnel, trapped and alone in the dark, and the muck and finally you see it; there's a light, and so you run towards it screaming, arms spread wide, only to discover that it's a *diable* train. Maybe that's why I feel like I do. Crushed. Flattened. Utterly destroyed.

Aidian was waiting on the platform when the mono pulled in. He was, amazingly and blessedly alone and that fact in itself was such an incredible relief that I actually grew lightheaded. I expected Facility representatives at least, oficiales maybe. They can track my movements using the software they installed in my brain. I cannot run. I cannot hide. Not if they truly want me with them. I will continue to put my faith in the fact that, as they can also download a great deal of dada my physical being, the part of me that's they spent all weekend marginalizing, is just more trouble to them than it's worth. So, when we came around the corner and the platform was empty except for Aidian, I nearly cried. I thought that he was safe, that I'd returned to my harbor and I was out of danger. I flew out the doors and into his arms before the mono had even completely stopped. He held me close, a I won't' deny him that, he held me there on the platform while I sobbed in relief, sobbed and wailed until my knees felt weak and I'd left this giant disgusting patch of tears and snot and spit on his chest. At some point, Daisy ran from my pocket to his shoulder, and I could hear her squeak excitedly. When I was ready, he led me to the cab and started guiding us home. About halfway there, I started crying again and he pulled the cab to one side and put it in neutral. The dam broke again, and I told him everything, the words nearly tripping over each other. I told him how they'd pushed me around, how they'd referred to me as a "true member of society," how I'd not been allowed to even *fikfek* speak. I told him how dirty I felt, used, like some sort of *prostitutino*. And I told him how afraid I was that I'd lose everything. Technically they hold the lease on my home. They put my stipend in my account. And what they've given they could just as easily take away. I could go home to a locked door at any minute, and then discover that I don't' even have enough left to get a room for the night. And I'm scared. I 'm just so damned scared and I needed him. I thought he'd tell me that everything would be all right. Better

yet, he'd somehow make n
tell me that he could make
with their records somehov
how. Easy, neh? A tiny, hop
he'd offer to marry me. T
Circle hall and this godfor:
my wedding dress. What I
never expected, was that he'
puling, lackey for the Facilit
everyone knows that inner-c
aĉas la kacos of the governm
But still, I would never have
why, I guess, I thought that
"What did you say?" I asked.
"Maybe it's not too late," he
the stress, yeah?"
"And go back?"
"Well, yeah, not to the confer
Those aren't so bad, you coul
week or so and you could kee|
My mouth opened and closed
able to choke out my words. "
to them, hands out, begging
you'd do? Go back like I owe
where to go, how to act, who t

like some
owe them
"Charlotte
His words
seat, coulc
"You bast.
"Ea
made me
"Shut up!
enclosed i
" I am, Lo
"It's just n
like he'd h
of his sho
that just n
But at leas
I could ha
drove hon
tried to go
and it hur
betrayed r
him arou
then" he s
So weak. V
thought th

"No," I called after him, "you won't." I saw his shoulders slump, but he kept going. I turned and noticed my front door for the first time. I don't know how I missed it. The *diable* thing was lit up like a Christmas tree. StickyTiks, like micronotes but topped with flashing red and blue lights, were stuck all over the door. There must have been a half dozen of them. I rushed up the stoop, suddenly terrified. Had someone gotten hurt? Was this how the Facility had decided to deal with me. As I got closer, the smell hit me. Puke and pee, beer, smoke. So, not the Facility. Vandals, maybe? I started to read the tickets. Noise violation. Noise violation. Public Indecency. *Jesuo!* What do you have t do to get cited with Public indecency in Flower Town? So, not vandals either. A party. Seriously? A *fekanta* party. Suddenly I was exhausted. Whatever was beyond that door, I didn't want to deal with it. Still, I turned the knob, it wasn't even locked, and went in. The smell was even worse inside, and I gagged a little as a wave of it hit me. I quick glance in the living room was enough to tell me that it was completely trashed. I could pick out bottles, and take-out containers strewn everywhere, and bodies that belonged to neither Tawny nor Dmitri. I hurried through the living room. That was nothing I wanted to deal with tonight. I just wanted to get out of this gown, grab a shower, and go to bed. For a week, maybe. Even that, though, was too much to ask. The toilet, shower, and floor were covered in foul, red, vomit and filth and who knows what else. Drops' vials were spread on the sink and there was even a needle behind the toilet. I set Daisy in her cage, so mad that my vision had narrowed to a needle point, and tossed on some Utilicothes. God that rough fabric, the baggy folds felt amazing, and set to work, one hand clenching a towel over my nose and mother, the other using the shower sprayer to wash the worst of it down the train. It was well after midnight before I was able to actually use the shower myself. I stood under the scalding spray, scrubbing until my skin was tinged with pink and the water ran cold. I threw on a second set of Utiliclothes that were identical to the fist, and started to my room. N o one in the living room had moved. Part of me wonders how long the party had lasted for them to be this exhausted. The other part of me doesn't care. Now I'm lying here trying to sleep. The thing is, I've gotten in the habit of lying in bed, daydreaming about Aidian and I and the future I thought we'd have. With that destroyed the goneness of him, the humiliation of this weekend, the betrayal by my friends, the fear of my future are all rushing to fill the void. To relax enough to sleep means to risk letting that in. I can't. Only in small sips. Sometimes, insomnia is self-preservation. This is one of those times.

AUGUST 20

My eyes are grainy, my whole body aches, and the day isn't even done yet. Still, enough has been accomplished that I feel like I can breathe, so we are going to take that as a win. Sleep eluded me last night, only to spring out every now and then and grasp me. It wasn't restful, tough, more of a battle of wills for my consciousness, and I was afraid to yield, I kept finding myself sitting up in order to wake back up, screaming my gasp for air, trying to escape the dreams that had been tormenting me. Nothing concretes. No storyline. Just paid and dread and loss. On the plus side, by the time I was driven from my bed at about down I had a plan. I had determined that it was possible, not probable but possible, that the Facility *kunuloj* had been so busy doing damage control at the conference that they hadn't gotten around to my punishment yet. They kept flashing me, Basanti more than most, and that led me to believe that they still hadn't sorted out exactly what had happened. Once they did, I imagine, the flashes will cease. You don't reveal your position to your enemies after all. So, there was a chance that I could mitigate he potential damages. This game I knew well. For the poor, the sick, your whole life is a game of staying one step ahead, ducking and dodging. If you wanted to live, that is. Mostly I didn't.

Back then. But I saw the life I'd be living at that price it didn't seem like that great of a deal. Now though, it doesn't. Even in the face of all that has happened I know that something in this life is worth fighting for, even if I don't know what it is. Maybe it's hope. Wouldn't that be an amazing change? I charged through the living room, nearly running over some sallow blonde dude wearing nothing but stained boxers who at least had the decency to look embarrassed as he slunk out the door and down the street.

I might have gone over time, to watch that *blanka kuniklo* run if nothing else, if I hadn't seen my SimCenter. It was tipped over on its side, the screen shattered. "*Fekanta bastardoj,*" I yelled. Slowly. Groggily, Tawny lifted her head. Her hair was tousled, matted to her head with sweat. She had a hickey on her neck.

"Hey Charlotte," she said, her voice slow and scratchy.

"Hey nothing," I said back. " I want this cleaned up by the time I get back.

"Chill, Mami," she said, and reached for a small vial on the nightstand. "Here, have some Drops."

"*Forgesi* the Drops," I said, and I slammed the door behind me.

I grabbed the StickyTiks off of the door, they were flashing slower now, their colors duller. A sign that their batteries were running low and I was running out of time. Before I did anything, these had to be paid. For minimum infraction, if you pay before the tickets run dead, it's like it never happened. They are officially registered once the battery runs out. If I'm going to have to get a new place, I can't have this *merd* on my file. Eight. There were eight of them. *Jesuo!* I ran four blocks inland, towards what passes for "downtown.," and started taking rights and lefts randomly. I didn't go down town often, so even though I knew what I was looking for, it had been a while since I'd been there. Finally, I saw it, the flashing digiboard, one of maybe five in the entire rim, with the ugliest man I'd ever seen. Tiger stripes were tattooed on every bit of his skull, and metal studs sprouted everywhere they could be anchored. He only had one eye, even though he had plenty of money to get another implanted. Rumor had it he liked it better this way. Crazy Eddie of Crazy Eddie's Bail bonds. There was a giant arrow pointing down and to the right. That was it. I didn't have to talk to Eddie himself, which was great. The way he looked at me made my skin crawl, and it was fairly well known that several people who'd jumped bond on him hadn't shown up again, at lost not intact. Still, he had a machine outside of his shop, and that's what I needed. I fed the tickets into the machine, and pressed my thumb to the payment pad. It came to more than a week's salary at

Don's and I cursed Tawny and Dmitri again. Still, the payment cleared and I couldn't help but breathe a sigh of relief. Next to the ticket machine was the ATM. I pressed my thumb against the payment pad again, and pulled out as much as the machine would dispense, twice. It was more than I'd ever held at one time, more than enough to cover everything I'd need for a month or more. Most places in the Centre circles don't take cash, they feel like it encourages criminal activity, but out here it's still the standard. Of course so in criminal activity so I'm not sure what that means. I stared at the money in my hand for a second, wondering exactly how much the Facility paid me as a "modest living stipend." I decided to try to pull out the same amount again. It worked and I determined that it was time to vacate the area. There were always eyes, especially on these kinds of machines, and I suddenly felt vulnerable, exposed. I ran down to the market, checking four or five times to make sure I hadn't dropped anything, and bought a money belt that I could fasten right against my stomach under my clothes. After that , I felt better. Some. My microcomp kept flashing, though, even though it was off, which meant someone was flashing the emergency override and it was driving me nuts. I really don't' have it in me to deal with anything more than the immediate, but my heart rate climbed every time I saw the flash. So, I stuffed the comp in the belt as well, and grabbed a bite to eat and headed down to the old amusement park and that's where I've been ever since. Eating, staring, and writing in my journal. Trying to avoid going home. Avoiding Tawny and Dmitri and whoever else may be there. With the crisis averted for the moment , I can actually feel something other than tired, and what's coming through is rage. Sheer, unadulterated, rage. I keep practicing my speech and it devolves every time into shrieking. I can feel my jaw clenching and my hands forming into fists and she's not even yare. And I'm afraid. I'm afraid it will take me over. I'm also afraid with will wane and I'll have to face what's behind it. Despair. More than I can take. Still, I've got to deal with them at some point, and I'll be damned if I'm going to let them drive me out of my own home. After all I've gone through to have it, it's mine and I'll be damned if they keep me away.

AUGUST 20

I expected to find the house at least a little cleaner by the time that I got home, and in that I was disappointed. If anything, it was worse. Someone, several someone by the look of it, had gotten hungry and had heated some Simplsoys. Just helped themselves to my food as well as everything else. *Porkoj*! The wrappers and boxed, filled with a mushy congealing mess, were scattered all over and the heat of the day had intensified the stench. It was rancid. *Fikfek naŭsa.* There were less people at least. They may not have much by way of manners or common sense or even humanity, but self-preservation they have in spades. Only Tawny and Dmitri were left and they had touched nothing. You would think that they would have at least made a *fekanta* effort, but no. I'm sure they just sat around laughing at me and what a *naiva tromp* I am. Trying to figure out how they can screw me even harder. I wish that I could talk to Aidian. He would know what to do. He's great with people; I'll give him that much. I can't though. That traitor. For all I know he's sitting with his friends right now, bagging on me and laughing at me, too. Or worse finding solace in the arms of some *franzia* center circle debutante. Too much. I can't think about that right now. Small sips. I can drink on only small sips or this will drown me.

I was also expecting a fight when I got home, and in that I wasn't' disappointed. She may not have had time to get any cleaning done, or figure out where she was going to go – she actually said that, that it was my fault for coming home early and leaving her with no time- but she'd apparently had ample opportunity to get herself good and *furiozis* at me. At me! It's as if all of this is my fault. Dmitri left soon after I got there, his eyes half-lidded and insolent as he strolled onto the stoop. Rolling a cigarette as he went. It was the smooth, practiced move of a professional charlatan, a coward. A conman. Stay for the party, leave for the shouting. And shouting there was. Shouting until her knuckles were white with it. I was overreacting. Overreacting she yelled, tossing her hair. "It's not that big of a deal," she said. "Where will we go?" "How can you do this to us?" And finally "you like to party just as much as we do."

"Not at the expense of others!" I cried.

She looked at me for a long time, then. Just stared with eyes that were simultaneously dead and burning with hate. I also realized this was nothing new; she had hated me for a while. Love me, too, perhaps. Once.

"You lie, Lotta," she said. "You think you're so much better than us now. Strutting around. You're so damned special with your house and your doctors and your brain. You've forgotten what you are. You've forgotten that you're nothing but trash. You'd better got off of your high horse before someone kicks you off. It might even be me."

That hurt. I could feel it in my gut, and I felt like yelling back. But there wasn't a point. It was the fight that she wanted, needed even. If she yelled loud enough and long enough it would silence her conscience. It never does, though. Not really. I could have told her that if she'd have listened. Somewhere, sometime, in the quiet times, there is a part of you that will whisper to you what you've done. There's a part that needs to confess if only to yourself. But instead, I gave up.

"Just be out, tomorrow," I said. That got her attention like nothing else had. Suddenly, the fight went out of here and the wheedling began. Sure enough, Dmitri came back for that part. "Lotta, *sestra*, you wouldn't toss us out. We will clean it up, look," and she started running around, picking stuff up. "We can make it up to you, lovely," Dmitri added. "You want a new SimCenter? I know a man who-" How like him. Replacing vandalism with theft. "Just stop," I said, after a minute, "get your stuff, and get out." "Where will we go?" she wailed, crocodile tears starting to slide. "We don't have any money. We don't have a place. I thought we were family."

"Me too," I said, stone-faced. "Looks like we were both wrong." I turned and walked, forcing myself to move slowly, to my room, shutting the door behind me. There, finally, I could cry.

AUGUST 22

I went back to work at the Café today. I wasn't due back, not for another week, but I couldn't take it, not staying home while Tawny leaves, not waiting for the oficiales form the Facility to show up, not seeing all of the holes in my life where Aidian isn't. It seemed easier jut to go in, lose myself in the ebb and flow of the day.

Don was happy to see me. Surprised, but happy. God he looked tired, though. He's probably gotten used to an extra pair of hands. "Hey it's my girl," he yelled, and folded me into a hug. "How'd it go?" he asked. And I should have lied to him. I should have told him that it was great, that I had a wonderful time. I should have spared him the worry. Still, though, I needed to tell someone. I deserved that much at least. So, I opened my mouth just to tell him a little. A summary, neh? Instead it all came out. Like, all of it, this unending flow of words. And he was amazing. Listening and nodding and "poor baby" in all of the right places. He even teared up once. And I hated that I hurt him but I needed that. Whenever a customer came in for whatever reason, they were pretty sparse this morning, he would wait on them, moving with his slow, shuffling step, and asking questions about their family, their work. I stayed in the back and stared at my hands wrapped around the coffee cup. I think I'll just have to work in the back for a while. I thought that I could do it, could work with people, but feeling the way my heart starts to pound, that I'm irritated just by the presence of others, leads me to believe that maybe I'm not ready yet. Now that I'm here, it just seems like too much; making small talk, pretending to care, afraid they'll ask my how I'm doing and I don't' know what to say. Besides, I'm sure most of the rim will have heard by know what happened with Tawny and Dmitri and will be lining up to put their two cents in. So I sat, feeding Daisy bits of cookie, and when Mr. Don was done with the customers he would come back.

"Go ahead, Darlin'," he said time and again, and I would. It felt nice, to be heard.

Eventually, the café got busy and I did as well, heating up soups and making sandwiches. Setting dough to rise and mixing batter. I had to take a little while to clean the machines first, they seemed dirtier than usual, bits of dough and whatnot crusted on the outside of the bowl and caked in the gears. I settled into a rhythm and time passed faster than it has in quite a while. I was incredibly glad I had come. So glad, in fact, that I didn't want to go home, especially as I didn't know what was waiting for me. I didn't know if Tawny would take me seriously, even after our "talk," and I had no idea what I would do if she hadn't. Call the *oficiales*? Somehow I can't see that going well. Fight her? I wanted to avoid that if I could. I always run from fights, hide somewhere if given the chance. I've been hit enough in my life, and I never knew if a blow is going to lead to a flashback. It's incredibly hard to do well in a fight when you're shivering and crying in the corner, neh? Tawny, though? She took the opposite approach. Instead of running away from a fight, she'd run towards. Sought them out, ken? I think, in some strange way she enjoyed them. It wasn't worth stitches, a broken bone. Yell? I couldn't see that doing any good. Yelling is just a way of life here.

Luckily, by the time I drug myself in, around midnight, I didn't have to deal with her at all. They were gone. They'd left a giant pile of filth, broken a couple of things for good measure. She'd even left my door open; an invitation for someone else to do more. Luckily no one did, and I can deal with the mess. I consider it a small price paid to just be done. I can only hope the other cleanup goes just as easily.

AUGUST 26

God, I'm lonely. It's not fair that they did this to me. I've spent most of my life avoiding people, keeping relationships light, superficial, ken? I didn't want to care about anyone, not really. Part of it was self-preservation. If you don't care about anyone, they can't hurt you, and with a brain that is hell-bent on destroying you the last thing you need is people on the outside with the ability to do the same thing. You'd just end up afraid from both directions. And also I know, I've always known, what an utter and complete disaster I am. I didn't do a great job of hiding that. I know that, but I think I did better than I would have if I'd actually allowed anyone to see me. So I didn't. If they didn't actually see me they couldn't judge me. I couldn't disappoint them. The other part of it was just Flower Town. Just the Rim. People move a lot, they don't have a choice. They move, or they die or go to jail or go on a trip and never come back. I don't blame them. Survival is inherently selfish, and when survival is the focus the rest kind of falls to the wayside. So, it's not been a big deal. But I came out of the hospital wanting-ready- for something different. If relationships were part of being healthy, then relationships were what I wanted. So I let them in; I trusted them. Aidian. He seemed so different from the rest. Kinder. Gentler, neh? Tawny and

Dmitri- they were Rim, sure, but they were some of my oldest friends and I thought they just needed a boost, a little help. Even the *anusuloj* at the Facility. I didn't have any ideations about Wu or Stevens, but Basanti? Dr. Alyce? Even some of the aides I thought actually cared about me. Not my franzia new brain. Me. So I opened myself to them, the best that I can anyway. Depended on them. Gave them what I thought they wanted. Let myself care. Then they left me. They just turned their backs. Used me and hurt me and then just (fucking0 disappeared. I feel their absence more than I ever felt their presence. It's with me all of the time. Reminding me of the places in my life where there's nothing, no one. I've spent hours and hours with Daisy, playing, snuggling, I've even found myself talking to her more than once. And she's great, she really is. I never would have thought that I'd get this attached to a little robotic rat, but I have. She's really something special. Still, she's not human; it's not the same. I find myself seeking out crowds. I go down to the old amusement part, but the clique down there isn't mine anymore, if it ever was. This crowd is younger. Harder, somehow. So suspicious of someone new. I tried a couple of times to join in, but they were having none of it and so I'd just climb up on some of the decrepit old rides and let the wind and whirl of conversation swirl around me. It's better than nothing, but not by much. I've gone down to the black market as well, come home with armloads of *merda* I don't need just to be able to talk to the shopkeepers. My living room is getting jumbled. I even tried going back to the club once, but I was so jumpy, looking around for Tawny or Dmitri or any of their crew that seem to hold a grudge against me for them trashing my house, that I couldn't relax. I didn't even make it an hour.

Then there's work. Listen, I'll admit that my schedule has been a little erratic. I can't work all of the hours I usually do. I just . . . can't. I'm dealing with two much of my own stuff right now, trying to process, come up with a plan. I have to be my own first priority. Don needs me, I know that. In all honest, I think that's the problem. He needs me physically; he can't do everything that needs to be done at the café anymore. He gets tired easily and he can't lift anything that's heavy. He's gotten even slower, can't keep up with the meager crowd that we have. So he needs me there to pick up the slack. He relies on me mentally. I don't know what's been going on, but he's been distracted lately, not really there. And so he's forgetting things, making batters wrong. Last week he forgot to lock the door when he closed up and the next morning people had broken in. They didn't take much-food mostly- so my guess is that they were hungry an desperate buy my God I can't be expected to remember everything. And talk. God, he seems to want to talk all of the time. About me. About Daisy. Mostly about himself, though. His daughter who died. His wife. His childhood, His dad was a Juju man and his mom died when he was young from using too much of her own product. I know what he's doing, I do. He's trying to make me feel better. Empathize, neh? But It's not like I don't know that other people have it rough. It doesn't make me feel better to hear about it. In fact, it hurts, makes it worse. So many lost people and it looks like I'm destined, no matter how hard I try, to be just one more. He's told me ten times at last about how he built the café from nothing. How he started by selling baked goods from the stacks, then worked up to a burnt out old hovertruck, and finally scraped and saved enough to buy that build. That's all fantastic, it really is, but I get it. I do. You built something and you're proud and I love it to, but I can't be there for him right now. I don't have anything to give him.

I respect him. I admire him so much and I'm grateful and I love him in my own way, but I'm downing right now, I can't be concerned with saving someone else. He doesn't get it, so I just stay away as much as I can without feeling guilty. I go in and help, like I've always done, take some of the load, but that's it. The rest of my time has to be about me. I'm going to keep searching until I find. . whatever it is that I'm looking for. Whatever it is that will fill this whole. Whatever it is,

that is me. I know it's out there. I know I am. I have to
be.

SEPTEMBER 6

I'm actually writing this journal entry, instead of keying
it in. It feels weird. Foreign. The scratch of pen on paper;
the cramping in your hand. I didn't realize how long it
had been since I'd actually written something longer
than a sentence or two. I also didn't realize how much a
security blanket my microcomp had become. I'm used to
it's weight in my pocket; the beeps and clicks. I'm used
to having it to find out what time it is, who is looking for
me, where I am. It's an extension of my arm, almost, my
connection to the rest of the world which is, I guess, the
problem. I must have reached for it a hundred times or
more in the last day and am surprised each time when it
isn't there. But it isn't. It's gone. For all I know, the tides
have taken it far out to sea. Or maybe not. Maybe it's on
shore, mixed in with the needles and the trash and the
oil. In any case, it's not with me. I just couldn't take it
anymore. It was looming in my pocket all the time, just
waiting to beep, waiting to reach out for me, and I just
couldn't take it anymore. I would jump every time it
made a noise, stare at the people trying to get ahold of
me, and my breath would come short and my heart start
to pound every time, even though I couldn't ever bring

myself to read their flashes, let alone answer. The Facility. Tawny. Don. Aidian. Aidian most of all. With him,though, I couldn't tell which was worse, afraid that it was him or afraid that it wasn't. That he'd forgotten me already. That I never mattered at all. When it was off, though, that was even worse. I was afraid of all of the flashes that would be waiting. I was afraid of what I was missing, that my world could be crashing around my head and that I wouldn't even know. Finally, I couldn't take it anymore. It was just too much. That's what they do, though, neh? They just pull and pull for whatever they can get from me, they drain everything out of me and they don't' even think about what it's doing to me. It's all about them all of the time. What they need. How they feel. What they want. And if it hurts me, so what? I'm just some little gutter rat. Some machine. So yesterday I took a long lunch from Don's and went down to the harbor. I just stood there for a long time, letting the breeze blow in my face, listening to the bustle and the sound, hoping that it would just wash it all away. I must have watched five boats come in, my hands clenched together so hard that I left little crescents in my palms, waiting for some sort of peace to come. It didn't, though. It may have done, if not for the beeping, but every time I would start to calm, every time I would start to think that everything might actually be okay, the damned thing would make a noise and it would all start all over again. Finally, I couldn't take it anymore, and I just threw the thing as hard as I could, out into the water. It barely made a ripple before it sunk. For a second I panicked, wanted to jump in after that. I had pictures of Daisy on that. Holomessages from Aidian, the first pictures of my little house. Then I decided just to let it go, just let it all go. Daisy is still with me. Aidian never will be again and my house doesn't feel like my house anymore. They took that from me as well. Tawny. Dmitri. The Facility. They made it so my house doesn't feel like my home. I can forgive them a lot, but not that. Never that. But we will build a new world, Daisy and I. One that their fingerprints aren't all over, and getting rid of that damned thing is the first step in that. I must have been gone a lot longer than I thought, though. Don was upset by the time I got back. I mean, he didn't say anything, but he was sweating, busy, and kept shooting me these disappointed glances. He'll just have to be disappointed. I love him a lot, I do, but I'm working through a lot of stuff right now and he needs to understand that. I don't' need to work there anyway, I have enough to get me through, but I am. So if I need to take a little bit of space every now and that he has to understand that. I'll come back, I'll help when I can, but I have to think about me right now. No one else will.

SEPTEMBER 11

I got to work mid-morning and I knew something was wrong from a block away. The kitchen lights were on, but the café itself was still dim and empty. A few of our regulars were standing outside, grumbling amongst themselves and I just about pushed the out of the way running to the door. I pulled out my keys, but I was shaking too badly to get them in the lock. Finally, I made it in, the bells clanged as they slammed against the door, and there he was, Mr. Don, lying on the floor. I threw myself down beside him, laid my head on his chest, but I could tell even before I got there that I was too late. Dead. He was dead. I could feel his ribs through his skin, Why didn't I notice how thin he'd gotten, and he was dead and cold and he'd shit himself. It wasn't enough that he'd died. No. He'd died alone, lying in his own shit. How long had he been there? How many hours? Three? Five? More? I don't know, but he was there alone and he shouldn't have been. I should have been there with him. I should have been here to help him, here to do something instead of wandering around the docks feeling sorry for myself. I can't believe I failed him like this. Don, of all people. Which probably explains what happened next.

I called for Emergency and they actually got there quickly for once, which is ironic when you think about it. The paras came rushing in with their gurney, running full speed even though I had told them when I flashed them that he was dead. A couple of police followed right behind, looking oh so stern and official. They pushed everyone out the door, which while I didn't much care for their tone I was pretty grateful for because by that time a crowd had gathered and they were standing there, jostling each other and staring. I wanted to ask them to leave, wanted to scream at them to the get hell out, it just seemed so damned rude and disrespectful and seriously who does that. I didn't feel like I had the right to say anything, couldn't find my voice, so I was glad that someone did. Anyhow, eventually the coroner arrived, dressed in his old-fashioned black suit. I'd seen him before, of course, we all had, if never this close. Gaunt and pale with buttons all the way up to his chin, no wonder people called him the Angel of Death. Anyhow he pulled out this bag of tools and equipment and did everything the paras already had, before nodding to his assistant. The young man sprang to action, wrapping Don in a large bag. I couldn't watch. The coroner started asking all sorts of questions. "Name of deceased?" "Age" "Next of kin?" I don't know why, but when he asked me that I told him it was me. I just. ..

somehow the thought of Don ending up without any kind of funeral or remembrance or anything, of him ending up in one of those numbered slots, of the café just sitting empty and falling apart, it didn't seem right. So, I told them it was me and I guess we looked enough alike or maybe they just didn't care enough to look too far into it, but whatever his reason the coroner just nodded and took my information. So now I guess I'm planning the funeral and who knows what else. I don't want to. I don't know how, but it's the least I can do. That man did so much SO MUCH for so many people, ken? Kept us from starving, gave us a place to get out of the cold, jobs, everything. He gave me chance after chance and after all that I just let him lay there dead. I knew he was sick. I tried to pretend that he wasn't because it was Don and he just seemed, eternal, but *fek*, I can't believe I did that. Now that it is over I can't believe I was so stuck in my own head that I couldn't be bothered to do more than stay an extra hour here and there. So this is too little too late. It won't make up for it. I know that. But at least it is something.

SEPTEMBER 14

I am exhausted. Mentally. Physically. Emotionally. I have spent the last three had in this haze of caffeine-fueled perpetual motion. I have burns on my arms from the oven and my face is chapped from snot and tears and I don't think I have it in me to hug or shake the hand or comfort another living soul, but it is finally over. Mr. Don's memorial was today, and even though he'd have been embarrassed, he'd have shuffled and grumbled at all of the attention, I think underneath it all he would have been proud. It was a simple enough funeral, such that it was. I had him cremated, it was really all that I could afford and I couldn't bear the thought of him in one of the stacked Rim graves. He'd worked so hard to get out of the stackflats that he, that most of us, were raised in that I just couldn't bear the thought of him spending the rest of eternity stuck in another version of them, rotting away in his little room until the time came to push his bones back with all of the thousands of others to make room for more. It was just, I couldn't. So I made the arrangements with the mortuary and then I want back to baking and good God it was beyond horrible. Sitting there surrounded by ovens when I knew that miles away Don was. .. *Jesou*. I vomited so many times I lost count. But I did it. I just focused on all the things that I didn't do for him in life, and all the things I could never do now, and I remembered that this was the one thing I could give him. Even though I must have said "I can't" out loud a hundred times, the reality was that I could. I blacked out the curtains of the café, and but signs up as to when the funeral would be, and then I scrubbed the space until it shined. I knew that word would spread, and sure enough it did. Within a day or two the sidewalk in front of the car was covered in flowers, whiskey bottles with candles stuck in the top, imagine both because everyone knew that Don favored whiskey and because it was something that most people had on hand, handwritten notes, marigolds, coins. I went this morning to pick up the creamains, which has to be the most fikfek ridiculous word I've ever heard, and whoever thought that would sound better than ashes is *freneza*, but I picked up the cremains in the run I had selected. It wasn't anything fancy. It was plain, simple, sturdy, kind of like Don himself ,which is why I'd liked that one in the first place, and by the time I got to the café there was already a crowd gathered. It seemed like all of Flower Town had shown up and even after all of the baking that I had done I was nervous that there wouldn't be enough. More than that, I was worried that I wouldn't be enough, All of those people knew Don, loved him as best as they could, and they were looking to me to do well by him. To comfort them even though I was every bit as devastated as they were. And I just didn't feel strong enough. So even though they were all waiting I sat there for a moment with the lights off, cuddling Daisy under my chin. Her whiskers tickled my skin and I could feel her heart beating under my fingers. She is alive, or whatever the Cynimal version of living is and, for that matter, so was I. So were all of the people waiting outside. If I could do this, if I could just cross the five feet to the door, maybe together we could keep Don alive, in a sense, a little longer too. So, I put Daisy on my shoulder, *testikoj* to anyone who took offense, turned on the lights, and unlocked the door. I must have shaken a hundred hands, found myself wrapped in a hundred tear-soaked hugs. Offered and accepted condolences over and over again as people filed past me and stopped to pay respects at the small shrine I had built. I'd rolled out one of the baker's carts. It was small, utilitarian, but it seemed appropriate, and I'd put on it he urn, some candles, and a loaf of fresh bakes bread. On the specials board I'd chalked a verse from the Bible, something I'd remembered from one of the few trips to church that we'd taken whenever Mother started to feel guilty and tried to turn herself around. IT never lasted long, these spells, but I'd clung to them, these ports in the storms, and I'd never forgotten one verse it particular. "For I was hungry and you gave me something to eat," it read," I was thirsty and you gave me something to drink. I was a stranger and you invited me in. Above all of that hung the picture that I knew was Mr. Don's favorite. It was a much younger version of him with his arm around his daughter, taken just months before she died. They were both smiling and her head was resting on his shoulder. I don't know why I never noticed before how much I looked like her, and my heart squeezed every time I looked at her face and understood why he'd been so determined to save m. And I never thanked him. Not really.

Once everyone was seated I took a deep breath, rubbed my cheek one last time against daisy's fur brushing it backwards, which I loved to do but she hated, and would spend hours putting herself in order, and gave the eulogy. I don't remember what I said, though I must have rehearsed it a million times. Whatever it was it must have been okay because people laughed and cried and signed in all of the right spots and many of them came up to thank me afterwards. When I was done Roger, one of the regulars who was also a street preacher in his infrequent periods of sobriety, stood up and lead us in a prayer. It was slurred a little but no less beautiful for it, and after that everyone stood and ate bread and pastries and just chatted. It seemed like we all had a story about some kindness Don had done, how he'd helped us or saved us or made us smile, and I smiled a little myself as I wandered form group to group listening. After a while I got to thinking. IF I Died who would come to my funeral? Who would say these kinds of things about me? Would anyone? I don't think so. Don gone I couldn't think of a single person who would even miss me. Infereoj, Tawny and Dmitri, even though they came to the funeral, wouldn't even look at me, and I haven't' heard from Aidan in weeks. Most likely I'd just rot until someone found me and shoved me into one of the mass graves. Is that why I'd gone through all of this then? The surgery and the therapy? To live and die alone?

Finally, the last people left and I was able to clean up. Every muscle in my body ached and it took forever but finally everything was set to rights. I put the urn and the picture on the shelf above the cash register, the place of "honor" if there is such a thing, and I left. I want to go home. God I do. I want to go home and reset Daisy and sleep about a week. But I can't. I have one more stop I have   to   make   first

SECTION TWO

"I go through the motions again and again
But you are not here to see them
I go through the emotions again and again
And this time I actually feel them."

Unwoman "Herione"

SEPTEMBER 17

Aidan is sleeping. He looks so young when he is asleep, his white-blonde eyelashes are so long that they brush he cheeks and he lays there in complete abandon, on his back with one arm thrown over his head. So different from me. When I do sleep, I'm curled into a ball with my teeth clenched and my hands curled into fists so tightly that most mornings my cheeks and arms are sore. I know too well the terrors, the fikfek horrors that nighttime can bring. Police looking to tear up a tent city for kicks, nightmares and worse, much worse, and even though I'm past all of that my body remembers. Not right now, though, right now my body remembers the way his whole face lit up when he saw me at the door, how his eyes widened and his jaw dropped. My body remembers the way that he trembled when he folded me into his arms and the way that my face found that perfect hollow in his shoulder. How he kept reaching out and patting me gently, almost like he was checking to see if I was still there, and the sudden loss of breath when I realized that his man loved me, he loved me and he had all along. My body remembers how he covered my face with kissed, stopping me every time I tried to say that I was sorry and how the vibration of his voice tickled my ear after I had thought he was asleep.

"Hey Bird?" he said.

"Yeah?"

"Please don't leave again."

SEPTEMBER 19

It's time for me to go. It's past time. I should have been at the café an hour ago and even if I leave now nothing will have time to rise properly. But somehow, I can't. It is so, so important to me that Don't café doesn't close, that I keep it going and that means' not waiting to reopen. To go on as if nothing has changes and hopefully we will fall below the radar of the Powers that Be and the will just leave us alone, but still, I can't leave. And some of it is exhaustion. More sleep sound absolutely divine. And part of it is fear. What if no one comes if it is me running the place and what if the center circle folks discover I wasn't really next of kin and what if I just plain can't do it. But most' I just want to be here with him a litter longer. I want to be here in his arms while he holds me even while he sleeps. I want to be here when he wakes. Daisy just woke up, turn in a circle or two, tucked her head against her side, and went back to sleep, so I think she agrees. The café can wait just one more day.

SEPTEMBER 27

I know that Cynimals don't actually need sleep, that the sleep cycle was programmed in to further the illusion that they are real. Even so, I'd swear that Daisy is starting to look irritated when I scoop her up in the morning. Not that I blame her. I'm starting to feel a little irritable myself. On edge. Brittle. I get up every morning around three and mix the bread dough for the morning and set it to rise. Then I start the muffins and the doughnuts. Usually, hopefully, there are enough of those done in time for the morning rush. The fishermen headed out for the day or the factory workers headed home. Everything becomes a blur after that until about 10am. Usually at that point I've been slamming coffee for what is a workday for some people, so more than anything I have to pee. I've taken to staying in there for a minute or two after I'm done just to get a little bit of a break, without anyone talking to me. That's what I never realized about this place when Don was alive, hiding as I did in the back room; people don't come in here for the coffee or the food, no mattter how good it is. Don't get me wrong, they want those things, but what they really want is to talk. I don't know if I'd call any of the regulars my friends, but I know more about their healthy and their families and their dreams that I could every bring myself to tell anyone. Somehow I'm safe I guess . and at fist it made me really uncomfortable, and I'd entertain myself by mocking them to Aidan. The panting man with the too-moist lips. The captain trying to drink coffee with a hand missing two fingers and a thumb. The pseudo-geishas in full gear, speaking to each other in Spanish. The woman and her boyfriend who missed bumping into her husband by no more than 30 seconds. Now though I find myself almost protective. Worrying about them a little when they don't come in. Wanting to hear how the latest crisis resolved itself. Sometimes, though, I need a break. After breakfast I have just enough time to bake some bread and start the soups before it is lunch and the whole process starts all over again. And then again. Aidian has taken to coming in in the evenings and I'm glad because otherwise we wouldn't have any time together at all. As it stands, he sits at his table in the corner either banging away at his laptop, on what I don't 'want to know, or finishing some fabulous piece of art. We don't really get to interact much, grasp each other's hands for a moment when I bring him tea, or smile across the tables until about seven when we start to slow down. By then I'm either dead on my feet or so jacked up on caffeine that he says he can hardly understand what I'm saying. He tried to help me in the back a couple of times but he is clearly not maid for it and after three days of burnt break rock hard muffins and gelatinous soups I told him that he could help me better by just being there. I know he misses me, and I miss him too, and it's hard not to get short tempered when you're both exhausted and hopping from one place to another, and we've both been feeling the strain. That's why I was so happy to see him grinning when he came in tonight.

"*Kio okazas?*" I asked as he bent over the counter to kiss me. He handed me an envelope.

"What's this" I asked.

He just looked back and forth between it and I, saying nothing. I opened the envelope and shook out a stack of papers. I had no idea what they meant, though they looked very official, golden seals everywhere and sentences that rambled on forever. I asked him what they were again, and Aidian reached over and flipped through the pile until he found a piece that said "Deed" across the top in ornate script. My name was written underneath.

"I've been doing some, er, research," he said with a wink, so of course it wasn't research at all but hacking, but I'm not an *idioto* so I played along. "Turns out Don did have a will, and in it he left the café to his daughter."

"But his daughter di-" he put one of my fingers against my lips, shushing me. "To his YOUNGEST daughter. To you." He pulled out another paper. This one read "proof of paternity." "I thought it was a nice touch," he said quietly. I thought so as well. I never met my father, so Don was as likely as any and a better choice than most.

"So," he said, speaking this time so that everyone could hear, "this building officially, permanently, and legally belongs to you." Everyone clapped and I blushed.

"You mean the bakery," I said. "

"Nope," he replied, " S'what's fierce. Don owned the whole building."

And suddenly I remembered the apartments up above. They were, by Flower Town standards, absolutely immense, and in fairly good shape. and to be able to just walk up a flight of stairs and be home. I grinned. It would be amazing. The old Victorian place hasn't seemed like home since the debacle with Tawny and Dmitri anyway. My thoughts must have shown on my face because Aidian nodded. '

"Aye," he said, "we should do it."

"We." It was like a bucket of ice water being dumped on my and I found myself scared, uncertain. It was a big step. Too big. And I must have sounded a lot shaper than I meant to because his grin melted and he just looked hurt.

"Just think about it, Bird, yeah" he implored and I nodded. And I will. I'll think about it. It's not that I don't want him around. It's not that I don't care about him. I do. A lot. It's just that what if I wake up one more morning and he's gone? I don't think I could take that. What if he isn't the one and I'll just have to get over him? Maybe it's better not to expect him to be there at all, neh?

"Oh and one more thing," Aidian said. He motioned to the papers still in my hand. "That's all public record. They can find you now." I didn't have to ask him who "They" were. I knew. My stomach dropped and I was suddenly nauseous. "But they've always known. . " I started, but I couldn't finish. Things had changed. I wouldn't be able to hide from them much longer. I knew it. Aidan did too.

"But they'll come looking, once they see this. They'll have to . Might be best to beat them to the punch, aye?"

Reach out to them? And tell them what? That I'm sorry? Because I'm not. That I want to come back to the Facility? Because I don't. That it's okay for them to treat me like some Cynimal?

"I can't" I said out loud. Aidan nodded. I guess at this point he doesn't expect anything else from me but cowardice. I don't blame him.

"let me know what you decide. I'll help if I can," he said, and then he left.

He's not wrong. About any of it. I should. I should do both. Move in with Aidian upstairs and swallow my pride and call Dr. Alyce, he'd be the best bet, I think. I just don't know if I'm ready. For either. Not yet. I need just a little longer to just be me. To only have to report to me. Just a little longer.

SEPTEMBER 20

It's late. It's so late and I want to go to bed but instead I'm sitting here thinking about this girl. She came by this evening, near closing time, when it was just me, Aidian and a few of the regulars. And she didn't say anything at first. She just stood there in the door, blinking at the bright lights. It gets dark out there, the streetlamps haven't worked for years. Her eyes were huge. They were the kind of huge that speaks of hunger, and drugs, and fear. I knew those eyes. I'd had those eyes. She had on a man's coat that was easily three sizes too bit, and she was clutching it around herself like this thing was a *lana litkovrilo*, like it could protect her from anything that would harm her. She was thin. She was so thin. I could tell even under all of the clothes, and her hands were shaking and she was inexplicably and obviously terrified. But as vulnerable as she was, she terrified me.

My heart started to pound and my skin began to itch as the panic took hold. I turned my back on her without saying a word, partly to hid my face I could tell my nostrils were flaring and my eyes as wide as hers, and partly to create some distance, as much as I could anyway, between she and I. But I had to do something with my hands. So I wiped down the counter, gripping the washcloth so tight that my knuckles turned white. I stirred the soups; a cioppino made with some fish and clams gifted by a regular, and a broccoli-cheddar, synth but still tasty. I could near the noise quiet behind me, knew that people were staring, waiting for me to look at the girl, expecting me to do something. So, I grabbed a bag and started filling it with the morning's bread and muffins, old enough by now that I couldn't sell them. Once the bag was full, I approached the girl, holding it in front of me. "Here," I said, "these are for you." She backed up a step as if I held a snake and not food. "no," she blurted. " I mean thank you," and she grabbed the bag and held it close to her chest. "But I' not here. . I heard. .. sometimes. . . there was work here. . for people," her mouth opened and closed silently. . "Like me" she finally finished. I tried to answer her, I did, but for a minute I couldn't speak. I tried, but the thought of this girl, this intruder, in my place in my safe place was too much. I just couldn't. It would be like inviting my past through the door, horrible beyond measure. "No," I finally chocked out. "Not anymore. She shied away as thought I'd stuck her. I tried again to explain through the panic. "I'm sorry," I said, "I just don't need help." The girl backed away, trembling, and stumbled into the night.

The silence grew until the weight of it was bone crushing and I knew that somehow I'd failed.

I didn't know why. I'd fed her. But even Aidian looked disappointed, and stared at the the gears and wires blanketing what had become his table. It was Moses, an ancient man with skin so dark black with was almost blue, someone I'd known most of my life, who spoke, he deep voice rumbling though quiet. "It's a damned shame," he said. "When people forget. Don would be turning in his grave." And slowly, so fucking slowly, he grabbed his cane and walked out. Others followed one by one, dropping their cash at the register, until only Aidian and I were leff. Wordlessly, imploringly, I held my hands out to him. For a minute, he didn't move, and I thought that he was going to walk out on me too. My eyes began to burn and I could feel salt start to rise in my throat. After a second though he just sighed and pulled me close. "I couldn't" I murmured in his chest, "She just. . . I shouldn't." He stroked the back of my head. "I know" He said, "Some someday, you're going to have to learn to give, love."

He didn't see. How could he with his life of privilege, how could he know? We give out of our excess and when I have excess I will give. I just don't' have any, not yet. I'm still balancing on the brink. I'm still just a step, a half-step away from being her. I have nothing to give. Not yet.

SEPTEMBER 25

I finally got around to calling the Facility. It wasn't any act of bravery on my part. Instead, I'd gotten so paranoid, waiting and watching for some Official to show up, jumping every time anyone came through the door, that I thought if I just bit the bullet and did it maybe I could relax a little bit. AT first it seemed like my plan was actually going to work. I was waiting until evening to call, partly because it is slower in the café after dinner but mostly because I knew that Dr. Alyce would be at East, making the rounds and finishing up his paperwork. Somehow it was extremely important to me that he hear from me surrounded by the sights and sound and smells of East, as horrible as they were, rather than the prim and pristine Facility. I thought maybe it would help him remember the pre-surgical me. I don't know. He answered and was reasonably kind, though he didn't pull any punches about how disappointed he was in my actions. He asked if I would come into the Facility. I thought about it for a long time, long enough that he thought we had been disconnected before I said that I would, but only if I got to meet with him and Basanti privately before we saw the rest. I want the opportunity to explain myself to the ones I consider friends. Of a sort. Part of me was hoping for an apology from them as well, but I am realistic enough to know that I probably won't get one, even if they do have regrets. They may, but more than remorse they will feel the need to save face. Bur I suppose we will see. We agreed to meet tomorrow.

September 28

I thought I'd be relieved. That I would sleep well. I did fall asleep easily enough, but first I called Aidian and asked him to come with me. That hadn't been approved and will probably be frowned upon but I don't care. I need him there and they need to understand that he is a part of my life. Aidian said he would go, of course, and showed up around closing to walk me home. Daisy was thrilled. She loves him more than ever and prefers to ride home on his shoulder when she can, which really makes me happy though I have to admit to a bit of jealously. Of both of them. Being curled up on his chest is one of my favorite spots and well and I invited him to stay so soon enough I was there. His hand was stroking my hair and I was able to breathe.

Then my eyes opened to a blinking white light. Dr. Stevens looked down on my, a surgical mask covering the lower half of her face. "Finally you're back" and she turned and saluted to a group of people that I couldn't see. "Let's begin shell we," she said, and I knew what was happening. I tried to jump off the table but my arms and legs were strapped down. I tried to scream but just like the E.C. table my jaws were forced to clamp on to this foul-smelling disc, it even tasted the same, and there were all of these hands covered in blue rubber gloves and with green scrubs sleeves moving above me and there was the saw and it was huge. Dr Stevens kept moving it lower and lower and then I could hear it. I could hear it as it tore through y flesh and my skull and I could see the blood spraying. I arched my back as high as I could trying to break free.

"You must comply" Dr. Stevens barked, "calm down" and then I was awake and Aidan was holding me and murmuring "Calm down. It's only a dream, bird, Calm down."

I went into the bathroom and puked until the taste of the rubber was out of my mouth and aiding held me until I'd stopped shaking. I was tired. I was so damned exhausted and so I fell asleep and was on the table again and this time her fingers were in my brain. They were actually in my *fikfek* brain and she was making me move. I would feel her dig and my legs would kick. A jab and I would jibber in some language I don't even know. I woke up this time clapping and clawing the air over my head.

After that, we decided not to try to sleep anymore. I told Aidian that we should just get up and he heaved a giant sigh of relief. "Good" he said, rolling a cigarette. "I don't know that I could take another round. Too savage by half." So we just sat together, chatting and playing with Daisy and her color board, which is still one of her favorite toys. Aidian got his guitar out, playing quietly so as not to wake the neighbors. Soon. Soon it will be late enough to go to work. Just a little longer.

SEPTEMBER 29

I walked to work on legs that were still shaky from the night, and the first thing I did was hang up some signs to let people know what we will be closed tomorrow. (Holy Shit) you'd think that I was the local JuJu man short on candy. They're junkies, all of them, only their drug of choice is habit. This is what they do in the mornings. This is where they go, and to have that option taken away from them sends them into a panic. I'm grateful. I'm grateful to them and I'm grateful for this business and I'm grateful that I've helped keep this a safe place, something to look forward to. God knows joy can be on short supply around here, but I was not prepared for their reaction. Some people were worried about me, they knew that I'd had surgery and not why so naturally they assumed I was ill. I had to assure and reassure them that I was all right. Some very nearly cried. And I found myself saying over and over again that "It's just for one day. It's just for one day," and even then I don't think they believed me.

Others had oh-so-helpful suggestions. I should just reschedule whatever it was I had to do. I should be open for a half a day, the half that they wanted to come in, no doubt. I should open on the "honor system" because leaving a shop unlocked and open is a safe thing to do. And a dozen times if one, I need to hire some help. That last I might actually consider. Fekegalo, another thing to think about.

Sometimes I wish that I could go back to the way things were before. Not the depression or the anxiety. Hell, not even the poverty, just the. . .irresponsibility, I guess? Immaturity. Hell, I don't know how to explain it. I just know that I get so tired sometimes. Tired of having to make decisions that actually matter. I want to go back to when all that I had to do was show up for work and do whatever someone told me to do. When a relationship was just some random guy I hung around with until they realized I was never going to *maĉcast* them. It was so much easier that way. Hollower, too. I know that. I do see how much richer this life is. I do, it's just that I could really do with some hollow for a day . . or a week. . . or a month.

AUGUST 19

It never ends, neh? No matter how perfect, how amazing everything seems to be, no matter how well you think you know someone , it's only a matter of time until everything, every *fekanta* aspect of your life falls complete and totally to *merd*. It's like some giant cosmic joke, ken? You're staggering though this tunnel, trapped and alone in the dark, and the muck and finally you see it; there's a light, and so you run towards it screaming, arms spread wide, only to discover that it's a *diable* train. Maybe that's why I feel like I do. Crushed. Flattened. Utterly destroyed.

Aidian was waiting on the platform when the mono pulled in. He was, amazingly and blessedly alone and that fact in itself was such an incredible relief that I actually grew lightheaded. I expected Facility representatives at least, oficiales maybe. They can track my movements using the software they installed in my brain. I cannot run. I cannot hide. Not if they truly want me with them. I will continue to put my faith in the fact that, as they can also download a great deal of dada my physical being, the part of me that's they spent all weekend marginalizing, is just more trouble to them than it's worth. So, when we came around the corner and the platform was empty except for Aidian, I nearly cried. I thought that he was safe, that I'd returned to my harbor and I was out of danger. I flew out the doors and into his arms before the mono had even completely stopped. He held me close, a I won't' deny him that, he held me there on the platform while I sobbed in relief, sobbed and wailed until my knees felt weak and I'd left this giant disgusting patch of tears and snot and spit on his chest. At some point, Daisy ran from my pocket to his shoulder, and I could hear her squeak excitedly. When I was ready, he led me to the cab and started guiding us home. About halfway there, I started crying again and he pulled the cab to one side and put it in neutral. The dam broke again, and I told him everything, the words nearly tripping over each other. I told him how they'd pushed me around, how they'd referred to me as a "true member of society," how I'd not been allowed to even *fikfek* speak. I told him how dirty I felt, used, like some sort of *prostitutino*. And I told him how afraid I was that I'd lose everything. Technically they hold the lease on my home. They put my stipend in my account. And what they've given they could just as easily take away. I could go home to a locked door at any minute, and then discover that I don't' even have enough left to get a room for the night. And I'm scared. I 'm just so damned scared and I needed him. I thought he'd tell me that everything would be all right. Better yet, he'd somehow make me believe it. It thought he'd tell me that he could make it okay, that he could *forbati* with their records somehow. Interfere. He has to know how. Easy, neh? A tiny, hopeful part of me thought that he'd offer to marry me. That we'd drive to the next Circle hall and this godforsaken gown would become my wedding dress. What I didn't expect, could have never expected, was that he'd be a *fikfek* traitor. A weak, puling, lackey for the Facility. I should have expected it; everyone knows that inner-circle folk are weak, used to *aĉas la kacos* of the government in exchange for safety. But still, I would never have believed it of him. Which is why, I guess, I thought that I'd misheard him at first. "What did you say?" I asked.

"Maybe it's not too late," he repeated, "tell them it was the stress, yeah?"

"And go back?"

"Well, yeah, not to the conference, but the appointment. Those aren't so bad, you could fake it for an hour every week or so and you could keep living the way you are."

My mouth opened and closed several times before I was able to choke out my words. "Go back?" I spat. "go back to them, hands out, begging to Daddy? Is that what you'd do? Go back like I owe them. So they can tell me where to go, how to act, who to be. To parse out awards like some sort of achievement. To make demands like I owe them something?"

"Charlotte," he said quietly, "you kind of do."

His words hit me like an explosion. I rocked back in my seat, could hear the blood rushing in my ear.

"You bastard," I growled. "Take me home."

"Easy, Bird, I only meant-" hearing his voice made me nauseous.

"Shut up!" I shrieked, and my voice was deafening enclosed in the cab. "You're supposed to be on my side."

" I am, Love, it's just-"

"It's just nothing." I spat. I wanted to hit him. Hurt him like he'd hurt me. "Take me home." I snatched Daisy off of his shoulder and held her on my lap. He signed and that just made it worse. I'm making him weary, yeah? But at least he didn't say anything else. I don't think that I could have taken it, and shifted the car into gear. We drove home in silence. When we got there, he actually tried to go in with me. I sent him away. I sent him away and it hurt more than I could imagine but after how he's betrayed me, once I discovered who he is I didn't want him around another minute. "I'll see you tomorrow, then" he said as he turned back towards the cab. Weak. So weak. Why didn't I see that before? How could I have thought that someone that weak could ever protect me.

OCTOBER 3

I did it. I went back. I'm still not convinced that it was the best choice for me, but I am certain that it was better than watching and waiting for them to come to me. I had told Aidan not to come; love or not this part of my life is not his concern, but by the time the hovercab arrived I was in such a panic that I didn't think I'd be able to go through with it. I used the cab's microcomp to make a call. I started to dial the Facility, but called Aidian instead. I thought that maybe it would be better if I just had someone on my side. There's dozens of them, condescending, judging, staring, and just me and that's enough to daunt anyone. I asked him if he would go with me, and of course he said yes. He is so *diable* predictable in his goodness to me. So much so that it infuriates sometimes, especially because I don't feel like I could ever be there for him in that way. Still, not bad enough not to grab the comfort when and where I can, and if that makes me a bad girlfriend, so be it.

The meeting was. . . well it was everything I thought that it would be. Basanti and Dr. Alyce tried, they really did, but I'm still incredibly angry with that and they're angry as well. They think that I'm ungrateful, and even worse in their eyes indifferent to the results of the experiment and what it might mean.

I'm not. I'm very grateful. And I think it's fair to say that I'm more vested than anyone in the results. I just don't believe that gives them total dominion over my life. I also don't like their belief that someone they created me. They didn't create me. I was a person before they cut into me. I had value before they cut into me. They didn't make me. They didn't even make me well. Sure, they helped, but it was my determination, my will, my hard work that brought it to fruition, otherwise why did it matter who they picked to cut? The simple fact is that we are never going to agree. Someday, thought, I hope that we can move on. One thing that I wholeheartedly agree with is that I will progress farther, faster, if we work as a team. After we were done I was turned over to Nu, who ordered a dozen tests and then left and Stevens, who looked me over while saying as little as possible. I could tell that there was a lot that she wanted to say. Her eyebrows were jumping up and down and she kept opening her mouth and then closing it again. Apparently she'd been told to play it cool, though, and with the exception of a brief altercation when they wanted Aidian to leave the room, I said no, it was actually fairly perfunctory.

One thing does keep coming back to me, no matter how hard I try to push it away, but it keeps playing in my mind like a song that gets stuck. It was something

Basanti said pretty early on in the talk. "You've come a long way, Charlotte, but emotionally you are still very young. You are selfish, suspicious. You keep everyone at a distance. Those were functional behaviors, once, but you don't need them anymore." I denied it, f course, but now that the heat of the moment has passed, I don't know. I think of Aidian, how he's given so much and I've taken it, or not, based on what I wanted at the time. I thought about Don, laying there dead while I was mooning about feeling sorry for myself. I thought about the hungry girl with the huge eyes that I'd turned away. God, maybe I am as selfish as they say. I used to sit there, wrapped in a blanket that was freezing to the ground and watch people step on my feet without one even looking at me, and I used to wonder what the hell had happened to the soul of a person to make them do that. I remember how I felt after Tawny and Dmitri trashed my house. How selfish they seemed. Have I really become that? Have I really become one of those?

Another part of the day that stuck out was me snapping at Dr. Alyce. I don't remember what lead up to him, but I remember looking at him and nearly shouting "You don't know that. You don't know ME," and he touched my arm and said quietly, so quietly I could barely hear him, "Yes, Charlotte, I do." And I realized, he'd known me longer than anyone, had been with me through more than anyone. I trusted this man with my life more than once. Trusted him enough that when he suggested the surgery I took the chance without hesitation. When had he become my enemy? Was that part of my selfishness?

I asked the hovercab driver to stop at the café.

"What are you doing" Aidian asked as we walked through the kitchen and up the stairs.

"I thought we'd take a look at our new place" I said. I hadn't even known I was going to do it, until I did, but someone must have. I unlocked the door, and sitting there among what remained of Don's life, sitting then in the dust was a brand new SimCenter. A microcomp was attached to the side.

OCTOBER 11

Busy. Busy again. Busy always. I think if I were to die right now my eulogy would be that single world. Still, if I look past the exhaustion and the perpetual motion if I stop for a minute, there is happiness, excitement even.. I mean, I am building a life. No, not just I, we are, Aidan and I. That was incredibly difficult to get used to at first, the "we." The together. I came home one night and he'd moved a bunch of his stuff in, set up a work station filled with his computer supplies.,. He'd even hung some pictures on the wall. I was immediately, viscerally, furious. Who does that? Just takes over one part of the house where they are crashing? I never did that. When someone let me live with them, I always tried to live small, to not intrude. Even Dmitri and Tawny didn't redecorate. I opened my mouth to tell him that when it hit me, he wasn't crashing with me. He wasn't' sleeping on my couch until we got kicked out or he found something better, we were doing this together. It's our place, not mine. And so instead of yelling I just stood there and watched him for a bit. He was painting the walls in the tiny area off of the kitchen, just big enough for one of the extra tables from downstairs and a couple of chairs. The paint was this amazing soft yellow that looked almost gold when sunlight hit it. He had his earbuds in, so loud I could hear the music from where I stood and between his height and his long arms his strokes reached all the way to the ceiling. , covering the dark brown with these beautiful swathes of color. You know, I didn't realize it until then, but he'd been working as hard as I, keeping up with his clients, moving our things, painting, and dropping all of that to show up for me whenever I called. Suddenly, my chest ached and my eyes welled. It was like this door opened inside of me. I wanted him, in that moment. Loved and wanted him so bad that my arms ached with it. I crossed the room and slid my arms around his waist. I startled him and he jumped and the roller sprayed both of us with yellow. I didn't care, pressed myself as tightly against him as I could and kissed him, softly at first, but harder, hungry. I could feel his hands at the ticklish spot at the small of my back and pressed myself harder still. If I could have crawled inside him at that moment I would have and it still wouldn't have been close enough. It was morning before we let go of one another, both of us out of breath, our lips swollen, and even then I never slept. I just lay there in fear and wonder. So this is what it is like to love someone. To want someone. With no reservations. There's a part of me that's angry, a part of me that can't help but hate the people who took this and so much else from me for so long. But mostly I just want to wallow around in it, roll it on my tongue, and I will, for as long as I can.

OCTOBER 16

Tonight was catastrophic. It was horrible and I have no idea how it went so badly so quickly. I don't know what I did wrong or what I could have done differently, though I can't help but feel like I should have done something. It started out well enough. Normal, ken? Just the ins and outs that have become my day. Baking breads and goodies. Making sandwiches. Serving food. Bantering with the customers. About four o'clock I looked up and I saw her. Denae. Standing in the doorway and looking, for the first time that I've ever seen, uncertain. Small. Her whole face lit up when she saw me behind the counter, though, and if there's anything that will come back and haunt me, it will be that look, especially considering what came later. She was happy to see me. No, not happy, ecstatic. Relieved. And I remember. I remember what it's like to be back on the outside after you've been in East after a while. As insane as it seems, the horrors of being inside become normal after a while, comfortable even. You start to take a sick sort of joy from lining up in the mornings to take your pills. Standing there in the jostling madness among the murmuring, the head-slapping, and the vacant stares, chatting with the people you consider friends and wondering which nurses will be distributing the pills that day. Talking sagely about what they're making you take. "oh, you're on that one, that one gave me the *eksplodo lakso* so be careful." "you're on this one? I was on that for a while and I hated it." "250 of the other one, you lucky *inaĉo*, you willing to share?" The boredom, the routine, even the smells become a security blanket of sorts and even though you complain daily you look longingly through the bars at the world outside and talk about what it's going to be like when you get out you find yourself not entirely wanting to be released. Inside you're safe, relatively so anyway. But outside, the outside is a big *fikfek* world, even if it's just one ring of one circle its just so *kaduka kaj malnova*. No matter how big of a fish you are inside, outside you're just the freak, the unknown, another face. So I understood and my heart went out to my friend and God I was happy to see her. I charged out from behind the counter, didn't even care about the slam that the swinging door made. What's another scratch on the counter, yeah? It was Denae and she was here. I zigzagged through the tables and threw myself into her arms, squealing. She was trembling, I could feel that, but laughing too and she picked me up so that my feet were dangling in the air. "Hey baby, she said, you look good," and I felt myself blushing, preening under her words. She was here. She'd be proud of me at least. So I took her by her hand, perfectly manicured as always, as took her around the café. I was jabbering a mile a minute. I took her in the back and showed her my kitchen and everything I was making and she beamed as she saw it all, even though the machines were rusty and old, even though the paint was flaking she didn't see any of that. She saw that it was mine and that I was happy and she was happy for me. That's her greatest gift, Denae, too take the joy of others and take joy in it. I took her around then and introduced her to all of the regulars and they were great, shaking her hand and welcoming her and I could see her relax. I could see that my place could become a safe place for her and I knew that she needed that. Out here where everything was so big you need a sanctuary. She had been my sanctuary so many times, and I was ecstatic that I could return the favor. After a while I realized that she was probably hungry. `When you're released, you're given a stipend. "Reintroduction budget," it's called and it's a joke. Enough for a cab ride home, if you have one. Enough for a couple of meals. Maybe. I rushed around, filling bowls with soup, layering a sandwich with more care than I generally use. I brought the plate over to Denae and I didn't imagine the look of relief on her face. I let her alone to eat, but checked in often, sitting and chatting between customers. It was so amazing to have her there, and soon we were laughing like we always did. Late in the evening, Aidian came in and I drug him over by the hand to introduce them, almost like a child. Aidian was charming, shaking her hand. "I've heard so much about you," he said. Denae was hesitant. At first I thought it was the natural hesitation of one of us for an outsider; after a while I saw it for what it was; the protectiveness of a mother for her child. No wonder it took me a while to realize that, Lord knows mine had never cared. Once I saw it though, I kept having to turn my back to laugh. She grilled him like I never did, asking about his family, his upbringing, his jobs, his intent for me. After a while I started listening in. I couldn't help but feel a little guilty that I'd never asked him those things. I didn't know, for example, that he hadn't finished college, but was paying to help his five (five!) younger brothers with their education. I didn't know that his father had been hospitalized for a long time now, due to complications from the chemicals that poison our air after even this long after the war, or that Aidian went to see him every Sunday to play board games and chat. I didn't know that he had desired, at first, not to be a hacker, or an artist, but a teacher. But getting to find these things out, even secondhand, was this amazing window into the man that I loved. His honesty disarmed Denae, and his easy laugh, and soon they were chatting like old friends. We slowed down and I was able to join them and it was amazing. Then they came in. Two guys. Drunk. I didn't know them; they'd never been in before and had obviously just finished a night at the club. They were obnoxious from the get go, loud and abrasive. Tacky. Rude. I brought the coffee and pastries that they asked for, and then sat while they pulled out a wad of money, dumping half of the change on the floor. "Pick that up, would you?" one of them asked. I signed but did what they asked, and tried to ignore the comments they made while I was bent over. Aidian came and stood nearby, checking his microcomp so as not to appear threatening, but I knew what he was doing. Apparently, they did as well, because they quieted down and I went behind the counter to start cleaning up. Aidian followed me and grabbed a rag to help. "Are you going to ask her to say?" he asked.

"Probably," I said. "She'll need somewhere." We kept chatting and at first I didn't notice what was going on. You get used to certain noises and learn to just shove them in the background. After a little while, though, I picked up in a change in the voices of the drunks. I looked up, and they were standing next to Denae. They were making fun of her, calling her these horrible names. She had her head down, trying to ignore them, but I could see that her hands had started shaking a gain. Just then, one reached out and grabbed at her chest, taking her breast in her hand.

"Are these real titties?" he crowed, "they feel real to me!" Denae looked up at me, then, and I could see the pleading in her eyes and I – I just froze. I wanted to help, I did, but they were customers and I didn't know what to do. I'd never had to kick anyone out before. What if they got mad? What if they came back and destroyed the place? What if they wouldn't go? Aidian didn't hesitate, though. He leapt over the counter and had them by the elbows and tossed out the door before I could even move. The whole thing didn't take more than 5 seconds, but I could tell by the look on her face that it had been too long. I came over to her and tried to hug her. "I'm so sorry that happened. I'll never let them come in again," I said. It was like hugging a wall, she didn't move. "It won't matter," she said, and got to her feet. "Denae, don't go," I said, "you can stay upstairs and I won't let it happen again." She didn't say anything, but I could see her get to her feet. Large tears slid down her face

"I always took care of you," she said, her back to me. " I just want you to think about that."

I followed her, calling her name for three blocks or more, but she never answered. Never even slowed her step. Eventually, I gave up, and went back to the café. Aidian was finishing closing. He saw my face and came and hugged me close.

"I didn't know what to do," I said.

He kissed the top of my head. "I know," he said, "let's lock up." He didn't say anything, but I walked away feeling like I'd let him down, too. I guess that makes three of us.

OCTOBER 15

Another appointment at the Facility means another day with the Café closed. People seemed to do better with it this time, at least. I mean, there was still a good deal of grumbling, but the panic and anger weren't as extreme as before. I guess that they are starting to believe that I am here to stay, which is *granda*, but I have to admit to a little apprehension, I'm not sure what they will do if I can't regularly be here when they expect me to be. To make things work I had planned on opening around lunchtime, but my appointment ran way over. It all started when I flinched at the light that Dr. Stevens shined in my eye. I didn't mean to, it was just surprisingly painful and I jerked away. "What's wrong?" she barked. It told her it was nothing, just a bit of a headache. I'd had it for a day or so. I told her that I thought it was stress, or lack of sleep, dehydration maybe, but of course she didn't believe me and sent me for the full battery of tests, CT, MRI the whole dammed alphabet, and when she was done she handed me over to C.S. Nu. I never did get to see Basanti, the one I actually wanted to see. The one who helps me more than the others. She said she will stop by the café if she has time this week, but we will have to see. Anyway, Nu hooked me up to about a million electrodes and pretty much just spoke to his staff the whole time. It was after dark when they finally released me and I don't even know what they discovered, if anything. I'm sure it was all well though.

Anyhow after a day of being inside machines, as opposed to the machines inside of me I guess, I really needed some fresh air, so I had the hovercab drop me off at the harbor. I planned to walk home from there. The breeze was nice on my face. Daisy must have agreed because she stood on my shoulder, stretching her neck as far as it would go and wiggling her whiskers. It was cold, though. I could see my breath as I walked. Somehow, in all my busyness, autumn had come and winter wasn't too far behind. Could that much time really have passed? I saw the coat first. The oversized men's coat, and she was snuggled so deeply into it that only the top of her head showed. She must have been new to the street, then. During the day, this strip seems like a good place, sunny, full of people, close to all of the places where you can sometimes find work, but at night it is horrible. The wind form the harbor absolutely howls down the street and there's no break from it, no shelter. JuJu men and woman prowl, looking or clients. Pimps, too, and they're not all above taking a girl against her will. But, we all stay there at first. We are all too stupid, too green to know how bad a choice it is. Some of us are lucky enough to find someone who takes us under their wing, shows us the ropes. The rest? Well, experience breeds wisdom, or so they say. God, I couldn't leave here there. Even though she terrified me. Even though part of me hated her for what she represented, for the memories she dredged up in me. Still, I couldn't leave her there. I put Daisy in my pocket to keep her safe, and shook the bundle of rags that was the girl. "Hey," I said. *Vekiĝ!* Wake up. She came to life like one of these children's toys with the box and the spring and the clown. I'd never seen a clown with a knife, though. I had to jerk away to dodge her and almost fell. I smiled, though, a hard smile. I guess she's learned something after all. "*Malstreĉi, karulinon*" I said, holding up my hands. I was ready to grab her if I had to, though. She wasn't worth dying for, no matter how much I sympathized. Slowly, oh so slowly, her eyes focused, the knife sunk by inches until it hung by her side. "It's not safe here," I told her, "let me take you somewhere that is."

Aidian's eyes widened when we walked in. "It's just for the night," I said, and grabbed her one of the blankets from the bedroom. She was asleep in an instant, twirling her hand in her hair like a child. Aidian walked over to where I watched her in the doorway, pulled me close, and kissed me on the forehead. "you did a good thing, Bird," he said. And maybe I did. Maybe I did in fact.

OCTOBER 23

Fekegalo Cakisto, how could he be so inconsiderate! I word hard all of the time. He gets to set his own hours, and that's incredible for him, you know? But not all of us can do that. We don't all have that luxury. A could of weeks ago, we heard that one of our favorite bands, Industrial Otter, was coming to our circle, one two or three levels in from us. I wanted to go so badly. They are amazing. This heavy industrial sound with this brassy beat and gears grinding all on top of amazing harmonies. I've been a fan for years, have wanted to see them forever. So Aidian came home with tickets one night, at first I was really excited. Giddy, ken? Then I starting thinking about it and I don't feel like I can shut down for something like that. For necessities, sure, but for frivolity? Neh. I tried to tell him that weeks ago. He was irritated. He thinks I should close shop whenever I want. "you're the owner, aye?" But it doesn't work like that. The café isn't some hobby, something I do to take up my time. I don't feel like he takes my business seriously. So, then he started going on again about me hiring someone. "If you had some help you could go out more." "Maybe you wouldn't be so tired." Maybe. But I'm not ready. I don't have anyone I trust and I'm not in a place where I feel like I could gamble on someone. It would slow me down, and who knows what they would do. Flake out and quit or stead or. .. . all of the things I used to do I guess. How did Don ever put up with me? Maybe I should follow his example; the regulars certainly think so. Moses hasn't been back since the night I turned that girl away. What they don't understand is this café is everything to me. It's the first time I've succeeded. the first time I've had something that belongs to me. I can't just let some stranger in. I can't let some random (foreigner) get close, get inside, take away part of it. Anyway Aidian and I went back and forth for a while, but then one day he just let it go. He seemed sad, but at least we weren't talking about it anymore. So, I thought he understood. I thought that he got it. Apparently not. He wasn't at the café by the time I locked the doors, which was strange because he has been there every night lately. it's become a bit of a tradition for him to help me wipe down and then walk me home, even if home is just up the stairs. I was a little worried. Not much, he is a grown man and his job sometimes lasts longer than we expect. Then midnight rolled around and he still wasn't there. I fished him a time or now and nothing. fikfek nothing. Not a "Hey, Bird." Not a "Home in a bit," nothing. Finally he comes strolling in at like 2am; his breath smelled like beer, and his face was painted bronze and gold. God he looked good, too. I didn't want to notice, but I couldn't help it. His eyes stood out so much they nearly glowed. His face was gorgeous and I wanted to punch it.

"I can't believe you went," I yelled. I thought he would look sorry at least. Repentant, neh? He wasn't. He was as mad as I was. "Why shouldn't I then?" he shouted back. "You're the one who wants to hide in the café, not me. I asked you to go, Bird. Begged you!"

I couldn't. I wanted to go with him but I couldn't. That's not the same as not going. I told him that dozens of times. Why doesn't he see?

"Then hire someone," he snapped. So, it's back to that again.

It's like everything has to e his way or not at all. I don't want to hire someone. I'm not ready to hire someone, but him going to bully me into it. That's all this was. Sheer bullying.

"Wash that *merda* off before you come to bed," I said. I slammed the door behind me so hard that it seemed like the whole building wrong. I've been in the room, playing with Daisy, ever since, waiting for him to come in and apologize. You know what's (absolutely insane)? As furious as I am there's a part of me, a larger part than I care to admit, that thinks that maybe I was the one who didn't understand.

OCTOBER 25

It's been two days. Two days of tension between Aidian and I. we're not actively fighting; no one is yelling or making sideways comment. I've been finishing the painting while he unpacks the last few boxes. In different rooms, yeah, but still. We've even been sleeping curled up together in my – our- bed. There's a distance, though. A hesitance that wasn't there before and I hate it. I absolutely *fikfek* hate it. So, I guess that's why when Aidian suggested we celebrate being officially and finally moved in, I agreed. I want to see him smile again. I want us to start our lives together doing something wonderful and together. I think, also if I'm being honest, I wanted the distraction, something to provide a bit of a distance while we heal.

Saturday night is usually pretty slow at the café. The regulars are off work, actually spending time at home with their families, or catching up on some much needed sleep. The other's are out with their friends, drinking their paycheck, laughing. I envy them sometimes, especially when I see the line from the club down the street. I miss the bouncer, that first "friend" I made after surgery. I think about that night in the club a lot, losing myself in the music and the lights. I wish I could do that again sometime. Or better yet, I wish I could get some music here in the café. Obviously I couldn't do anything elaborate or large scale. I wouldn't want to anyway, that's not the vibe this place has. Still though, some life music on the weekends would be (fantastic). For now though, there's hardly enough time to do all the things already on our plate. Even so, I'm closing early next Saturday. We are inviting the customers and our friends. Friends, I have a few from the café, but no one that Aidian doesn't know and this will be the first time I've met most of his. I'm more than a little terrified at the prospect. Sometimes I'm sure they're all be incredibly (sophisticated) and trendy. Computer types and artists and typical inner circle kids covered in black vinyl, dripping in gold and gem inserts, scowling at the way we live here. Other times I believe that if Aidian likes them, I will as well and I picture them relaxed, welcoming. I guess we will find out either way.

Aidian wants to have some food catered. At first, I resisted. No one ever had events catered around her. Ordering a pizza or some takeout, sure, but catering? That's too *franzia* for our taste. Still, eventually he sold me on the idea. It is a special occasion, and besides if we had it catered I wouldn't have to do any more work. That, more than anything, was the deciding factor. I like the idea of just showing up and there already being magical food on the table. I wish there was some way I could arrange that in the café. I'm going to have my hands full. See, I want to do something to make it really special for him as well. For us. It's time and past time. I find myself thinking about it, worrying about it, fantasizing about it more than I care to admit. There are so many nights that I can't even sleep, I'm just so aware of him being there. I think of the way he touches my back or kisses my neck and I can actually hear the blood pumping through my veins. I just want to have it done and over with so that I can have my mind back, my body back. No. That's not all. I want to say it is because otherwise it's just too big, this thing that I'm planning to do and the reasons it's all too much, but the simple fact is that I WANT to give him this. For the first time in my life I want to give myself to someone. I just hope that I can.

NOVEMBER 1

I should have known it was going to be a disaster. I was a wreck before the party even started. Trying to make sure everything was perfect, worrying about the people, running back and forth from the apartment to the café. Finally, people started to come. My friends. His. A couple of regulars. And I think it would have been nice, if I could have relaxed. But I couldn't. Everyone was great; calm, mellow, but I don't think I could even remember their names. They must have thought I was such a *inaĉo*. Or insane. I kept finding myself in the middle of a conversation and had no idea what it was about. I kept going to the kitchen, presumably to check on things, but really to hide. And to think about after. Our guests must have been enjoying themselves because it seemed like they'd never leave. They just stayed. Chatting. Singing. But finally, finally it was over and then I didn't even know how to start. Should I take him by the hand and lead him to bed? I just didn't think that I could do that. It seemed contrived. Do I strip down to my new underclothes and wait? But what if he doesn't come? Do I just lay there and keep waiting? How long? *Fek*, how would I know. I've never done this before. I wished I could talk to Denae. She's the one who taught me, I don't know, everything girly. How to do my hair.

My makeup. How to deal with my period. How to deal with the men who hit (and sometimes hit) me. I know she could have told me what to do. She's at East,though, at least I assume she is, and so I was on my own. Disastrously on my own. I was so worried about it that I don't even remember the party and by the time the last person had finally left I'd talked myself out of it. But all I could think about was how proudly he'd introduced me to his friends, how hard he'd worked getting ready. I walked over to the couch where he was sitting and straddled him. Kissed him until I was lightheaded and had to come up for air. I moved my hips against him. Slowly at first, but then quicker. He kissed my neck and I buried my fingers in his air and I remember thinking "I can," as I rocked, " I can and I can and I can" Our shirts ended up on the floor and he laid me on the couch and I drew him down (I CAN) and that's when it happened. Brief at first *tre rapide* just a flicker Aidan's hair grew dark and a moustache , sparse and mangy, sprouted on his upper lip. I gasped. I swear I could even smell the *bastardo.*

Aidian pulled back and looked down at me, panting, "what's wrong" he asked. I couldn't say it. I didn't want to say it, and so I pulled him down again and closed my eyes. That just made it worse. God, I was ten. I was ten years old and it was him, that first one, forcing himself between my legs and I screamed. I couldn't help it. I screamed and I brought my knee up, hard and I think I bit his lip but I don't' know because after that I ran. I ran, blind to the bathroom and slammed the door. It wasn't until I'd gotten my breath back, that I opened my eyes and realized what had happened. God, I'm such a *azenulo*. And a tease. And a fraud. I've never been so humiliated in my life. I wish that tonight had never happened. And I don't' know how I can ever leave here, how I can ever show my face again. Maybe I won't. Maybe I will just stay here on the cool tile, the thick door at my back forever.

NOVEMBER 3

I have to get down to the café. I have work that has to be done. There are people depending on me. But to do that I'd have to leave the bathroom. I still don't want to leave, am not sure that I can. It doesn't help that Aidian is still outside the door. Sleeping I'm certain, but I can hear the rustle of fabric when he rolls over or shifts. He can stay out there as long as he wants, I'm still not coming out. Why is he doing this to me? He isn't the one who was humiliated, neh? No, that was me. Me who made a *tromp* out of myself. Me who can still feel that *bastardo* crawling all over me like a million cockroaches. No, cockroaches don't eat you live. Sewer rats do. I heard about n old man who fell once and broke his leg in an alley. They say they could hear his screams for blocks while the rats bit off bit at his flesh. Killed him a little bit at a time. That everyone heard but no one did anything. My mom used to use the rat man as a threat when I was little. God, but then it became my reality anyway didn't it? She let them kill me a little at a time and no one did anything. *Fikfek* rats. Oh God. Rats. Daisy. I have to reset daisy. But I can't. I can't go out there, not even for her. What do I do? It isn't' safe out there. It's not safe outside of this door I thought it was for a while but it isn't. I need to stay here. Here where I don't have to see anyone and where no one can see me. He, but oh, my Daisy.

NOVEMBER 4

It was the smell of burning bread that finally drove me from the bathroom, strong enough that it crawled up through the vents. For a minute I thought that the whole building was on fire. I snatched a town from the tiny cupboard under the sink and soaked it in cold water before I charged out into the hall. I must have looked like a *freneza*, my makeup smeared all over my face, my hair wild, even wilder than usual, my face red, that stupid towel that read "Flower Town Villas" third-hand at least, held up to my mouth, coming through the door. There was no one to see it, though.. I was glad. I would have probably scared the hell out of anyone I'd encountered, looking as I did and shrieking Aidan and Daisy's names . I was almost all the way down the stars before I realized what was really going on. Aidian had tried to run the café for me. The customers were trying as well, they were being as good of sports as you could ever ask for, , but they were wrinkling their noses and trying to fan away the stench, chewing forlornly at doughy muffins and burnt bagels. Aidian was red-faced and sweating, and he had a large blister along one forearm. It was the closest to out of control, panicked than I'd even seen him, and it did more to melt my heart, to break the spell than anything else could have done. I love that he's so solid. He's my rock, ken? And I need that. But sometimes I get so (shitting) sick of his perfection. Of his unselfishness that I want to do something, anything to make him waver. Damn it, why doesn't he feel? Still, I couldn't look at him long. Just the sight of him made me want to vomit, to run and hide in the corner. It made my skin itch. So I walked up behind him, staring at the countertop. "I need you to leave" I muttered. He had been so intent on the task at hand, getting the charred bread out of the ovens that I scared him and he almost dropped the tray. "I'm sorry," he said, backing away. He was backing away like I was going to hurt him and I couldn't blame him because I had, I had. "They don't work. I've been trying." "What doesn't work," I asked. I was shaking just being near him. "Baking." He said. I looked up some recipes and followed them but they just won't'. "Sometimes it doesn't," I said. "Sometimes the ingredients are there and you do everything right and it just doesn't work. It's not a machine, Aidan." I looked down at my hands, the ragged cuticles. "Lots of things aren't' machines." He started to cry. He actually started to cry and reached for my shoulder, "Bird, I never thought-" but I ducked out of his reach. "I know you didn't But I still need you to leave."

And he did. God help me, he did. And I spent the rest of the day watching the door, simultaneously hoping and dreading that he'd come back.

NOVEMBER 10

Fek the nightmares! Every time I close my eyes they return and each one is worse than the one before. Last night was horrific. There were demons chasing me. Huge and black and their flesh was rotting off of their bones. It hung there in these long stinking strips and drops of poison fell from them. everything the drops would touch would start to, I don't know, burn? Rot? Everything. The walls. The floor. Mr. So soon everything was this blistering, festering pool. And their arms. God, their arms. Twice the length of human arms. Three times. Their fingers were even longer and they were white hot. The hot of *fekanta* machines that have been pushed too far, that are about to explode and they were grabbing me with them, tearing my clothes, running them up my legs and along my face. But their faces, those were the worst. Every face from my past was there. My mother. The men she sold me to. Dmitri and Tawny. The fortune teller. Even Denae was amongst them, her face a twisted and rotten caricature. Dr Stevens. I woke up tearing at my own face and it took a minute, an hour after the last before I realized they weren't really there. I sat up in bed rocking, trying to slow my breaths the way I'd been taught., relaxing my muscles one at a time. Murmuring over and over "not real not real not real." Oh, but they are. They are always with me, those demons. Hiding. Waiting for the chance to pounce. And I guess I should be grateful They want to rule me all of the time. Every step I took, everything I ever did was guided by the demons one way or another. Still I thought they'd be gone by now. I thought that I would finally be free of them. Sometime I think this is even worse. They hide and wait, the *bastardos*. They wait until I'm asleep or happy or my guard is down. When I'm not looking for them, yeah? And then they attack and remind me of what I really am. You see, I think I'm a business owner, a baker, a lover, a friend. what I really am is a sickness. I break everything I touch and I don't mean to it is just inside of me. This messed up version of the Midas touch, the *merda* touch. I wish I could get rid of it. I wish I could be as good, inside and out, as I try to be, but sometimes just don't know if it is possible. Maybe it was never my brain that was broken, maybe it was my, I don't' know, my soul. How do they fix that? How do I fix that? After a while, I wrapped up in my blanket and went to look for Aidian. He was, as I'd asked, neh, demanded, keeping his distance. Staying out long after I came home, sleeping on the couch when he did get in. I was thinking I'd hold his hand for a minute while he slept, maybe even lay on the floor. I can't bring myself to talk to him, not yet, but I miss him. Sometimes

I just want to be close. I got to the end of the hall and I saw him sitting up. His eyes were bleary, unfocused, so I knew I had been the one who had woken him, and seeing him awake stopped me, like I'd hit a wall. So for what seemed like an infinity I stood there, starting across the, what, 15 feet that separated us. It might as well have been miles. Damn it. I might as well have been forever.

NOVEMBER 12

Today, after the lunch rush I was icing cookies. It is intricate work, using the frosting to create psychedelic swirly. Japanese characters, even simple pictures. It is one of my favorite tasks, both exhilarating and soothing, yeah? Daisy watched intently from my apron pocket, and every now and then I'd slip her a taste of the sweet icing. She lies it, but I get the impression that what she really wants to do is try her hand, or paw, at painting. I've come really close to letting her, too. I think, though, that customers would flinch at a rat-decorated cookie. Cynimal or no. I've often thought that I should buy her some paints and paper. I keep meaning to do so, but somehow it never gets done. Anyhow I was painting and I hear the brief tinkle of music, Industrial of course, that Aidan programmed to play whenever a customer comes in. It's been nice having something more than the old bells. That means I can work in the kitchen without feeling like I need to rush up front every couple of minutes to see if anyone has come in. He wants to install thumb pads that would allow people to self-serve from the pastry case, too. It seems like an amazing idea. God, Aidian. I wish that I could go just an hour without thinking of him. Without something reminding me of him. It hurts. Every time it hurts. I'm no t mad at him anymore. I got over that part pretty quick. I mean, I was the one who initiated it and let's be honest, he couldn't win. He goes along with it and it goes bad and I'm devastated, but if he'd refused me I would have been crushed. And he wants me. I want him too. I just, I can't look at him, ken? It's like there are weights on my eyes and it makes my skin burn and itch. But I miss him . *Multe.* Anyway I slipped Daisy one last piece of icing and walked out front. Basanti was waiting at the counter.

"What do you want?" I asked.

She was playing coy. "I think I'll have coffee and one of the sticky buns." I crossed my arms and glared.

"What do you really want, Basanti.?"

She sighed. It seems like she spends most of her time with me sighing. Sometimes I wonder what she really thinks of me.

"I came to talk," she said, "but I really would like a sticky bun. I haven't had lunch yet. I slid open the case and pulled out one of the gooey pastries. I went to the carafe of our darkest coffee, so think it was nearly syrup, and pulled her a cup and then pushed all of it across the counter. "Did Aidian call you?" I asked. I was already planning my speech to him, something about betraying me, minding his own damned business. "No, Charlotte," Basanti said, and my argument died before ever being born ,which always leaves me disconcerted. "Your journal entries." She said simply. Right. The microcomps. I'd gotten so used to keying in entries that I'd forgotten that anyone else, let alone a whole group of anyones, was reading every word I typed. Suddenly, I felt a little sick to my stomach. "So they sent you to check in on me?

"I came because I knew you must be hurting, Charlotte. I care about you."

"You mean you care about your investment."

"I'm not going to pretend that everyone at the Facility is your friend," she said. "We all know better. But Ken and I (Ken I assume is Dr. Alyce), we care about you more than any results."

I snorted.

"Remember, he fought for you. To help you. As for me? All I can tell you is that I' not on the clock right now."

"So you won't' be reporting to anyone?"

"Not unless I fear that you are in immediate danger."

Something in me broke then, the dam that I'd been trying so hard to keep intact just shattered. "Oh Basanti," I sobbed, "it was awful."

NOVEMBER 15

Aidian and I sat in the backset of the hovercab on our way to Center Circle. It was the closest we'd been to each other in a week, and we were both feeling the strain. He didn't seem to know what to do with his hands. He kept putting one arm across the back of my seat, then snatching it back, reaching for my hand, and then pulling away. "I miss you, Bird," he said once, but I was pretending to be fascinated by the skyline as we approached and so it was easy enough to just pretend I didn't hear him. Still, it hit me like a punch to the gut. I want so much to go back to the way things used to be, and I know it was me who screwed it up. My issues, anyway. What I don't know is how on earth to fix it. Which is part of why we were going to see Dr. Alyce. We, or at least I, were hoping to be told something that could help, I don't know, Bridge the gap? Go back in time, maybe? Half an hour later, we were seated in Dr. Alyce's office. Still next to each other. Still silent. Aidan spun the gear he wore on the first finger of his right hand around and around, and I chewed on the skin around my thumb. Finally, Dr. Alyce spoke.

"I understand there has been a setback. I know what I read on the microcomp[s. Can you tell me more?" And I didn't want to talk. I didn't' want to cry like I knew I inevitably would. Didn't want to make a fool of myself again, but I had to say something. That's why we'd come all this way, why Dr. Alyce had cleared an entire day of his schedule. So I spoke.

"I'd been having . .. feelings for a while," I started. But I couldn't seem to figure out where to go next. I sounded so childish. I felt so childish.

"What sorts of feelings?" Dr. Alyce prompted. "Love?"

"No." I said, and Aidian flinched.

"I mean, yes, that too, but I'd had that a while. There were different. I-" *Fek* why was this so hard? "I wanted to be with him."

"Sexually" Dr. Alyce asked. I nodded.

"Well," he said, and he pushed his glasses up his nose, "sexual desire is normal. Healthy even." I nodded again.

"And so one night I tried to. . . I tried. At first it was good and then Aidian turned into. . " I paused so long I could hear the clock on the wall ticking. "Him." I finished, choking out the word.

"Who, Charlotte?"

God, didn't he know? Couldn't he figure it out? Why was he doing this? "The first man my mother sold me to." I mumbled. A tear, hot so hot that it burned, rolled down my cheek. "I mean, I knew it wasn't really him, but I could see him, smell him,' I started rubbing my arms on the arms of the chair, "Even feel him, and I just. .. I couldn't go on."

Dr. Alyce said nothing. Just pursed his lips and leaned back in his chair and I wanted to jump across the desk. I wanted to rip his smug face off.

"And how did that make you feel?"

Really? I really had to do this? I swallowed and my tongue clicked in my throat.

"Dirty. Terrified. Humiliated. Furious."

"Furious? At Aidian?" Dr. Alyce asked.

I nodded again. "At him. Mostly at myself. But then that wore off and I just didn't want to see him. Seeing him reminded me of what I did, and that reminded me of what I am."

"What you are?"

"Broken. A cock-tease. And Aidian was so mad at me-"

Aidian drew in his breath and took my hand. "Not mad, Bird. Sad. Confused. You. .. " his jaw worked for a minute but no sound came out, " you acted like I'd raped you and I, I would never hurt you like that."

"I know," I said, and I realized in that minute that it was true. Aidian infuriates me sometimes, and confuses me at others. He can be pushy and I can't forget for long that he's inner circle. But he would not hurt me. God, it felt good to feel that about a man. To trust a man to not hurt me.

There was a lot more talk after that, but that was really the moment that things started to turn around. A lot of tears, his and mine, but for the first time those tears felt like they were truly helping, like they were getting the sick and the shame out somehow.

When I'd calmed down, Dr. Alyce made some suggestions. A tranquilizer, a pill, just mild one, to help me sleep. "Nightmares can teach us a lot," he said, "but not these. These will just hurt and you need some rest." I agreed. I don't like the idea of medication, but if it will make the dreams go away so be it. I liked the next idea even less. Dr. Alyce is going to talk to Stevens and Mu about the possibility of making a few adjustments to my internal programming. Not to erase the memories. Not just so I can have sex, obviously, but to see if they can counter some of the PTSD. "It is even more profound than we'd thought" he said. Hell, I could have told them that. I don't want to go under the knife again, not at all, I want to do this on my own, but I guess I'll consider it.

I suggested the next step. "I wish I could see my mom," I said.

"Why can't you?" Dr. Alyce asked.

I gaped at him. Was he *stulta*? "I don't know where she is. I haven't in years."

Dr. Alyce and Aidian shared a look. "Oh, it bet we could find her," he said. Aidian nodded. For all I know, he already had.

"I'll warn you, Charlotte, it may not go well." I know that. How could he think I didn't? When had my relationship with my mother ever gone well. Still I feel like it's something I need to do. So, I'm going to have the surgery next, and then I will.

We left the Facility three and a half hours after we arrived and I felt like a ton of concrete had been lifted off of my shoulders. It's still hard, looking at Aidian, having him look at me, and that's going to be strange for a while. Still, though, I napped on his shoulder on the way home. It was nice. Not amazing. Not as peaceful as it used to be, but nice. And for now, I'll take nice. For now, nice is good.

NOVEMBER 20

My surgery is tomorrow. I'm not at all sure that I'm ready, but I have become convinced that it might help. I've come so far, but I feel like I'm being held back. I'm ready to take the next step. The dreams have been held at bay as long as I take my pills, but I'm still having flashbacks during the day. I just want this part to end. I'm amazing at how quickly everything has gone. Two days after I saw Dr. Alyce I got a phone call from Stevens. It turns out that they believe that there is a "a chance for significant' improvement in quality of life," and that doing so would "increase not only my day to day functionality but also the validity of the experiment. I have a feeling that it was that last part that convinced her to expedite. I think that I could spend every day and night covered in creepy oldmen, real and imagined, and she wouldn't care if it didn't affect her results.

Daisy will be going with me. Partly for comfort but also so that she can get some routine maintenance. I think that I'm more nervous about her than I am about myself. Some intern tried to tell me exactly what they were going to do, but I waved them off. I don't want to know the details. All that I wanted to know was that she'd be there, alive and well and still here, when I woke up. They assured me that she will and that they won't take her until I fell asleep, so I guess that I am okay with that.

I was really worried about the café, too, but Aidian had a really good idea. I'd been wanted to make a couple of changes for a while now. Nothing major, just a little stage so that we could get some music in. The thumbpad for the self-serve. If I have room in my budget I'd really like a synth-soy processor so I could save a lot of time and money if I don't have to shop. So, since I don't want to *fari iu kolera* or scare them by letting them know that I'm having surgery, we are just going to "close for renovations" and kill two birds with one stone. It's not really a lie, right? Aidian says that he will be at the hospital most of the time, that he has "people" who can do the majority of the work for us. I'm not surprised. He seems to know people who do all sorts of things, and most of them owe him a favor. He's promised me it won't change too much. I want it to stay "Don's I want it to still be my home, but I'm excited to see how we can improve it.

I guess the silver lining of all of this, the only one that I can really seem to cling to anyway, is that they aren't going to shave my head. This time they are just going to thread some wires through holes at the base of my skill, and while that seems horrifying beyond words, it does mean that I don't have to deal with stubble and scars. Anyhow, my eyes are gritty and I'm so tired I'm starting to shake. I'm going to try to get some sleep, tomorrow is going to be a big day.

NOVEMBER 22

Daisy is okay. Oh thank god, Daisy is okay. She was waiting for me, her nose twitching, when I woke up in recovery. She was the very first thing I saw. I guess the fact that I woke up means that I'm okay, too. I don't feel okay. My head hurts and it keeps hurting no matter how much I hit the little button. I don't' remember it hurting so much last time. Of course, last time I was unconscious for days afterwards so I guess I slept through the worst of it. Other than the pain I don't really feel any different. Then again, I haven't had the chance to encounter any of my triggers, either. God, I hope I'm fixed, though. I'm tired of feeling like I'm constantly walking through a minefield, like that dream I had is real.

Aidian has been here, just like he said he would. He has been amazing, bringing me ice chips and helping me arrange pillows. Mostly though, we've just been talking. I didn't realize how long it has been since we just talked. It's always a quick conversation here and there, between customers, or before we fall asleep, or while we are getting ready in the mornings. But not anything substantial, not in a while. I forgot show charming he is, and how funny and how damned smart. He is completely without conceit, so low key, but he knows so much about so many things, and he's just offhand about it. Like it's not a big deal. He told me all about growing up with five brothers and how that didn't happen much in the Inners, very into population control there, and everyone looked down on them. He told me about the first time he hacked something, how he didn't even realize he was hacking it was so easy, until some Oficiales showed up at his door. I was laughing so hard that I had to tell him to stop, it was making my stomach and my head hurt.

Dr. Stevens came in late this afternoon, and told me that if my pain is under control I can go home tomorrow. I can't imagine that I'll feel well enough, but I'll have to see. I've been surprised before. One thing hasn't changed. It is impossible to get any kind of good rest in a hospital. If I can leave, I will; I'm looking forward to getting home to my own bed.

NOVEMBER 25

Incredible. This place is incredible. I'm so exhausted; so ready to go to sleep, but I have to take a minute to get this down while it's still fresh. Amazing. The Café has never looked this good, as *belega* as it looks right now, never, but the great thing is that it is still absolutely and wonderfully Don's. God, he would love this. The self-serve station has been installed and it is unbelievable. I was really afraid that we'd have to get some of the harsh, industrial looking cabinets to make it work, but somewhere Aidian's "people" found some giant antique wood and glass cabinets and just rigged them with the components necessary to make them work. The thumbpad is small, discreet, offset a bit, so it's not right in your face, but easy enough to see that people should be able to figure out how to work it, ken? There are still regular doors in the back so I can serve people out of the same cabinets, which I didn't think would be a possibility. I thought I'd have to have two different cabinets, so that's a bonus. They did, in fact, install a SynthSoy processer and even though I have absolutely no idea how to use the *diable* machine, if they are anything like I've heard it is going to be fun. I'll be able to make things that I could have, never buy. Like carrots. Root vegetables don't grow well in the soil, not after

Unification, and they just don't taste the same when they're grown in the hydro gardens. And, of course, people want them and since they're impossible to get fresh they cost an arm and a leg to even get synth. Supply and demand, neh? But now, now I can have carrots. Potatoes. Blueberries. That's what I'll make first, blueberry muffins.

But the thing is, even that isn't the best. The best is that they cleaned the whole place, really scrubbed it top to bottom. I didn't realize how much dirt and grease had accumulated over the years, in the kitchen, on the walls. I mean, I clean daily, a couple of times daily, but years of accumulation on the walls, under the tables. It looks new, so new that I thought they'd painted it. Oh, and the kitchen, they fixed the one oven that goes wonky all of the time. In its place is a whole new contraption, top of the line, computerized and everything. I don't even want to know how they got it or how much it cost, but it is taking everything I have in my not to go down there right now and start playing with it. I guess it's a good thing that I'm not moving around incredibly well, still sluggish and tired, because I'd overdo it for sure. Hopefully I'll feel better tomorrow, because I'm going to play it my kitchen either way.

NOVEMBER 26

I didn't go to my kitchen today. I didn't rest either. Instead, I got a call at 8am on the dot, with this high-pitched Cyber voice telling me that I needed to report to the facility right away. I flashed a hovercab only to realize that there was already one on the way. And that was it. No explanation, no one telling me not to worry, that this was just routine. Nothing. What the hell is wrong with these people? Every time I start to think they might be human they prove me wrong. And I'm the one who's theoretically a hybrid. *Diable.* So I'm rushing around, walking Aidian up, thrown on clean clothes, trying to do something with my hair and I'm getting dizzy and my head is starting to hurt. Even so the cab was honking before I was even halfway done. We climbed in out of breath and rushed and I immediately keyed inn s top of coffee. The cyber cabbie complained. I swear they program them to sound perturbed. I didn't care, though. I was perturbed, too.

I got to the Facility and was met at the door by a Cyber. At this point I am freaking out. My hands were shaking and I had to hold back tears. I was convinced that I was going to die. They never treat me like this, ever. So they led me to the room and everyone is in there, the whole treatment team, and I couldn't hold it in any more. I started crying and clutching at Aidian's arm. And it wasn't good news that they had for me, but it wasn't as tragic as they led me to believe. I don't know. Maybe it is. I don't know what it means, but apparently while they were "restructuring" the other day they found that some "nodes" had grown along some of the conduits. I'm not really clear on what these nodes are, if they're tumors or corrosion or some weird combination of the two. Whatever they are, they were, in the words of Stevens, "concerning." They had send them away for analysis and had just gotten the results back this morning, found out that this was, in fact, not anticipated. Not "normal." And I had about a million questions. Why did this happen? What did it mean? Was I going to die? And they hemmed and hawed and went back and forth and in the end they didn't tell me anything. I think because when everything is said and done they don't' have the first clue, this is all as new to them as it is to me. I forget that sometimes. They seem so larger-than-life, so, what's the word, omniscient. It somehow made it worse that they didn't have the answers. I thought I could have taken definite bad news better than this ambiguous possibly good possibly nothing. But they are going to keep an eye on my and in my and think that everything should be okay. Should. Not incredibly comforting.

I'm not the praying type. When I was a teenager, I spent two months praying to a different deity. One every week. God. Buddha, Diana, all of them and I really didn't notice any different on my quality of life. Of course, Roger, the street preacher told me it was because God knew I meant him all along. I don't know. What it meant to me was that I was done praying. Until today. Aidian believes, he doesn't mention it much, but he wears a small medallion on a chain and has gone to Mass a couple of times since we've been together. So, I took his hand and asked him to pray with me and today I prayed for the first time in a very long time. It wasn't particularly inspired or even articulate, just "please" over and over and over. Please don't' let it all be taken away. Please don't let me die. Please don't let the nodes come back. Please and please and please.

DECEMBER 2

I feel so beat up. So wrung out, and I will spend the rest of my life trying to get over what happened today and I don't' know if I will ever get there. The guilt. *Jesuo!* The guilt alone is enough to overwhelm me, to drive me to my knees, ken? Add to it all the rest and I'm surprised I'm still standing.

I had wanted to wait a while, preferably a long while, before I went to see Mother. But after my talk with the team at the facility I don't' know if I'll have a long time to wait. I don't' know how to function in this uncertainty. Most days a large part of me just wants to curl up in bed. To snuggle with Daisy and have Aidian sing to me, and pull the blankets over my head and just shut it all out. The rest of me, though? The rest of me knows that if I-I can hardly even write it without gagging- if it does all fall apart I'll have all the days in bed that I could ever want and then some. So it's up to me to soak in every minute that I can. To do everything that I've ever wanted to do someday. To grab life by the fikfek throat and demand my fair share. Because I've never had it. Fair. What's mine by right. No kid should have what I had. No adult neither, neh? But no one who had what I did has ever been given a second chance, neither. And I was. I have to remember that, especially on days like today. I was given the keys to my cell.

Dr. Alyce had mother's address. Turns out they'd had to find her before the surgery to found out some medical information. Pre-existing conditions, childhood records, as if she'd kept up with them. Information about my father, though if she even knew who he was she had never told me. Sure, she'd moved three or four times since they last talked to her, but they'd tracked her pretty easily. Turns out, she's only five blocks from me; five blocks and an entire *fikfek* world. Not one I wanted to visit, either. Aidian wanted to go with me, of course, but I wouldn't let him; some *blanka sinorjon* from mid-circle? He wouldn't do anything but set them on edge. He didn't like it, but he understood, and so I left him sitting on the curb, rolling a cigarette. I walked in the front door of the stacks and the stench hit me like a wave. It was the smell of every stack we'd ever lived in, the kind where the owners don't much care how the rent is paid or how many are paying as long as it keeps coming in. Where no one bothers with the formality of a lease, and the scrap men have a standing contract to stop by and clean up the picked-over piles of trash out on the curb. Spilled booze. Stale take-out. Cigarette smoke and the sweeter slyer smoke of things a bit more dangerous. Sweat. Piss. *Ejakul.* It was like a hand, beckoning and pushing me away all t the same time and so I stood there paralyzed for what? A minute? An hour? I don't even know. Eventually I willed my feet forward, up one flight of stairs, then two. I checked my microcomp for what had to have been the 20th time. Apartment 219A. I knew it was hers as soon as I got close. It was the music, mostly. Sitars and warbling vocals against this heavy beat. Indian. My mother always played Indian music when she was entertaining her "gentlemen." She said it made her feel sexy, exotic. She burned incense for the same reason and I could smell that too, underneath all of the other scents. My palms started to sweat and I wiped them on my pants. I knocked. I didn't expect anyone to answer. Mother never let anything interrupt a dollar and I figured I'd been let off easy. I'd come. I'd tried. It didn't work out. I knew that I wouldn't try again. The door flew open, though, almost immediately. The music, unrestrained now that the door was open, poured into the hallway. In the doorway stood a woman, a girl, really, younger than me anyway. Her legs were thin but muscled, and clad in patterned tights and her dress plunged so low that you could see the top curves of her breasts. Her lips, pressed into a pout, were painted *genera* pink. Her eyes were hooded, seductive, but as soon as she saw me her expression changed. It was like someone had flipped a switch,. She grew suspicious, hard. "What you want?" she asked. AS impossible as it seemed, I thought I'd gotten the wrong place. That Dr. Alyce had made a mistake, and I started to offer an apology. The girl squinted at me, and tilted her head to the side. "Lotta?" she asked quietly. I whirled back around, speechless, staring. Who was this girl? This *malfacila, singifi* girl who knew my name? It couldn't be. It couldn't, but somehow I knew that it was. "Daisy" I said, moving forward to hug her. Hard. She was so hard. It was like hugging a rock, a statue. After a second I couldn't take it any longer. I pulled away. "Can I come in?" I asked. She narrowed her eyes. Suddenly, she reminded me, not of a mouse, small and delicate and wide-eyes, but of an alley cat. Feral. Street smart. "Might not be good," she said. "Mama don't like interruptions." I flashed back to all of the beatings I'd gotten as a child when hunger, or fear, or dirty diapers had sent me knocking at her doors. "I know." I said. "You don't' know nothing" she spat, but she moved pack, opened the door wide.

I went in and sat down and after years of missing her, worrying about her, rehearsing what I'd say over and over I couldn't think of anything. My mind went completely blank.

I didn't expect to find you here," I said after a while.

"Where else I go?" She said, speaking in the thick street slang of my childhood. I didn't have an answer for that, so I fell into silence again. From the other side of the wall the voices rose in a crescendo. "Mama will be out soon." Daisy said. I nodded. I remembered that, too. Sure enough, a man came staggering out a minute or so later, still buttoning his pants, and Mother followed, pulling a sheer orange robe around her that left nothing to the imagination. *Inferi!* Would she never age? At first I thought that she looked exactly the same, though on closer examination I could see that it wasn't so. Tiny lined spider webbed out from her lips and the corners of her eyes, the whites of which had yellowed, and a small roll of skin, not fat, just tired skin, hung over the top of her panties. She looked at me and lit a cigarette. "
What do you want?" she asked. Just like Daisy. She had trained her well, it seemed. What did I want? AT that moment what I wanted was to run. Why had I thought for an instant that this monster, this chupacabra, had anything to offer me. She never had. "You know about my surgery?" I asked. "She nodded. "how come you never checked up on me?" She shrugged. "I haven't known for years if you were alive or dead. Figured it weren't no difference." Why did you come here, Charlotte."

I didn't answer. I couldn't. For a panicked minute I couldn't even remember. When finally I spoke it was the high-pitched, whiny voice of a child. I had no idea where it came from and it scared me. "I wanted to talk to you." She shot twin jets of smoke from her nose. "So talk." And I looked at her. This person who brought me into the world. Who was supposed to protect me. "Why did you let them do that to me, Mama?" I asked.

She laughed It was brittle. Humorless. "Why shouldn't I? Little queen, Lotta, that's you. Always thought you were too good for us. Too good to pull your wait. You ain't. You just trash and it's time you acted like it. Running to the cops on your Mama. Getting your brain taken out. You should have just learned to enjoy it like your sister. She a good girl. You? " she stood. "Nothing but a waste since the time you was born" and she stomped out, nearly naked, slamming the door behind her.

I stared at Daisy, stunned. "I didn't know she'd do it to you, too." I said. 'I'm sorry." She looked at me and her face was mother's face. Suddenly I remembered the dream from the Facility. Only it was different. Now I could save her. "What you don't' know," she spat. "Fill a book. Fill a library. Who you think gonna take your place when you ran?" And suddenly I had to save her. This time I could. "Come with me," I said, taking her hands." I have a home, and I own a bakery, come with me, now. You don't have to be like this I can take care of you. ' She pulled her hands out of mine and slapped me across the cheek, so hard that I saw stars. "Take care of me," she yelled, "Like you did before. You left me, you *inaĉo*. Get out!" I staggered, blind, to the door and felt my way down the hall to the stairs. I was almost there when she called to me from the doorway. "Lotta!" she yelled, and started towards me, her hand held out. I braced myself, somehow sure she was going to strike me again. Instead, she handed me a picture. It was old, paper old. In it, she and I had our arms around each other, smiling for the camera. Mother stood over us. "Here," she said. "Ain't got no use for good memories. All they do is hurt," and she walked away.

I made it to the stoop, where Aidian was pacing, his hair wild from running his hand through it. I guessed he had met Mother. He looked and me and took it in in an instant, the mark on my face, the tears, the picture, and pulled me close. "Oh baby" he said, "I'm sorry."

"Take me home," I sobbed. He did and I looked out the clock. I'd only been in there 15 minutes. How was it that I felt years older? I stared at the picture that I clenched in my hands. That poor baby. Poor Daisy. Poor 'Lotta.

DECEMBER 9

Somehow a week has passed. I'll be honest, I don't know where the time has gone. I spent the first two days replaying everything they said at the meeting over and over again, like some album from hell on the microcomp. I'd tell myself that I just had to hang on for one more hour, just one more, and look at the clock to see that only 5 minutes had passed. Or 15. Or three hours. Aidian was fantastic through it all. He was there whenever I needed him, but never pushed, and I made him carrot cake muffins in return. They remind him of when he was young and are his favorites. It was nice to be able to do something for him, as limited as it was. By the third days I was thinking of all the things I should have said. Somehow, that was even worse. If only I'd said this thing everything would have been okay. If I'd said that thing then Daisy would have come with me. If I'd said the other thing, then I could have cut them like they cut me and they'd be sorry. And I know on some level that it's all complete and utter *absurda*. What possible conversation would have made things okay? Did I really expect her to apologize? What to say to wound someone who thinks it's all right to sell her children, her own children? How to you even start with someone to whom you have to explain that not wanting to be raped by old men doesn't make me a snob? Still, knowing that doesn't make me stop reciting the what-ifs. There was no hope with Mother. Daisy, though? With her I think there might have been once. If I'd gone about it differently, not been so caught off ground, maybe there could have been a chance for us. That's the part that kills me, the guilt of Daisy. The guilt of leaving her. "Where did I think she'd be," she 'd asked. Truthfully, I can't answer that. I have always known that Mother saw her differently. Hell, be honest Charlotte, loved her more than she did me, so I thought maybe she'd spare her. I thought that maybe with all of the visits she must have received from the oficiales after I left, every time I was hospitalized, every time that I got into trouble, that they'd take my little sister away, put her somewhere she'd be safe. I can say though, with utter honesty, that I would have never guessed that mother would have made Daisy take my place or that, worse, Daisy would choose to stay there and abide it. And the guilt that I left her to it, that I sold her to buy my freedom is almost more than I can stand. Two days after I saw her I flashed Denae at East. Trying to make something right somewhere. It came back rejected. I'm not surprised, but it hurt. Which explains, I guess, what happened on day four.

It was getting dark when I saw her standing by the window. The girl in the coat. She had been gone by the time I woke up after bringing her home, and I hadn't seen her since and suddenly there she was. For a second I saw, above the huge lapels not her face, but Daisy's. This time, instead of ignoring her, instead of just pushing her away I charged out from behind the counter, leaving surprised customers behind but God this one, this girl maybe I could save and I had to. This girl I could help and I wasn't going to let her slip away.

"Hey!" I yelled down the sidewalk, and she flinched as though I'd hit her. She turned, though, and when she did I saw that if I had hit her I wouldn't be the first. One whole side of her face was marked with the imprint of a hand, black in the center, then purple, and a sickly yellow on the edges. The cops maybe? A john? Another homeless? I couldn't be any. I don't know. I still haven't asked. I did ask her though if she was still looking for work, and I know that I didn't imagine the look of relief on her face. She followed me back inside to the smiles and even the cheers of the regulars. Word had gotten around of my dismissal of the girl, Suri, her name is Suri, I have to stop thinking of her as just "the girl," and I know they'd seen it, somehow, as a direct betrayal of Don. I was glad that I could make them happy, could prove them wrong, but was even happier that I could do something to help her. Tom clapped me on the shoulder, "Good job, girl", he said, and I smiled. I didn't want her in the apartment that Aidian and I share; work has become such a huge part of my life that I don't want it literally following me home, but I did set her up in the small storage space. We don't use it anymore, not since we got the SynthSoy compounder, and there's no reason it should sit empty. It connects directly to the shop, which kind of makes me nervous, that's a lot of exposed equipment in there and she could strip me of every last piece of it if she so chose, but I guess I'm going to have to trust that she won't'. It wasn't that long ago that I bristled at the concept that because we are poor we are criminals and I won't, damn it I WILL NOT do the same thing just because I have lucked into having something worth stealing. It's just this tiny room, doesn't even have a window, but her eyes lit up like it was one of the palaces in Center Circle when I showed it to her, especially when I told her that the next day I'd get her a bed. Aidian came in just as she was tying on an apron. I told her she could just rest, but she wanted to get to work, and he grinned from ear to ear, pulling me close, and kissing the top of my head before staying pointedly out of the way.

So that's what I've been doing the rest of the time, training Suri. She's a quick study, just like they always said I was, and I have to admit that the place is staying cleaner than it ever has before. I think she's sneaking in to clean more at night, but she won't admit to it, just smiles. I'm going to teach her to make sandwiches next, and she'll be able to man the place, for brief parts of time, by herself. I'm terrified at the thought of leaving the café in someone else' hands, but to be able to get out, even for a little, would be amazing.

DECEMBER 13

My chance to leave Suri on her own came closer than I expected. I got a call from one of the Cybers at the Facility this morning, asking me to come in. Aidian had already left for the day, and I know that he was doing something that meant he wouldn't be able to be in contact. A ringing microcomp or unexpected transmission at the wrong time can be disastrous and so some days he has to 'go dark" Leave everything except for whatever it is that he's working on. Today happened to be one of these days. I asked the folks at the Facility if it could wait until tomorrow but the Cyber was no help. Just kept repeating "Your presence has been requested TODAY" until I gave up and gave the voice command to schedule a time. I told them that I would be there at 4:30, which meant I'd be at the café as long as possible. Knowing what I know now I wish I'd gone in sooner. It would have saved me one hell of a lot of panicking. There's nothing wrong with me! Nothing! Everything is going to be fine. Apparently they got the results back from the lab and they're been monitoring me wirelessly to see if any of the nodes have started to grow back and they determined that if they were growing back there would be this certain disturbance in the electric pulses or something. I'm not entirely sure how it works to tell you the truth. All that I know is that whatever would be happening if the nodules were back isn't and so they think that it was just this freak-onetime thing. They're sure enough that they're started angling for me to go to another medical conference, which would probably really irritate me any other day. Today thought it's just more affirmation. Certainty, neh? I mean, they wouldn't take the chance at being wrong and looking stupid, so they must really think that this has worked for good, that the chances are going to stick. I got out of there as quickly as I could and then nagged the hovercab driver to speed on the way home. I really wanted to get there before Aidian. I rushed through the downstairs and waved at the regulars who shouted "hellos" at me. Once I was upstairs I started going through all of my old boxes and bags, tossing clothes here and there. Daisy loved it, running into the collars and out the sleeves as I tossed everything onto the floor. Most of my wardrobe is Utiliclothes; originally they were designed for military use, they're a one size fits all sort of universal something that you adjust with buckles and drawstrings and maybe they were a good idea in theory, but to no one's surprised except those who ordered them to be created that no soldier or oficale wants to wrestle with folding and strapping down their pants just to get them on, and buckles aren't really great when you're crawling on the ground or jumping over fences or whatever. So there's' just masses of this stuff everywhere and it's cheap or sometimes even free. the cloth is rough and scratchy, some sort of all synthetic processed something, and I tend to tie them baggy. People look at you when you wear tighter clothes, like being able to see the outline of a person is an invitation to stare. Anonymity, neh. Tonight, though, I was in the mood to celebrate. A couple of years ago on the spur of the moment I'd gotten this crazy outfit at a street sale. It's this beautiful copper orange dress that shimmers in the light and feels slinky on my skin. It's old fashioned, knee length, not a buckle or a zipper or a bit of PVC in sight which is why I liked it. It hugs in tight at my waist and the back is cut really low. I still had no idea what possessed me to buy it and had never actually worn it, just tossed it in the bottom of my backpack and forgot about it, which is the only reason I still had it. So, I but it on for the first time and it looked every bit as amazing as it had in my mind, more so. I laughed and twirled a little bit and though a part of me desperately wanted to throw on one of Aidian's hoodies over it and maybe some pants. I probably would have changed if Aidian hadn't come home just then, carrying a stack of comps under one arm. I had just enough time to see his eyes widen before I ran, hugging him so hard that he staggered back a step and I heard him muffle a few choice words as the comps slipped and almost fell.

"Come on," I said, " lacing my hand through his and pulling on him, "We're going out."

"Oi," he said, laughing, "what's the occasion?"

"I'm going to be okay," I said. "I went to the Facility today and they said everything was going to be fine.

He put the cops down on the couch and kissed me, and when he pulled away I saw that his eyelids were wet. "Come on," I said again, "Let's go."

I took him down to Akaifūsha, that same club I'd gone to what, months ? Years? Ago. The bouncer didn't even recognize me at first, and that made me laugh again. I led Aidian out on the screaming jumping mass of the dance floor. I closed my eyes and raised my hands over my head and let the music and motion work its way into my veins, let myself disappear. Only this time I didn't' disappear completely. I was too aware of that one other body in the mass of bodies, too busy anticipating the occasional brush of his hand on my back or my arm amid the jostles and elbows, too busy sneaking glances at him. He dances like he does everything else, relaxed to the point of perceived boredom, if you didn't know him. Confident. Absorbed. I wondered for a minute if he would make love the same way and my breath caught in my throat. Not yet. I can't . Not yet, but now there' no rush. I have time. Time for love, for friendship, for leaning. For life? Ken? I have time to be alive. Tonight, though, was time for dancing and I grabbed Aidian's hand and pulled him close and we danced until the Bouncer ordered us out the door.

DECEMBER 15

You know, I've always known that our minds are traps. I mean, I've always known that mine was. How could I forget? But what I didn't realize is that even when we are sick, even when your brain isn't hell-bent on our own *fekanta* destruction, we can still get stuck inside it. Not a cage, necessarily, at least I don't feel the bars like I used to, don't have the same sense of this huge door keeping me blocked off from the rest of the world, to a room none the less. Sometimes a damned small room where everything we see and feel and believe is set by the view from the window. I've been in a room in regards to Suri. I see that now. She reminded me so much of myself that all I could see when I looked at her was a projection of myself and I treated her like she was the younger me, not as though she was a person in her own right. She was patient with me, grateful even in spite of it, which I guess should have been my first clue since patience and gratitude were never my strong points. Tonight, though, she finally snapped. I wanted to experiments more with the compounder. I've gotten pretty good at working the machine but there are still some things that come out wrong. Grainy or bitter of the kind of hot that leaves me standing there with my mouth under the faucet.

When I got downstairs I found Suri sitting in the kitchen, all of the light on, the dishwasher running, and the faucet on, the hot water had been running so long that everything was partially hidden in rolls of steam. She was sitting in the middle of it all, sobbing with her face in her hands. She didn't even know I was there until I'd shut everything off and then she jumped and the sudden silence and shared at me. Her whole body was shaking, she just looked , *me ne sci*, lost and broken and without thinking I wrapped my arms around her and hugged her. "It's okay, little sister," I said, "You're safe now." She went rigid for a second, just a second and then just exploded. She shoved me, hard, hard enough that I few across the room and slammed my hip on the edge of the sink. And her face,oh, she looked like a whole different person. She scared me. "I'm never safe," she screamed, "No one is ever safe!" And then she just crumpled. About 15 minutes later we were sitting at the table in the break room, the same table I had sat at so many times, crying. I'd brought Suri a cup of tea and she'd managed to collect herself a little. After a while she started to talk. Fuck. That poor girl. I'd assumed that she was like me, you know? No family, no career. Just another of the Flower Town's wilted blooms. She isn't, though. First of all, she's older than I thought. Nearly my age. She hasn't always lived on the street, either, I was right about that. In fact, the first time I met her she'd only been out for a couple of weeks, which really explains a lot, sleeping in the alley, jumping at everything, those are all (newbie) mistakes. As it turns out, she hid lived not too far from the house I had lived in. We may have even been neighbors for a little while. She shared the home with her husband and their child. Her husband owned, owns I guess, The Trapeze, one of the higher class burlesque parlors, a quirky place with fire-eaters, snake handlers, topless girls on unicycles, stuff like that. She'd performed there herself sometimes, playing the electrofiddle and singing. Then, her kid died. It wasn't Suri's fault, she wasn't even there at the time. I guess the sitter had walked down to the club with the boy, Suri never said his name, and I'm not sure she can. The family had had lunch together, she'd given the boy a kiss and sent them back home. It had been raining and I'm sure there were puddles everywhere, drainage is always an issue here, this close to big water, and the sitter and the boy were walking on the edge of the street. This hovercar came out of nowhere and hit them both. Hit and run the cowardly *bastardos*. The sitter survived, burns and a couple of broken bones, but someone who'd seen it came and got Suri. The boy died in her arms. After that, she and the husband just couldn't keep it together. They tried, but it was just too much. Too many memories. Too much blame and nowhere to put it. So one day Suri went out the front door and started running. She never stopped. She ran as far from the house and the club and her old life as she could get. She went a couple of circles in at first, thought that maybe her talent or her education would help her get established there. They don't do to well with Wanderers there, and life inside is more about nepotism than talent, so they shoved her back out to the Rim. Flower Town. That's when I met her, just a couple of days after that. God, that poor woman. How she even stands up under the weight that she is carrying is amazing. I couldn't. I DIDN'T. I always knew that there were other people who had it rough. Buy, you know, a selfish as it sounds, it always seemed that there was no one who had had it as bad as me. After today, though, for the first time I feel kind of lucky. Lucky and mad. Betrayed. There's so damned much hurt in the world and it shouldn't be that way. It's not fair. Someone should do something. God, or the oficiales, or something. They should fix what is hurting people. They should fix what is unfair. Or, I guess, maybe I should. I can't fix it all, not even a lot, but there has to be something I can do. If we all put one finger over one whole in the dam, eventually we will stop the flood, yeah?

DECEMBER 21

Basanti stopped by again today. I swear, she has this sixth sense of when to show up, she always walks in during a lull in business, when I can't come up with a good reason not to talk to her. Part of her job, I imagine. The thing is, I couldn't deny that I was happy to see her. There's something about Basanti that is just wholeheartedly good, I guess. I genuinely like her, no matter how hard I try not to, which I think is why I'm always a little angry with her. As much as I try to pretend she's just part of my Facility staff, I think of her as a friend. As much as she pretends she's my friends, I know deep down that I'm just another client and it hurts.

Still, we sat and talked for an hour or more. Nothing in particular, just life, ken? Suri. Aidian. The café. My mother. She was incredibly curious about Suri, and not a little surprised at her increased presence in my life. I can't blame her. I'm more than a little surprised myself. Surprised, and conflicted too, and I told Basanti so. There are so many similarities between Suri and Tawny and Dmitri, the homelessness, the draw to the Café, the choice to leave their families behind. Yet, somehow, it's different. She's different. Opening myself to Tawny and Dmitri, at least to the extent that I did, was not a wise or healthy thing to do. What I see equally as clearly though is that doing so for Suri is right. I know that there's a difference there but I can't see what it is, and that scares me. Basanti laughed when I told her that. It started to upset me and I told her so.

"What's funny, *amiko*," I said, "I'm being serious."

"I'm laughing because "I'm happy," she said. "That question you ask, it is absolutely and perfectly normal. I struggle with it every single day.

"It seems like it would be easy; that you could tell when someone was using you, when they were a *"fekanta anusuloj."*

Basanti stared into her coffee for a minute, then she looked at me, her dark eyes twinkling. Then, in her prim and proper voice she said, "Ah but then the *fekanta anusuloj* would just try harder." And it was so ridiculous, that word coming out of her mouth, that I couldn't help it. I started laughing too. That's when she told me that she had been struggling with that very concept in regards to me. Not that she thought that I was talking advantage of the Facility, which is what I'd expected. I know how much money they are giving me, how much they continued to give me even when I was incommunicado; I know the strings they've pulled, the laws they've allowed to be broken for me to be allowed to keep the Café. Rather, she was worried that the program, in asking me to attend another conference, was taking advantage of me.

"I've seen the videos from the other conference," she said, "and I can understand now how it must have seemed to you. Whether or not that was our intent. .. " she trailed off. "At any rate, I can understand if you don't' want to do it again. I will recommend that you be released form that publication, if you ask me to do so.

I damned near dropped my tea. I tried to say something, but couldn't and just sat there gaping like one of the fish that gets left on shore sometimes when the tide goes out. And I wanted to scream "yes." Yes, I would take her up on that recommendation. I would stare here on the rim with the shop and my man and the people who I love, who love me. Yes I would do Yes, I would stay here where I was comfortable, and safe, and in control. Yes, I would do anything to avoid the utter humiliation of being parade around and asked to perform like a little *hundido*. Then I thought about the people I could help by going. Not Stevens or Wu or even Alyce. Not the franzia, oh so interested doctors who would be there, but the others like me. People like Suri, or Denae, like Dasita. The countless others I've seen dead in the alleys or as good as dead at East. The people who, maybe, could be set free. .. like I was. I took a bite of muffin and chewed slowly, savoring the sweetness of the blueberries, and took my time answering. "No," I said at last, "I'll go. I will dress however they want and sit pretty and listen to them talk about how they made me a 'real human.'" She opened her mouth to talk and I held up one hand. She quieted. "But, I get to talk too. Nothing rehearsed, no 'examples of emotional development." I just get to look at the people who came and talk.

Basanti raised one sculpted eyebrow and the corner of her mouth twitched as she held back a smile. She didn't know what I had in mind. Hell even I don't know, but she was on my side. That felt great.

"Deal." She said.

DECEMBER 24

The past few weeks have been just beautiful. Sweet and lovely from start to finish. Officially, there is on Christmas, of course. That went away with Unification. Traditions die hard, though, especially on the Rim, and even 200 years hasn't been enough to completely do away with this one. It's nothing overt, of course. I think everyone knows better than that, but around the first of December you start to notice some changes As long as the winter isn't too bad, that is. People are more cheerful, there's a lot more "Hellos" and a bit of a spring in our slog back and forth. Every now and then someone stops by the café to show off some gift, some little treasure carefully scrimped and saved or bartered for, and everyone else will ooh and ahh. It's great. This year is different though. *Speciala*. I haven't had a family, not a real one, in *diable* has it been 20 years? It adds a while new layer, makes me want to do it right. We started planning weeks ago. They used to decorate trees for Christmas. That's no possible, now. The black market does a fairly steady business in replacements. Holos, sometimes, in any color that you could imagine. Mostly homemade synthetic trees, though. Bits of this and that fused to bases. I didn't want either of those, though, and was pretty hard-pressed to figure out what would make me happy. Finally, Aidian came up with an idea and it was perfect. He found a bunch of paint and has been spending the evenings painting a tree on our living room wall, and it's been magical. He's an artist- a real artist- and it's incredible to me to watch him take these piles of materials and his hands, those giant , square-fingered hands, and turn them into something beautiful. He starts by putting on music, something without any words, just a heavy thumping beat, and his eyes narrow and then the tree just grows. Watching him makes me ache. I can literally feel it all over. Pride. Admiration. Love. Lust. It's almost more than I can bear. Each night, while we are waiting for the most recent coat to dry, we've even working on our gift for Daisy. It's a house that's a perfectly-sized replica of ours, but even better. It's filled with all of these little tunnels and passageways, and Aidian is wiring it with buttons that make lights shine or little toys or treats pop up. Puzzles, ken? It's nice, working side by side. Chatting when we felt like it, sitting in silence when we didn't. All of that was fantastic, more than I could have ever dreamed of, but a couple of weeks ago I started feeling like it wasn't enough. I wanted to do more. It wasn't decorations; those never mattered much to me. For a while I thought about getting extra gifts for Aidian. I love spoiling him; he reacts almost like a child whenever I give him something that lets him know that I was thinking about him. But that wasn't it either. I couldn't figure out what it was that I wanted until Tom came into the café one day. His shoulders were more slumped than usual, and his eyes were red with unshed tears. It turned out that he'd found out that some of his family, family he hadn't seen in years, were coming in from somewhere else around the rim. That should have been a cause for celebration. As I understand, he hadn't seen them in almost ten years, but instead, it just left him broken hearted.

"I can't get them anything," he said. "I can't even afford to feed them. I'm down to the line as it is. They're gonna come here and I got nothing, nothing." And he put his head in his old, weathered hands. I stood there for a long while, laying my hands on his shoulder, just being there for him, then it hit me. I walked over to the register and opened it. We didn't have much in there, it was still early, but it would be enough. I pulled it out, all of it, and carried the bills and coins over to Tom. "Here," I said, handing it to him. He stared for a minute at the wad in my hands and for a while I was worried that he wouldn't take it. That damned Rim pride. *Inferi!* It was possible that he'd be so offended that I'd never see him again, but at that minute I didn't care. Then, after what seemed like an eternity, he reached out and took it.

"Why you do this, girl?" he asked. "Because you helped me see, once, you helped me see that what I was doing was wrong, that I needed to help other people. You could have just given up on me, but you didn't." He didn't say anything. "It's what Don would want." He was still silent and my heart sank, afraid that I'd lost my friend. Then I saw that He was crying. Large, fat tears were sliding silently down his face. I rose, slowly, and folded me into a hug. "Thank you," he said. "Thank you." And I swear I could feel my heart swell in my chest. That's when it hit me. That's what I was missing. I wanted to do something for Flower Town. For all of the people I cared about. I wanted to take care of the others.

Aidian talked a long time about what we could do. Our first thought was gifts. The thing was, though that we couldn't possibly get personalized gifts for everyone. By the time we got enough for as many people as could come it, the gifts wouldn't be of enough substance to help. It was the same with money. We couldn't give enough to everyone to do anyone any good. Finally it hit us, both at the same time. A dinner. We would make a dinner. We would feed anyone who didn't have a family to eat a meal with or the funds to cook a Christmas dinner.

So, that's what today has been. Decorating our tree. Finishing and wrapping the gifts, and baking.

Baking and cooking everything that I can so that tomorrow can work. It has been magical. I just hope tomorrow is everything that we so want it to be. I just hope the magic holds.

DECEMBER 25

It did. It held. It held and expanded and grew until it was so much larger than the sum of its parts. I should be exhausted but somehow I'm not. I'm happy, invigorated. My cup runneth over. My day began at the stroke of midnight. We had taken a hovercab in several circles to attend midnight mass at Aidian's family's underground church. I was nervous; I'd never met his parents, and I'd certainly never been to a mass. I had no idea what to expect, but was certain that I would say or do something wrong. Aidian was great, though, gentle, and reassuring and so other than my racing heart I was actually doing all right. I had spent the last three weeks baking an Irish Christmas Cake. I had no idea if it had actually turned out all right; I'd never done anything like that before, but it smelled good and had been liberally soaked in whiskey, bought at a pretty steep price at the Black market, so I figured that it couldn't be all bad. Going to the church itself was intimidating. We stopped a few blocks down, in a neighborhood, not really different in appearance from any other, and walked a few blocks to a tiny, nondescript house. We knocked at the door and were greeted by a pleasant–looking woman, dressed in a simple black dress. After exchanging a few pleasantries, the woman said, a touch too casually. "It's been a pleasant enough winter." "Aye," Aidian replied, "but it would be nice to get in out of the cold." I was puzzled, the weather was chilly, that's for certain, but not too bad. Still, it must have meant something because the woman let us in, and motioned to a staircase. We walked down some old, nearly falling apart stairs, and opened the door at the bottom and suddenly we were in a whole 'nother world. It was a sanctuary. Dark, covert, but a sanctuary nonetheless. Tapestries hung on the walls, people were gathered together in small groups, and a large crucifix hung at the front. Suddenly, we were surrounded by a whole group of faces, all looking slightly familiar. Aidian's family. God, I knew at he had lots of brothers, but there, in that space, there just seemed to be so many of them. They were lovely; friendly and welcoming, and took me into their arms as if we'd known each other our whole lives. We didn't have too much time to talk, because soon mass started. Aidian told me that these used to be grand affairs, but here there was no time or space for grand organs, for incense, for choirs. The whole mass was hushed, hurried almost, but to e that made it all the more beautiful. I didn't understand a lot of it; some was in different language, the rest was in English but talked about things I didn't understand. Aidian has promised me that he'll tell me more about it if I want him to, and I may, someday. After about an hour it was over, and we departed. I gave Aidian's mom the cake and she seemed pleased, and after another round of hugs we all went our own ways. I thought that I'd fall asleep as soon as I got home, I really did, but I was too excited. I could feel it bubbling up inside me, keeping me awake. Aidian must have felt it, too, because he was tossing and turning beside me. "Wanna get up?" I asked after a while, and he popped up, grinning. We shuffled ot the kitchen and made some coffee, and then it was time for gifts.

I was so excited to give Aidian his, been nearly vibrating with it for weeks. One was just okay, it was a special sort of very tiny soldering and cutting tool, slimmer than my pinky finger, that he'd mentioned several times he wanted for his art. But the other, oh the other. I'd found a ook at the Black Market, a real book,not digi, about an artist named VanGogh. It must e very old, before Unification, because I'd never heard of him before, and that was when all of the works of the old artists were destroyed, undesirable because they were a source of national pride, pride in the past. And while I understand that, I don't see how these works could be considered undesirable, they were gorgous. Soft and gentil and they spoke to me and I just knew that they would speak to Adiian as well. Sure enough, they did, he hugged me close and when we pulled apart I saw that hhiseye were wet. "it's perfect, Bird, he said, burhing th tip of my nose with his finger, "just perfect." I opened mine next. I wanted to let Daisy open hers, but Aidian insisted, I think that he was more excited than I was. We both laughted, because he'd found me an old book as well, filled with recipes for cakes and pies and cookies of all sorts. I sat there for fifteen minutes pouring over it before I realized that he was waiting, smiling and patient, for me to open the rest. He'd bought me a dres as well, an old fashioned one made of some soft fuzzy material that he said was wool, completely opaque with sleeves that went down past my elbows and a low, draped back. It was a bright, soft green, that perfectly matched his eyes. "May I have the next dance?" said a microflash that he'd put in there with it, and I could see us, together, with me wearing that dress. But the last gift, oh, the last. I still don't have any idea how he pulled this off. We had this extra room; one that we'd always used for storage, and afer I'd unwrapped my two gifts he made me close my eyes and then led me by the hand into the room. There I opened my eyes and gasped. Somehow, at some time he had cleared it out, fixed the holes in the walls, and painted it. The whole room was this deep blue, the blue of the ocean, and it had been coated withsome sort of topcoat that gave back light in little sparks like stars. One entire wall had been painted with a mural; it showed the three of us, Aidian, Daisy, and I on a beach, staring out at a sunset. Rose and gold shone out. "Oh," I breathed, reaching out to touch it. "Oh." We stayed in there for nearly an hour, wrapped in each other's arms, leaning against the gorgeous wall, before Daisy's insisten squeaks and rusltes reminded us that there was one member of our famly who had yet to get her Christmas gifts. It was full doawn by then, the light streaming in through our windows. We set Dais in front of her gift and pulled off the paper and it was everything that we had hoped. Daisy went wild with joy, running in and out, exploring the tunnels and coming out every now and then to nuzzle our ears or run an excited lap up and down our arms. I took a minute while petting her to reset her quickly, to thumb the little chip behind her ear. The last thing I wanted was to forget, in the course of all of the excitement. I could have watched her forever, but there was still a lot of work to be done, so I walked down to the Café. Aidian followed me, carrying the little house in his arms so that Daisy could continue to explore in the back room.

Soon, I was up to my elbows in batters and marinades, and all of the ovens were full. There was a knock on the door that startled me; we had been putting out word for a while that he Café would be closed until the big meal began around noon. Aidian's eyes locked with mine. Had some *oficiale* with an agenda found out about our free meal? Had someone reported us? Aidian motioned for me to stay in the kitchen and he went to the door. I heard the murmur of low voices and then he came back, followed by two young men, regulars who worked the electric lines, carrying a large something wrapped in plastic. They pulled the plastic free to reveal a large hunk of meat, pink and fresh. *"Kio estas ĉi tiu,"* I asked. "What is this?" Game is hard to find, there's not a lot outside of the circle for anything to graze on, but occasionally something finds a way. As it turned out, a wild boar had come snuffling around out where they were working that morning. They'd managed to bring the thing down and butchered it on the spot, hurriedly, before anyone could find what they were up to. They'd brought nearly half of it to me. It was wild. I knew that. Who knew what it had eaten, if it had gotten into radiation. But still, it was meat. Real meat. And it looked good. "Thank you!" I exclaimed. "They nodded, grinning, "We'll see you later, Charlotte, yeah?" they said. "Yeah." I answered. I looked at Aidian, my eyes wide, "Now I have to find a way to cook this meat."

I did. Somehow, I found a way to cook it all, and by the time we opened our doors every surface was covered with something to eat, and it only increased as people arrived. It seems like everyone brought a little something, and soon the café was bursting with people, eating, laughing, hugging, telling tales. It was everything I had hoped that it would be. I looked up at Don's picture, thinking of how much he'd enjoyed it. And he would have. He would have been proud. Midway through the meal, Tawny and Dmitri came in. I didn't know what to do at first, and I could feel Aidian appear noiselessly by my side. "You okay, love?" he asked. I nodded. For a minute I thought about turning them away, tried to think of a way to do it that would be unobtrusive, not disturb anyone. Somehow, that didn't feel right. I thought about ignoring the, but I knew that wasn't going to work either. Their presence would just grow, until it filled the room. So, I crossed over to them. I could feel them tense. I took a deep breath and hugged them, briefly. "Welcome," I said, "Merry Christmas." I could feel Tawny tense. They looked rough, hollowed, thinner, but they were there and they were at peace. I decided that it would be all right.

It was more than all right. The laughter and food and people held out for hours, long into the night. I wasn't about to turn anyone away. As I started to clean up, lot so people pitched in to help, and soon there was a mass of people moving about the café, washing dishes, carrying trays this way and that. Dmitri came up while all of this was going on, and I could see him fall into the cadence of the experienced con-man. "It's looks like you're doing well for yourself, 'Lotta," he said. I was guarded. "I guess so." "So, are we cool?" I looked at him for a long time, trying not to see the wreck that was my first real house. I took a deep breath. "Yes," I said, "we are okay." " I was wondering," he said, "Tawny and I, we've been on some rough times. I figure with you having so much maybe you could-" I reached out and grasped his arms, firmly, but without anger. "No, Dmitri," I said softly, "You can take food, all you want. You can come here any time you need some, but that's all." He tensed, and for a minute I thought he would yell, or worse, strike out, but he didn't. Instead, I saw all the fight go out of him. "All right." He said. "Thanks, Charlotte."

There really wasn't much after that. We finished the clean up and staggered upstairs. I talked Aidian into dragging our mattress, as weary as we were, into the new room and lay there with him, my hand making idle circles on his chest and talking quietly until he slipped away. It was a good day. Of everything I've been proud of, of everything that has brought me joy, this day is at the top of my list. A true gift.

DECEMBER 28

Aidian and I were sitting on the living room floor. Music was blaring from his microcomp and there were canvases scattered on the tile. "look," I said for about the 50th time. She's doing it!" "Another self-portrait. Aidian replied. She's quite the narcissist." We'd been letting daisy paint every not and then, usually one color on a napkin down at the café, and she seemed to be enjoying it, so tonight we'd gone all out, set up three or four pallets of paint and a dozen canvases and just let her go. She absolutely loved it. She would dip her paw in a color, limp three-legged to a canvas, and smeared it in tiny, precise strokes. After the first color she had stopped and just stared and me, and I thought maybe the experiment was a bust. She amazing and incredible, but she is a Cynimal after all. It was Aidian who figured it would. He reached out and rubbed the leftover paint off of her tiny paw. She nodded, I swear, and went right back to it. So, I wet a little rag for her to use to clean herself off, and she's been at it ever since. the first couple were abstracts, different colors and shapes capering across a canvas, that must, to her, have seemed like a city block. The last several had been self-portraits, and *sankta merd'* I never realized how self-aware this creature was. One showed her as an old-fashioned robot, silver and gears and square-shaped. In another one she looked almost human. No matter what they looked like, though, they delighted me. Delight me. I squealed and clapped my hands and described each one to Aidian as if he weren't sitting right there. It was wild. I felt giddy. Accomplished. Proud, ken? At one point I glanced over and saw Aidian staring at me with the strangest look on his face He unfolded himself and crawled over behind me, moving awkwardly around the canvases. He pulled me close and kissed the tender skin under my ear. "you would make an excellent mum," he said. At first I laughed. *Jes ĝusta*. No one had ever said anything like that to me before. The opposite in fact. It was well known, I think that I would be a disaster. "He took one finger and lifted my chin until my eyes were inches from his. "hey," he said, "I'm serious. You would be brilliant." And he pressed his lips, warm and gentle against mine until I almost believed him.

Kids, me, that's crazy right? I can't imagine ever having it in me, ever being enough to be able to take care of a child. Still though, if I could, if I was, that would. . that would be amazing. Not now but someday, I think I might like that someday. For not though, just the fact that someone thought that I wasn't like my mother, that I was whole and healthy enough to take care of someone, that I could, for now that's enough.

DECEMBER 29

I fell asleep last night thinking about the children I might someday have, it seems both predictable and *kaduka kaj horora* that I'd spend the night tormented by my mother. This time, I WAS her, looking at the younger version of myself through her eyes. I kept trying to break through the wall of selfishness, of black, vicious hate that was her mind, her body, but she'd twist my action and my words. A caress would become a slap, a smile a sneer, and after every insult, every blow my "child" was diminished, disfigures, until finally this little shrunken gnome like creature was all that was left. Aidian woke me up then, shaking me gently and calling my name. He help me close for a long time after that, and the warmth and nearness of him steadied my heart but still I couldn't sleep. I found myself staring at him, his face, the curve of his arm, the blonde hair that grew downward from mid-stomach. I kissed him there, in that batch of down, and again on his ribs. My mouth opened against his and soon we were both breathing heavily, my head thrown back while Aidian trailed kisses down my neck, murmuring "I love you" after each one. Suddenly, my microcomp blared, blasting Industrial Otter into the room. I groaned in frustration and Aidian flopped over on his stomach, burying his face in the pillow. "Call in sick," He yelled, muffled. I slapped around the nightstand until finally, by sheer luck, I found the comp and hit the button to turn the alarm off. I smiled, " I can't, my boos won't allow it." He reached out and pulled me back into his arms. "Go in late then." I laughed. "I can't do that either. I advertized lemon meringue pie." "So?" He raised an eyebrow. "That means I have to make lemons," I said, rolling out of bed and onto the floor.

"Bollocks to lemon" he said. I leaned over and kissed him one last time, a quick peck. "Come spend time with me there," I said.

Ten minutes later, he came strolling, freshly showered, down the stairs. I was standing next to the synthesizer, trying like hell to figure out the right combination for Lemon SynthSoy. It had to have not only a specific flavor, but it had to be as close to liquid as possible or else the pies would be too dense. Aidian grabbed a cup of coffee and one of the leftover cupcakes from the night before.

"We need to try to get you past your nightmares, Bird," he said, I hit the last few buttons, praying that I'd gotten it right, and turned to face him. "Dr Alyce made a suggestion that he thought would help, but it seems kind of *ridinda*," I said. He shrugged his shoulders. "Might be worth a through though, yeah?" I signed deeply and nodded. "Can't hurt," I said. "I'll try to get out early some night this week. And I will. I just wish I believed myself when I said it couldn't' hurt.

JANUARY 3

Yesterday I finally followed through on my promise and took off the afternoon. It is still so amazing to be able to just leave like that and I can never repay Suri enough for that freedom. To still have my shop but not be bound to it every waking minute. Aidian and I walked hand in hand, down the length of Flower town. As we neared the harbor, I could see the skeletal fingers of the boardwalk pointing skyward. We passed the docks and the fishmongers, until the ruins towered above us. Aidian stopped for a moment and shivered. "Where going up, yeah? " he asked. "Yeah," I nodded. I watched as his eyes travelled upwards for a moment, talking in the rotting beams, the layers of graffiti. Towering above everything else was the Behemoth, or so said the falling down sign with the broken light bulbs. Everyone called it Aokigahra, though. While the old coaster hadn't seen as many suicides as the fabled Japanese forests, still a body, sometimes two, hanging from the beams or lying crumpled at the bottom was not uncommon. "IS that where we're headed Bird," he asked half in jest. I nodded. "but don't worry, we're coming down." His eyes widened. "Slowly," I added. He chuckled. It was a nervous, barking laugh, but it was still a laugh. I took his hand and we started walking again.

We got closer and with every step the Behemoth seemed to grow, so by the time we stood at the base even my heart was pounding. I couldn't see the white in a complete ring around Aidian's eyes. "Your Doctor prescribed this, huh?" he asked. "He prescribed the ritual. I picked the place." I answered. "Right. Brilliant choice," he said. Still he didn't hesitate. "Up we go," and reached high over his said and grabbed one of the beams. Rush fluttered down and I saw a flash of his stomach a few swings of his feet and then he was up, reaching his hand towards mine. We didn't go all the way up. The higher we went the worse shape the metal was in, until there were rusted holes as big as my head and the wind, just a gentle breeze on the ground, was much stronger, shaking the beams back and forth. We were a little more than halfway up when I chickened out. Symbolism was well and good but if I died he with would completely undo the *fikfek* point, yeah? "This is far enough," I yelled. The wind sucked the words out of my mouth. I didn't' imagine the look of relief on his face. "Now what," he asked. I wrapped my legs tightly around the crossbeams closest to me and leaned forward. The beams groaned and shifted but I squeezed my legs tighter, kind of pointless if the whole thing gave, and fumbled in my pocket for the item I'd put in there earlier. Finally, I pulled it out. The picture was ragged on the edges from where I'd torn Daisy and myself out of it. Only Mother remained. I leaned back, putting more faith in the beam behind me than I had, and reached into my pocket for a lighter. I flicked the wheel over and over again, but couldn't' get it to light. Wasn't that just perfect? Even here, even now, I couldn't rid myself of that *inaĉo*. Suddenly, Aidian was leaning towards me, handing me a long thin silver device I'd seen him use before while fixing microcomps and the like. "The button on the side," He said. I pressed it with my thumb and the tip of the device glowed blue. I touched it to the picture and a flame erupted immediately. The flame crawled across the surface of the paper, and I watched as mother's face blistered, then crumpled and blew away. Soon, there was nothing left in my hand. Instead, I watched as blackened bits danced in the currents and eventually floated out of sight. "Ready, love?" Aidian asked when he hadn't seen anything for a long while. I nodded and we made our way down.

I was quiet on the way home. Disappointed, hen? I'd hoped to feel different. Free. Instead I just felt like I'd wasted my time. Burning a picture I'd only gotten a month before? How could I have felt like that would do anything? It was stupid. Pointless. And I wished I hadn't tried. At least before I'd had hope that someday I would be free. I just felt heavier than before.

The sun was setting and the street vendors were staring to pack up. I stopped to chat with a few that I knew, that I had bought products from before, and that's when I saw it. Senora Ruiz was an old friend of mine. She was kind, had always given me conchas when I was poor and hungry. I bought a few from her and made some small talk while looking over the table of things that she had for sale alongside her baked goods. Junk mostly, but tucked in among it all I saw a calavera, its dark eyes staring out of the swirls and dabs of brightly colored paint. "Quanto qesa?" I asked. "How much?" She named a price and I paid it, tucking in a few extra dollars before she could notice. We strolled on, the painted skull under my arm. A few boots down I was able to pick up some marigolds, and we went home to where Daisy was waiting as patiently as ever. Aidian put her on his shoulder, and started pressing buttons for some quick dinner. Meanwhile I carried the skull and the flowers to the living room, where I arranged them on a shelf. I rummaged through a drawer and found a flameless candle and flipped the button that caused the holoflame to appear, floating above the wax base. And with this ritual done I felt the band around my chest loosen at last. I felt lights, even though my heart had never been so full. This was the answer. This was right. No psychobabble, no manufactured emotion, just the peace and comfort that comes from a much-loved ritual of honoring the dead. "Rest in peace, Mother," I said. "Finally, FINALLY, please let me go and rest in peace." And you know, I think maybe she will.

JANUARY 16

I had decided to hang Daisy's pictures in the café, decoration ken? Suri suggested that we make a party out of it. I liked that idea. Something different, fun. So we baked some sugar cookies and frosted them yellow and white, and set of carafes of free coffee. Aidian somehow programmed some lighting so that it highlighted the pictures. Everyone was having a great time, oohing and ahing over the art and making a fuss of Daisy who was quite the belle of the ball, running from painting to painting and then looking at us as if to say, "Do you see this?" Yes, love, I see. I see. Aidian was there with me, his arm around my waist, or talking to the customers and describing how Daisy had created each piece of art. H sounded every bit the proud papa, and I stared at him, remembering his comment from a couple of weeks ago. Parents. Maybe he was right. Maybe we would be good at it. I crossed the room and hugged him fiercely. "I love you, Aidian," I whispered. "Thank you. Thank you so much." He looked down, surprised. "Sure, Bird," he said.

Just then laughter burst from the group in the corner. Two of our regulars, girls from one of the brothels down the street, and still in their tiny versions of geisha ensembles, had attracted a circle of admirers.

The girls had their arms around each other's shoulders and were in full form, telling jokes that had even the shadiest characters blushing and singing songs that went way beyond ribald. The crowd loved it, clapping and hooting for more. I nodded at Aidian and he walked the closest of the girls and whispered in her ear. Soon they had moved over to the stage. The patrons, without being asked, started moving tables and chairs so that everyone could see and enjoy. Soon we were all whooping and clapping along. They were up there for the better part of an hour before they bowed exaggerated bows that allows the tops of their obis to gape, which of course ted to more cheers. They had hardly shuffled off of the stage before someone else jumped on, a trio of pale young men dressed in Utiliclothes that they'd buckled tight and crooked. One of them pulled out an airccordion and began running short melodies while the others started tuning the strings of a digitar. The third reached into his cavernous pockets and pulled out what appeared to be a pair of real bones. With a somber nod they launched into a song, a jarring discordant piece that was somehow heavy all at the same time. By the time they had finished, people were clamoring for their turn and I found Suri at my shoulder holding the shop's microcomp and a plate of our daily cookies. "You're brilliant" I said, giving her a quick hug. She circled the crowd with cookies and coffee while I got all would-be performed signed up. Aidian, used to it from his job and his friends I imagine, became a sort of instant roadie, ushering people on and off of the stage and doing what he could for sound and lighting with whatever bits and pieces he carried in his work bag. It was busy, crazy busy, but I could tell by the incredulous looks that we kept shoots each other that we were as happy with it as the customers. It went on like that for hours. An earnest young man, who recited poetry until Aidian had to guide him by the elbow off of the stage, old sailors with shanties that rivaled those the girls had sang. Dancers, including a b boy and girl that challenged each other to a panting, sweaty draw. It was near midnight by the time that the list was done, and while the crowd hadn't thinned much, people were getting tired. The lights had been turned down low and even Daisy had stopped running back and forth from her paintings to whoever would reward her with a pat and a bit of cookie Instead, she was curled in a small ball on my shoulder. Aidian walked onstage and started strumming his own digitar, an acoustic, low and slow and mellow. Eventually the strumming became chords and the chords became a melody. One that sounded familiar but that I couldn't' quite place. It was beautiful, though. At the first chorus I heard someone behind me start singing along, quietly at first, hesitantly. The voice grew stronger and (my god) was it amazing. Haunting and pure. Heads started to turn as people looked for who was behind it. I saw her first, standing behind the counter and gripping it for all that she was worth. Her face so pale that she looked almost ghostly in the light. Suri,. People started motioning to her, trying to get her to move to the stage, but she wouldn't. I don't even think that she saw them. The song spun on and it was like they were casting a spell and we were all under it, silent, our hearts simultaneously swelling and breaking. When it was over the spell lasted for a few minutes more and the café was utterly silent. Then it exploded. People clapped and cheered, jumped up to hug Suri and clap Aidian at the back. I kissed him, briefly and then nodded towards Suri, who hadn't moved. He nodded. I fight my way through the throng to the counter, where I saw that she was crying, grinning, but crying. I held out my arms out and she came into them. "You did good (sistger) I said.

JANUARY 28

I can't believe that the conference is almost here. When I said that I would do it, it seemed a lifetime away, something abstract, too far in the future to be worried about. Then, in a blink of an eye, it is almost here. I have programmed the specials boards to alternate between the soups and goodies of the day and a "help wanted" notice. After the impromptu performances the other night, we are busier than ever, and what used to be our down time now has more customers than early morning, though a distinctly different crowd. Suri and I are both feeling the strain. It's no longer just serving during the day, but also baking a whole new set of food, the evening crowd favors cookies and sweets heavily. We've had a dozen or more people apply, but so far no one that we think would be a good fit. We are going to have to find someone, anyone, soon, though,. I can't leave her to deal with all of this on her own.

Then there are the things that don't have to do with the café. I need to get some new clothes, for example. They don't want me there in Utiliclothes, and I get that, I really do, but I'll be damned if I'm going to let them doll me up in the franzia clothes that they buy for me. I'd been thinking about getting a couple of things after the night of the dress and the dance club, anyway. I'd hoped to make an event of it, ken? Take Suri or Basanti and go rummaging in the funky old second hands stores. It's not going to happen, though. So, I scanned a holo of myself into a shopping app, and in the few breaks that I get every now and then I've been scrolling through different online shops and the items that they think would be best for "my personality and body type." I have no idea what kind of program they use for this, but it needs some tweaks because I haven't been impressed so far. The clothes people wear now are just so, I don't know, without character. Or taste. Or style. Or practicality. Hell I don't know how they even move in half of them. *Sankta merd'!* Even finding something that covers my body is becoming a challenge. I'll figure something out, though. I have to.

On top of all of this the Facility has had me coming in two-three times a week. I understand it. They don't' want a repeat of last time. Hell, neither do I, but they've got me going through everything over and over again. What to expect, what to do, when we go where, what I should say. It's endless. Exhausting. After hearing about the "exhibit" of Daisy's work at the Café, they want to include that, which is the one bright point. They want to show off our "attachment" and our "bonding" and Wu wants the opportunity to show the incredibly advances Cynimals that he and his interns have been churning out. I'm actually pretty excited about all of that, but the other side is that they sent out a bunch of staff that spent hours tripping over customers and moving tables while they pulled down each canvas, wrapped it, and then packed it carefully in a box. Which means we are down to bare walls. After having gotten used to all of the color, it looks pretty horrible. So, I asked Aidian if he'd make an art installment to put in their place. He teased me a little bit about playing second fiddle to a mouse, but he's actually pretty pleased. I can tell by the sudden reemergence of gear sand bits of wire, the way her keeps showing me the works in progress almost expectantly, like he's looking for approval. That's unlike him, but this is his first real show, such as it is, and I think he's nervous. Then days to go. And ten minutes until the next set of interviews for the Café. Here's hoping one of them works out.

FEBRUARY 5

And then there were three. Three days until I leave and still no end in sight. *Diable,* I swear I'm going to be going break neck right up until the second I leave. Still progress is being made. The staff at the Facility has apparently decided that I'm as well-rehearsed as I'm going to get and I need a break more than I know more preparations. Still I'm getting about 10 flashes a day from them, I don't have to go into Center Circle any more. My now clothes finally arrived. I don't even remember what I ordered, and didn't bother to check. I just stacked them, still in their packages, into my suitcase. Best of all, we finally hired someone at the café. He is the grandson of a regular, I've known most of my adult life, and I think he will do well. In fact, I don't' think he'd dare do otherwise with his granddad checking in twice a day. He's a sweet boy, conscientious. Suri agreed and we have already started training him. She's a quick study.

Still though, with everything going on it's been impossible to spend any real time with Aidian. We try. We've both been trying but it seems like we're always moving in opposite directions. When we do come together, it's just been too much for us to really connect. Too much stress. Too many distractions. Too much exhaustion. I couldn't ask Suri and Akhiro to run the café, not with the crowds that we've been getting, so I decided to close it down altogether for the day. I can't do that often, I know that, but it was amazingly freeing just to look at everyone and say "we are taking the day off." Suri and I spent all day yesterday talking about what we would do with all of our time – we planned out enough for a week's worth of time off, if not more. More than anything, though, we both just wanted to sleep. I really planned on it, too, but Daisy woke up at our accustomed 3:30am. I heard her rusting back and forth on and off for a couple of hours until finally she came to check on me, squeaking and nudging me with her nose until I opened my eyes. It was a little after six and for a while I thought about rolling over and going back to sleep, but as I lay there I could feel the day, my day, slipping away. I grabbed the sting that I kept on my nightstand and sat up, stretching it between my hands. It was an old trick, far too easy now but I enjoyed it because of that as opposed to in spite of it, and I think that Daisy did too. Eventually we tired of it, so I coiled the string and rolled out of bed. The hot water felt amazing. How long had it been since I was able to just take my time in the shower? Weeks? Months? So I made up for it, letting the water wash over me until it ran cold. Aidian had woken by the time I got out and was making coffee. His hair stood up in the back, almost like a child's. He handed me a cup, lots of soysweet, just how I like it, and kissed me. I slid my hand sunder his shirt and grinned as I felt the muscles jerk. "That tickles, Bird," he breathed into my neck. I curled my fingers under, slid them beneath the waistband of his pants instead. "How about this? I teased, "Does this tickle too? " Eventually we made it out of the house, and started our day.

"Kie?" he asked. I thought about it for a minute. Nothing particularly appealed to me, not in Flower Town anyway. "Show me something new" I said. Aidian raised his eyebrows. I might as well have asked him to take me to the moon. "Might as well get used to it." He hit a couple of buttons on his microcomp, and his hovercab appeared, gliding in silently. He opened the door with an exaggerated bow, "your chariot m'Lady." He said. Together we climbed in, he put the car in gear and off we went. I'd asked for something new and *infero* I got it. First we went to the Interactive Adventure Center, or Incen. It's this crazy place where they put you in these suits covered in sensors,. Then you put on a helmet. The comps take your feelings out of your mind and project into the goggles and you, I don't know, you are really in it. At first he idea terrified me. I pulled off my helmet and handed it back to the worker, a cyber who just looked confused. God, I know what my mind can do. I know what it's like to be stuck in a world your mind builds, and I wanted no *diable* part of that. But Aidian told me that he'd take the lead, he'd done this before, and so even though I was hesitant I decided to give it a try. It was an incredible experience. He built us this amazing maze of giant gear and turbines and steam billowing out from everywhere. We took off into it, together, jumping off of platforms and sliding down conduits. Finally, laughing and panting, we made it to the end. It felt like we had been in there for hours but Aidian told me that really it had been a standard 30 minute session to me. That blew my mind and I wanted to go again, but there was more of our day waiting. We were really hungry and thirsty so we walked a couple of blocks to a café. That place was such an inspiration. It was all about taking what you know and turning it upside down. Some of the stuff would never work on the rim; the waitress with the fake beak and the birdcage over her head, or the crystallized rattlesnake venom – harvested,or so they said, from the snakes that lived behind glass by the register – there's' just no way. I imagined serving that to some of the grizzled old fishermen, or some of the late night drunks, and actually lighted out loud. Other elements, though, were brilliant. There were shelves of books, real books not digis, that people could sit and read, and the food – oh the food.

There was custard served inside these dyed and jeweled eggshells and soup that they'd formed into balls that warmed and melted on my tongue. That stuff? That I could do. I was so excited, grabbing Aidian's arm and jabbering into my microcomp that I caught the attention of the owner. Aidian introduced me as a fellow restaurateur and I nearly died. Somehow I never saw myself like that, and I was so sure that the owner was going to see through me, to think that I was a fraud. The thing was, as he and I spoke I realized that I knew quite a lot about running a business. He was amazed that I had my own SynthSoy producer. It was a great talk and he even gave me the recipe for the soup. We ended our night at a club with a bunch of Aidian's friends. I'd met some of them at the housewarming party, and they seemed happy to see me. The club was having a Battle of the Bands with a bunch of local groups. Some of them were truly awful, screeching and of tune or with lyrics that I knew they'd intended to be trendy or profound but that were really just, well, terrible. Other's though, had a huge amount of talent. I found myself leaning against Aidian, considering them not just as something to listen to but as groups that would sound well in the café. Aidian must have thought the same thing, because as our favorite of the evening had left the stage, he excused himself and I saw him handing out micronotes.

I hope it works out; I've been wanting to have a bit of an event after I get back, the reveal of Aidian's installation and a special menu, and some of these bands would make a great addition.

I was so exhausted by the time that we headed home. The good kind, though, not the drawn and stressed version that I'd been feeling lately, and I held Aidian's hand in both of my own and watched as the bright lights of mid-circle gave way to the spotty dark that made up the rim. "Mi amas vin, mian karan," I said. Aidian programmed the cab to a stop, hovering in the air, and took my face in his hands. He kissed me and then just looked at me for a long time, a searching look that made me more than a little nervous. "I love you too, Bird," he said, " "I always will." He but the car back in gear and we went home.

FEBRUARY 9

Another dream. Not about Mother, *danki al Dio*. Time will tell, of course, but it really feels like this time I have finally laid that *fantomo* to rest. Still though, a mother was featured pretty heavily. In my dream I was in one of our old stacks, sitting on the bathroom counter the way I used to do, so that I could see into the cracked mirror. The sink was filled with mother's make-up. I'd tried to put some on, tried will all of the skill and delicacy of the child that I was. It hadn't turned out well and I was frightened, scrubbing at it with wet toilet paper. Suddenly the door flew opened and I jumped, certain that it was mother and that she was going to beat me again. Instead, Denae stepped inside, her bulk nearly filling the bathroom. She took one look at me, and her face softened. "Not like that, sweetheart," she said and took the sodden wad out of my hands. Gently, so gently, she washed the smeared mess off of my face and then set to work. The brushes looked so tiny in her hands, and yet she worked with an artist's touch, tilting my chin this way and that, humming lilting melodies. I was starting to fidget a bit with impatience when she got done and together we looked in the mirror. "There now," she said, "don't you look fine." And I did. I looked beautiful. I flung myself off of the sink and into her arms and that's when I woke up, smiling. How long had it been since I'd thought of Denae? Then that really hit me and my smile faded. (Holy shit) How long had it been? The memory of that horrible night in the café had faded and I hadn't a spared a thought since then?

Denae really had taught me how to do my make-up and how to dance, swinging each other around the recroom, and what nurses to avoid. She had taught me about straying strong and loving. That woman, who had been given no reason to love anybody instead unabashedly lovely everyone. And I had forgotten her, had stuffed her in the box labeled "before" and had just cast her aside. How could I have done that? I was a wreck all morning waiting for it to grow late enough for me to contact Dry. Alyce. I flashed him the second it turned 8. "Charlotte," he said, his voice as pleasant as always. "Can I help you with something?"

"How's Denae?" I blurted. There was a long pause and for a second I panicked, fearing that she was dead. "She's. .. fine" he said, hesitantly. She is back with us, and pretty much the same as she's always been."

"Then what's the problem," I asked, " I can tell by your voice that something is wrong."

Dr. Alyce signed and I could picture him sliding his glasses up his nose. "She' misses you Charlotte. She's angry because of your last meeting and is even more upset to have not heard from you.' A lump rose in my throat. " I miss her, too." I said. "Will you – will you tell her that? And that I'm sorry. And that I'll come see her as soon as I can. Please." There was another long pause and then he replied. "yes.," he said. I can tell her that but Charlotte. . " "Yes" "You'll need to follow through. You don't need to be told how important it is to make good on your word. Not before the conference, of course, but as soon as you get back."

February 10

Well, we're off. My bags are stuffed in the storage compartment along with absolute scads of charts, holos, computers and who knows what else. The techs and aides are gathered together in a clump in the back of the communal compartment where they have set up some sort of portable SimCenter and are playing a game. I have no idea which, only that it involves lots of hooting, cheering, and the occasional argument over the properties of some creature or another. We are well beyond the rim already, outside of the boundaries of the circle altogether as far as I can tell. *Jesuo* it's bleak. I understand now why people congregate in the circles. Unfair they may be and filthy they are, they're still better than this waste. The earth is littered and scorched after all these years, and with no plants to hold the soil it hangs in this hazy dust in the air. There's these little towns scattered here and there, no more than shacks tacked together and peopled with scrawny animals and settles that all have the same sun-leathery skin and hardened expressions. I know I should be scared or sad, and I guess I am a bit of both, but right this second I'm just relieved to be done with the preparations, with training, with rehearsing, with goodbyes. For better or for worse, I'm out of time. I've done all that I can, and it is out of my hands. I don't like that, not at all, but there is a certain finality about it that is soothing. Besides, I trust the people I'm leaving behind. I didn't think that would be possible after what I came back to last time, but I really believe that Suri and Akhiro love the café like I do, and I know that Aidian does. I'm shocked to find that I trust the people I'm going to meet as well. Don't get me wrong, I don't harbor any romantic notions of their regard for me anymore. With the exception of Dr. Alyce, I think it would be fair to say that I will not have any friends or admirers waiting to receive me. Still, even though our motivations are different, I think we all want the same thing, namely for me to get as healthy as possible and to stay that way, and to pave the way for them to do the same for others, and so far that's not good enough. Also, this time we all know what to expect. We have negotiated and rehearsed to the point that I think any of us would hesitate to sneeze out of place. For right now, though, I'm hurtling along in the space between goodbyes and hellos, between those I love and t hose to whom I am indebted.

FEBRUARY 11

I've been surprised at Basanti's chattiness on the journey. It's as if, away from the pressures of her job in the Circle, she can relax. She saw me stroking a necklace that Aidian had made for me, *diable* I miss him, and opened a small locket to show me a photograph of her fiancé, a thin almost boyish-looking man named David. Somehow I'd never pictured her as having a boyfriend. I told her that and she laughed her bell-like laugh. "I have had many," she said, "much to my parent's dismay." Then, she told me about her first boyfriend, how her parents had planned on a union between Basanti and the son of their dear friends, and how she'd shocked them all by sneaking out and then steadfastly refusing to end her relationship with a young man from her school That relationship had ended, but a pattern had begun, one that led her nearly down the path of so many of us in Flower Town. She found herself midway through college with no funds, no support system, and no actual knowledge of the real world. It would have been so simple, we both agreed, for her to give up, to flee, and to become bitter or reckless. Instead she tightened her belt and lived in a young women's home, washing her clothes by hand each night to go to class during the day to finish her degree in a subject that her parents hated.

Eventually they relented, and through the years have become as close as they ever were, but I think it was that time that gives Basanti the compassion and heart for people like me. "Actually I admire you," she said, "I'm not sure that I would have done as well as you, in your position." I actually laughed out loud. "Which did you think was my smartest move," I asked, "sleeping in the north-south running streets or the fourteen suicide attempts." She looked at me seriously. "Going and getting help." She replied. "Signing up for this study. I really admire you for that, Charlotte. I don't' know that I could have done the same." I didn't know what to say to that, so I just sat, stunned.

After a while the early morning caught up with us. Basanti fell silent and then fell asleep. I tucked Daisy in the hollow under my chin and stared out the window. I'd better rest now; I know in a matter of hours I won't have the chance. Already I think I can see the light of the next circle hanging in the air. Already we are almost there.

FEBRUARY 13

On the mono again, this time going the other direction. Going home. In some ways it seems like weeks have passed since the last time I wrote, in others I feel like I did nothing more than take a nap and awoke to find the sun on the other side. I know that I should sleep. I want to sleep. Heaven knows everyone else is. the aides, hungover on self-importance and cheep booze, were out before the mono even left the station. Basanti tried to stay up with me, but I know for a fact that she has had far less sleep than I, has dropped me off late in the night only to go on to strategy meetings, cocktail parties, and the like. Even Daisy is depleted, and it didn't take long before she snuggled down, wedged between my hip and the seatbelt where she could be comfortable, and curled into a ball, sleeping with her tail wrapped around her face. Not me, though. I can't. Six presentations, one press conference, two question and answer periods, three luncheons, and two formal dinners in three days and I still can't. I'm too busy rehashing everything that happened, and anticipating what will happen when I return. I want to get it all down now, before I forget anything. We arrived at the conference Thursday afternoon and the techs immediately sprang into life. They nearly flattened me in their frenzy to get the job done before the Facility staff caught up with us. They didn't make it. We had barely started shaking and stomping the feeling back into our feet before the sleek ebony cab pulled up and the familiar faces piled out. They bustled past, pulling us into their whirlwind, a measured chaos that kept on until we got back on the mono. I really hope that others were able to find, I don't know inspiration, information, something out of it, because with the exception of a few brief moments it all seemed boring as hell to me. I mean, it all went as planned, I respected the team and they me and I'm incredibly grateful, but it had all of the joy and creativity of a newsflash, ken? I don't see why they couldn't save the hop fare and read a textbook. I didn't see anything that would make someone want to rush out and throw gobs of money at the program or try to figure out how to repeat the procedure on a larger scale. Basanti's presentation was good. As promised, she featured Daisy's art and interspersed that with recordings from my nurturing aptitude tests, the original ones where there were people calling for help as I ran right by. Those were hard to watch. I remember how I felt then, but it seems so disconnected and disassociated with who I am now, like it was happening to someone les. I guess, in a way it was Then she talked about Suri for a little bit, how I went from terror of her and apathy for her to where we are now; and Daisy of course quite a lot. She referred to her as my "surrogate child," and I certainly don't disagree, though it's strange to imagine her as such. She ended the presentation with a photograph of Aidian and I together, she must have taken it on one of her visits to the café because I'd never seen it before. It was gorgeous, though. He was standing behind me, kissing my forehead, and I was looking up and smiling and oh it made my heart hurt. Below it was a copy of my journal entry, " I might like to have kids someday. . ." "I do not posit," Basanti said, "that the maternal desire is the ultimate sign of mental health." So, she must have heard the grumbling in the certain sections of the crowd. Our eyes locked and I saw one eyebrow go up just a touch, so I know she must have. She is astute, I'll give her that, "Simply that the development from someone who tested as having very little compassion to someone who cares for others in her community and is considering bearing children is striking, and is demonstrated and reflected in her relationship with the therapeutic Cynimal." After that, there was a question and 6answer session and when a couple of people wanted to address me she allowed that, we were there together as a team. The others, not so much. Dr. Alyce had a series of holos, old men who I didn't recognize, bearded and wearing these *malnovstila* suits, and every now and then he'd play recordings of things I'd said or done or whatever. I didn't get it, but the other psychologists seemed to eat it up. Then there was C.S Nu, and something went wrong with his. I don't know what. The assistants had everything set up right, I think they did anyway, I stood where I was told and did the movements and responses rehearsed, but something must have gone wrong with the equipment. He was doing a "live mapping" of my brain when the machine malfunctions and the screen bloomed with white blotches, looked like snow for a minute. It was just for a second, but Nu, he's so dependent on his computers that he doesn't' really have the ability to just roll with it. Improvise, ken? So he was stuttering and staring at the machine, and then had to flip through his notes until he found his place. He recovered, but I kind of felt bad for him. No one else noticed, but he was in a foul humor for the rest of the conference.

At the close, they let me give my speech. I knew I'd never be able to remember it all, so I wrote it down. Here it is.

"Ladies and gentlemen I stand before you fully present. For most of my life my greatest ambition was to escape. I would stop at no length to distance myself from my thoughts, my feelings, and my life. I tried self-mutilation, drugs, sleeping for weeks on end. I filled my life with temporary places to live and superficial relationships. Every day that I didn't give in to the voices of my past or the anxieties of the present and end it all was a victory. It was the greatest contribution I could make to the world around me. But now, now I know joy. I can face my life unafraid. I can put my past behind me. I can pursue my passions. I can love and be loved in return. I can contribute emotionally, physically, and practically to my community. I give full credit for this to De. Stevens and her staff at the Facility, and look forward to their innovative approach being used to give this same freedom to others like me. "

The applause, well it wasn't thunderous. I wasn't performing surgery or showing off gadgets. I was just a woman telling them how I feel. Well, close to how I feel, I might have laid it on thick regarding how much credit goes to Stevens, but I felt like she'd earned it. I really think they heard me. Even Stevens smiled. A little. I can go home knowing I did my best and I can't wait to get here. I flashed Aidian and he says that everything is fine at the café. He sounds as excited as I feel. He says that he has a surprise for me. I can't imagine what it would be, though I plan to spend the rest of the trip home guessing. I can't think of a better way to spend the time. Suri send me a message saying that Akhiro is doing well, but that they're ready to have me back. Soon, everyone. Very soon now.

FEBRUARY 14

Aidian was waiting on the platform when the mono pulled in, I could see his hair from a mile away. In the early morning light it burned like fire. He snatched me up before I was fully off of the train. Hugging me close while my feet hung by his shins. "You're not going to disappear this time, are you, Bird," I kissed him. "Never." It struck me for the first time then why he'd seemed so drawn, so on edge. It wasn't me leaving, it was the fear of what would happen when I got back. Funny, I'd almost forgotten. "Never," I said, more firmly. He drove me home then. I didn't think I'd be able to sleep, but Aidian pulled the shade and led me to bed. There he started stroking my hair, long caresses that started at my temples, and before I knew it it was afternoon. I shuffled out of the bedroom, wincing at the light. "Good morning, gorgeous," Aidian said. "Afternoon," I replied. "Evening" I wasn't sure. "Afternoon," he said. I flopped down on the couch beside him, stretching. "hey, do you want to go out," I asked, " I don't feel like cooking. Or cleaning up after." "I can take care of all of that," he said. "Neh, I'd like to get out a bit, while we can." "Aye, Bird," he said, standing up, "if you like." I grinned. "Good. I'm starving." So we went out and grabbed a bite to eat, and

I thought we'd come straight home, but instead we headed in the opposite direction. "Where are we going?" I asked. "Somewhere you've never been before," he said, "I haven't been in a long time either, but was thinking about it this week. I think you'll like it." I could see them miles before we got there, the huge structures marching like sentries all the way to the horizon. I squealed and grabbed onto Aidian's arm. "Oh look," I said. "Look at them Aren't they amazing." And they were. Thousands of wind turbines, huge, taller than any building I'd ever seen, so white they almost glowed, ghostlike, in the dusk. "They're beautiful," I breathed. "Can we go closer?" "Of course." Aidian steered the car closer and as soon as we landed I was out and running. Aidian was right behind me. We crested the hill and then we were in amongst them, the arms whooshing above us. The whispers and creaks joined together and the noise was both hushed and deafening. I stood at the base of the turbines, pressing my back against the cool surface, and looking straight up, still laughing. Aidian sauntered over, grinning, and I pulled him close. We kissed and I could feel it again. The knots in my stomach. The wanting. I slid my hand below his waist and stroked the hardness there. Aidian groaned deep in his throat but pulled away. "you don't' have to, love," he said. "That's not why I brought you here." "I know," I said, "I want to. He asked if I was sure, twice, and would have kept asking if I hadn't pressed my mouth roughly against his, kissing away his words and fumbling at his belt. Soon we were naked, standing there with the wind currents playing against our skin. Aidian's fingers slid between my legs, but even while I shed and pressed against them They were there. The others. I squeezed my eyes tightly shut, willing them to go away. "Open your eyes," Aidian said, "Stay with me, Bird." And I did, I opened them and it was so hard, I just knew that I would see his face, but as soon as they were open, as soon as they focused the others were gone and I was with Aidian again. "Do you want me to stop?" he asked. "No!" I said, more firmly than I'd intended. "No," I said again, softer this time, while I pulled him to the ground with me. And then he was there. We were there and it was him and it was me and then he was inside me and it was like nothing I'd ever known. It was love and joy and safety and this delicious pressure that built and built until I found myself laughing and weeping and crying out his name over and over as we rocked, loving one another there while the sentries stood guard overhead.

MARCH 1

Every now and then I start to feel like I've reached the depth of Aidian. That I know him as well as is possible, that I understand his goodness. That I've memorized the planes of his body and the beat of his heart and that I could not love him more. Every time, I find out that I was wrong. Those moments are like watching an artist at work. You think that the painting is complete. It must be, and then they add a shadow here or a highlight there and what you thought couldn't get better suddenly does. Those moments are excrutiatingly wonderful. My skin starts to tingle and my limbs ache. It like, in that moment I am filled with everything that is him, everything that is us, but instead of leaving me sated I find myself hungry for more. That happened again today, in the unlikeliest of places.

I had mentioned to Aidian a while ago that I wanted to meet his family. He was surprised, excited, but nervous as well and so I let it go, didn't mention it again. I figured that he'd let me know when he was ready. This week, he asked me to go with him when he visited his Grandfather. Of course, I agreed and he picked me up at the Café after the breakfast rush. I've decided to keep Akhiro, and I know that he and Suri could handle it. We climbed into a cab, and headed into the Circle.

From the outside, the Extended Care Facility looked like a nice enough place. Industrial, yeah, but well-cared for, synthflower landscaping and all. They tried on the inside as well, but there is no escaping what the place really is; it's East for the old. A place where no disinfectant can truly get rid of the smell of piss and death. The murals on the wall can't cover the despair. I found myself rubbing my wrists on my thighs and checked myself quickly. I took a few deep breaths to calmed my heart. This wasn't East. It wasn't. Still, it was hard. It's even set up like East, the corridors lines with room, the rec areas, the nurses' stations. The nurses, they all loved Aidian, you could tell, coming around the station to give him a hug, asking about his art. And me. They knew who I was. "You must be that special girl he's been talking about" one –woman said, taking my by the hand and smiling. I could feel myself starting to calm.

"How's he doing today," Aidian asked the nurse. She kept smiling but I could see her eyes droop. "he's been a little scattered," she said. Aidian's face fell, the way they downplay things, they think it makes it easier but it doesn't. I crossed to him, slipping my arm around his waist. I could feel his hand tighten on my shoulder.

"go get your visit, honey," the nurse said. "Maybe it will help. You know how he loves you." I could see the muscles in Aidian's jaw working, and he stared at his feet for a second. "Aye. All right then." He smiled at me. "Let's go meet Samathain."

We turned down one of the sideshoots, our shoes clicking on the tiles. Three doors down we knocked and then went it. It was kind of surreal to be on the other side of that maneuver. The room, oh it was gorgeous. The white sterile walls were gone, covered with these stunning murals, Aidian's work, I could tell. Green craggy hills, fields of purple-pink flowered, and a perfect blue sky. Here and there people strolled, they could only be Aidian's family. After a bit of searching I found him, a younger version of him, anyway. I walked over and touched it, running my hand over his chubby arms, his green eyes. I was so lost that the spasm of coughing from the bed startled me, jerking me back to the present. Aidian rushed to the bedside, grabbed a tiny stericoth, and started rubbing at the chin of the shriveled, old man who laid there. I ran to the other side and grabbed the wrinkled hand that was flailing about, looking for something to hold on to. I rubbed the skin gently, watching it flatten and then recrinkle, and after a minute the panicked motions whopped. "Who are you? " querulous voice demanded. "I don't know you."

"It's okay, Sanathain, she's with me," Aidian crooned and his voice, it was so soft. Soft and smooth and sweet, like melted chocolate. "I don't know you, either," the man replied. Aidian said nothing, just continued to gaze in the man's eyes, eyes that were blank and angry at the same time. Then, just like that they cleared. "Aidian?" he asked. "My boy!" He laughed rustily. He was old and tired so, so tired, but there was no mistaking the joy on his face. Aidian reached down and stroked the man's face. "How have you been?" he asked.

"Oh, 'bout the same," his grandpa replied. " I have my good days and my bad." He turned and looked at me, startled, as though he hadn't seen me before. "Who are you" he asked again, but gentler this time, more relaxed. "That's my Charlotte," Aidian said." "So you're his lass?" I nodded, smiling. "Aye," I said, and Aidian's word sounded strange coming out of my mouth. "Aye, I am." "Good," the old man said, nodding, "that's all righ' then." They chatted for a bit, but his Grandfather got tired quickly, and soon he was sleeping fitfully, jerking and moaning. I thought we would leave then, but we didn't. Instead, Aidian pulled his digitar from his pocket and started playing, low and slow. After a moment, he started to sing. It was a beautiful song, plaintive and soft. Old. Nothing I had heard before. It is, he told me later, an old Irish song, five hundred years or more. His grandmother had taught it to him when he was small. "I slowly rise and gently call, goodnight and joy be with you all." Tears began to slide slowly down my cheeks as the old man calmed, stilled. It was just so *diable* gorgeous. I crossed the room and took Aidian's face in my hands, covering it with tiny, butterfly kisses, lightly running my lips over his brows, his cheeks, his jaw. "I love you so much," I whispered fiercely. "Thank you for this." He exhaled a long, shaky breath. "I love you too, Bird," he said. We walked to the door. "See you next week Sanathain," he said quietly, then closed the door behind us. I don't' know what I've done to find a man so kind, but whatever it is, I'm grateful. So, so grateful.

MARCH 12

Suri has a boyfriend. It happened sooner than I thought it would, and certainly sooner than she thought it would, but still, I think it's sweet. There is a stillness about her now, a peace. I swear, it's taken ten years off of her. She seems almost girlish now. I'd suspected it for a while, suddenly it seemed like Akhiro's older brother Hideo had taken an awfully big interest in his younger brother's work performance. We decided to keep Akhiro on, it is so much easier when he is around, and he fits in well. On the day that we told him that he was permanent, Hideo came in to congratulate him and, to be honest, to check us out a bit. When he and Suri saw each other, you could almost see the sparks fly. Since then, he's been around quite a bit, and their peals of laughter often rang out, even over the noise of the crowd. I asked Suri about it once or twice, gentle, playful questions, but she always clammed up. She'd blush a bit, yeah, and smile, but she wasn't ready to say anything. I couldn't blame her; it had to bring up a lot, Joy at what she never expected to find, guilt at being happy again, fear that tragedy would strike. I got it, I really did. I'd felt much of the same. So, I let it be. Tonight, though, I woke up to go to the bathroom and thought I'd go downstairs to check on things. I do, occasionally. I don't know why I chose to tonight intuition, I suppose. Sure enough, there were lights on. Suddenly, I was worried. Had something happened? Was something wrong with the equipment? Had there been a break in? I charged through the back door, barely keeping myself from calling out, and I found them in the prep room. Suri's head was thrown back and Hideo's hands were in her hair as he trailed kisses down her neck. She saw me and her eyes widened as she gasped. Hideo looked up and his face changed instantly. He became shy, sheepish. Suri started to stutter. "I-Charlotte-we-" I let her hang for a minute, just a minute, before I grinned. "Have fun, kids," I said over my shoulder as I walked back towards the stairs. Suri let out a squeal of mock indignation as Hideo grabbed her and pulled her close again.

This morning Suri was meek, almost embarrassed. "Charlotte, *amiko*," I was going to tell you-and I didn't mean to disrespect you by allowing him in, I-" I hugged her close. "Stop worrying, *fratino*," I whispered, I'm happy for you." I could feel her relax in my arms. "So," I said, leaning against the table and rubbing Daisy behind her ears, "tell me all about him." And once the floodgates were open, she did, talked and laughed until we were almost late opening the café. Finally I hugged her again. "I'm so happy for you," I said, "so, so happy." And I am. I wonder if there would be a way that we could all go on a double date? She deserves some joy; it's way overdue. And I'm so glad that I got to join her in it.

MARCH 29

Wonders never cease, do they? Whenever I think that I can't be surprised by anything, that I have seen or experienced it all, something happens to prove me wrong. It has been a while now since the conference, and nobody has said much about it. After weeks, months of planning and preparation it was over in an instant and then, seemingly, gone as if it had never happened. I've even called the Facility once or twice to see if they needed anything; I'm so used to them doing so, ken? Everything is fine, though, They're getting most of what they need form remote downloads and journal entries, the rest they can follow up on during our once-monthly appointments. That's why Dr. Stevens and the rest were about the last people I expected to see belly-up to one of my tables at the Cave. But there they were, and Basanti as well, smiling in the sun that streamed through the window. Dr. Alyce stood when he saw me. I crossed the room and gave him a brief hug, then held Basanti in a longer one. Dr. Steven and I merely nodded, cordially enough. Quickly, though, my surprise turned to nerves. They had never been in here before. None but Basanti. Never. My hand flower instinctively to my head. "What's wrong? What's the matter with me?" Dr. Alyce reached out and squeezed my arm reassuringly. "Don't worry," he said in a smooth voice, "everything's fine. We would like to tell you something though." I went behind the counter and grabbed a platform full of various goodies, sticky buns, cupcakes, muffins, and poured a carafe of coffee. Daisy scurried up my arm to her favorite spot, perched on my shoulder. Suri and I exchanged a long look and she nodded almost imperceptibly. Then, finally, I sat down. My heart was absolutely screaming in my ears. "What can I do for you?" I asked. I tried to keep my voice light, but it cracked on the third syllable. Dr. Alyce and Basanti looked to Dr. Stevens. This was serious business, then. And it was. They've selected another candidate for the surgery. For my surgery. They were given extra funding – tons of it, by the sounds of things –after the conference and my success had convinced them to move forward again. That's why there's been so little contact. They've been busy. Reading applications. Holding interviews. Finally they found someone they feel like will be a good fit. They can't tell me much, not without breaking about a million privacy laws, but he is a young man, a few years younger than me, and he's from a circle in and a whole other quadrant. He's had it rough-can't keep a job, string of abusive boyfriends, in and out of the hospital for a decade or more. Sounds familiar, neh? But he's smart and eager. He found out about the experiment and submitted himself, as opposed to the others who were mostly referred by one doctor or another. At any rate, his surgery has been scheduled for a month from now.

I can't tell you how ecstatic that makes me. But it's more than that. I'm proud. Hopeful. It was enough, ken? It was enough that I was healthy. That I was able to have my life and find that joy that I could. That I could reach out and help others in the meager ways that I can. Suri. Akhiro. Even Aidian. That I could take care of Daisy and together we could build a life, a family. But this? This is so much bigger than all of that. It's like I was a pebble, tossed into the sea, and the ripples are spreading a little farther each day. It's incredible, and not a little intimidating. All we do, all humans but especially those of us on the Rim, all we can hope for is to leave the world a little better, our part of the world anyway, than when we found it. It was all that I ever hoped for, and more than I expected. But this changes all of that. In five years, ten, depression and anxiety could be all but gone and how amazing would that be? What could we, as a people, achieve? What if he had the brains and the ability, and the opportunity to really reach out. Just think of it. Oh, just think of what it could be. And I had a part of it.

APRIL 8

Merinda! Merega! I was late getting started, today. Again. That seems to be a pattern lately. I wake up every morning on time, but then I see Aidian and I get. . distracted. I had no idea that it could be like this. That you can be wrapped around someone and realize that – mind, body, soul, you complete each other. It's not that we become one; it's more than that. It's that Aidian, Aidian alone is the piece that's missing from me and me from him and together we each become more. I had no idea that I could even like sex, let alone that I could be taken up to the peak over and over and then, at the end, find myself more hungry, not less. Suri and Akhiro know why I'm tardy of course, and they tease me a little, but mostly it's just small smiles and knowing eyebrows. I hit the ground running today, though. I had to. Tonight was the event we've been planning for a month or more. It started out small, another party to celebrate Aidian's art installation. And then we were able to book the band that we liked in the Inners. Then I wanted to show off the techniques I learned from the other café. Soon, we were hosting a concert with a catered mean and art show beforehand.

"You don't' do anything small do you," Basanti said. I told her that I never saw the point. Anything worth doing, ken? She came, too and brought David and he was every bit as fabulous and delightful as I would expect him to be. A little shy, but he obviously loves Basanti very much. But anyway, starting right after lunch we had the crew come in and start working on sound and hanging art and stuff. I had fought hiring other people, but I ended up being glad that we did. Aidian was nervous and distracted all day, worried about his art I had thought. He was in absolutely no position to be programming sound boards and running wires. Not that he had anything to be afraid of. His sculptures were, as always mesmerizing. I found myself spending more time than I should following the crew around, staring at the pieces. I'd seen most of them in progress, but there was one that I had no clue even existed. It was a portrait of me, three times as large as life, and more exotically beautiful than I could ever be. Coiled wire made up my hair, and my Utiliclothes were made out of circuit boards but my face, he'd painted my face by hand. I found myself staring at all of the tiny strokes that had gone into it. Aidian caught me looking at it and came over to me. "I'm not a machine," I said stupidly. It was the only thing that came to mind. "No Bird," he said, "you never were."

Meanwhile in the kitchen things didn't go as smoothly as I'd hoped. I followed the directions for the soup but it was a whole new process. At first I was really frustrated, almost in tears, but by the time Suri, trying to pierce the rock-hard shell sprayed soup all over her face, and we dissolved into laughter. Once we relaxed, everything fell into place.

The crowds were incredible, three times as many people as we anticipated. They flowed out of the café and onto the sidewalk, and I found myself enlisting people to carry tables and chairs out of storage and outside so that there would e somewhere for people to sit. All of Aidian's friends were there, and a bunch of *franzia* gallery owners from Center Circle surprised us all and seemed very impressed. One of them even bought a couple of Aidian's pieces. Akhiro had brought his younger siblings to help serve, so once the exhibit kicked off, Suri and I were able to circulate and enjoy ourselves. I spent most of the evening on Aidian's arm, and I've never been prouder to be there. He looked incredible and was grinning from ear to ear. At eight o'clock the band started playing, and I could tell from the first chord that they'd been the perfect choice. Then, halfway through the set, I just. . I still don't' have the words. the band had just finished this really mellow tune, a love song, when a spotlight hit me, so bright it blinded me for a minute. I was scared, that hadn't been planned, at least I didn't think it had. But when my eyes adjusted I saw that Aidian was down on one knee. *Sankta merd'* my heart dropped to my toes. I'd always laughed at the girls who got all fluttery and waved their hands when they got engaged. I found myself doing the same, though. I couldn't help it. There was no speech, he's not the type for a lot of words, but he just pulled out a box and said, "Be mine forever, Bird?" God the ring, the ring is incredible. The stone matches his hair almost exactly, and he'd put it in this old ring that I'd admired one night when we were thrifting. He must have sn-

SECTION THREE

"And though I've been spoiled by pretty privilege
I am no child throwing a fit
I could write the book on disappointment
And you'd be the final chapter of it."

Unwoman   "Heroine"

??????

I woke up with a piece of rubber in my mouth and electrodes on my temples and for a single horrifying moment I thought I was on the ECT table at East. That everything else had been some sort of delusion or hallucination or some *merdá*. I panicked. I panicked and I screamed but all that I could hear was my blood pounding in my ears, and I was almost completely out of the bed before I saw him. Aidian. Steady and tender and real as always. And if he was real, then the rest of it was real, too. Somehow even in my mindless flight I knew that, and it calmed me. A little. Enough to stay in the bed, anyway, though I found myself touching his face, his arm, over and over. I'd done a bit of damage in those first excruciating seconds, though, and the machines were screeching. I'd ripped out my IV. Blood was pouring down my hand and leaving bright red drops on the bedding, drops that I found strangely hypnotizing. The nurses swarmed the room like some demented flock of geese, white and squawking and I was shoved back in the bed, wired and tubed and strapped in before I could get a word out. Not that I had any words, anyway. Other than maybe "what." "What happened," "what are you doing," "what's wrong with me," "what day is it," but I couldn't seem to get all of that out in any sort of order and just found myself chanting "what" over and over again. Aidian tried to explain, but I couldn't hear him over the nurses. Dr. Stevens came walking in just as the nurses were leaving and I didn't think I've ever been so happy to see her as I was just then. The nurses briefed her first, of course, the first evidence that I saw that they were, in fact, not actually deaf, and then Stevens turned to me.

The answer to my question was worse than I'd feared. I'd had a grand mal seizure, it seems, one that lasted nearly an hour, which explains why I'm so fikfek sore. I feel like I've been beaten with a baseball bat, and I can feel a tiny line of stitches marching along my cheek. I've had several more seizures since then as well, shorter, thank God, but Stevens says that she thinks they are finally under control. I haven't had any in the past 24 hours, or so they say. They ran dozens of tests while I was unconscious, and they can't find the cause. They have *tunoj* theories, of course. That's one thing I have noticed they are never short on here at the Facility, theories, but there is rarely anything to back them up. I've talked to Aidan extensively and I've come up with a theory of my own. It was just a one-time thing. It was a power surge or a reboot or something like that. It was horrible and painful and terrifying, but ultimately it doesn't mean anything. Aidian disagrees. Pretty much everyone disagrees. And I understand. I can't possibly comprehend what it was like for him, to watch me in that condition and not be able to stop it or do anything, but it's been days and days that they've had to figure it out and they don't know anteing. I have to believe that if it was relevant the cause would be apparent. And I have a life out there. I have my café to run and a wedding to plan and Aidian's microcomp hasn't stopped flashing since I've woken up, people who want to see his art mostly, and I'm already sick of being there. I want to laugh with our friends and bake and play with Daisy and make love to my fiancé, not sit here in this bed worrying over what is most likely nothing. Twenty-four years old and I finally have a life. I want to go live it. I want to go home.

APRIL 15

A.M.A. Against Medical Advice. Unauthorized discharge. Freedom. Call it whatever you want. All that I know is that our apartment has never looked as beautiful as it did today. The colors, *Jeseu* it doesn't take long in stark white walls before you start to feel like you're going insane. I can't wait to get in the café in the morning. I want to make some more egg shell custards; they take forever, but *diable infero*! I'm also going to compound some lemon. It's tricky, lemon, but so bright and tart and cheerful. That's what I need. Lemon. And to knead some bread. Just dig my hand sin and feel the dough form itself in my fingers. I want to call a couple more bands about coming in, and see if Suri has started playing again. I want to build a maze for Daisy, something three dimensional and beautiful and fun. I want to look at wedding dresses. Not now, though. Right now I'm going to lay my head on Aidian's chest. The poor man, he was exhausted, fell asleep nearly as soon as his head hit the pillow, but not until after I'd coaxed him into loving me. That was like coming home, too. Suri came up to check on me before we went to bed, I had just gotten out of the shower and was drying myself off and heard them talking. They're worried, both of them. I'm worried, too. I'm not trying to be reckless,

I'm not. I just refuse to believe this is as bad as they say. I have to have faith that there's more waiting for me than that. I have to believe that everything is going to be all right. The staff at the Facility, as much as I despise them, are the best in the Circle, in several Circles, at what they do. And I'm due for a break. Overdue. At some point the odds have to fall my way and I'm determined to believe that this is the time.

APRIL 25

God, it happened again. *Fek.* They say that this time was even worse than the last. So bad that they had to put me in a medically induced come. They started bringing me out of it three days ago. I couldn't talk until yesterday. I still can't seem to stay awake. I need to try, though. I need to understand. Because they finally found it, the glitch that's been causing all of the problems. It's deep, I guess, much deeper than the nodules from before and one hundred times worse. The primary chip has malfunctioned, which is what has been causing all of the corrosion, nodules, growths. I still don't really understand, but there are more than before and they are pressing on some of the soft tissue in my brain. That's what's been causing the seizures the headaches, all of it. They say that we are going to have to discuss options, but I've asked for a few more days. I can't focus right now and I'm going to need to think. We have to come up with a plan to fix this, because I won't lose my life. I can't. I have so much to lose. For the first time in my life I have so much.

MAY 5

We knew as soon as they marched in all in a row that the news was not going to be good. I saw Aidian's eyes fall, and the muscles at the side of his jaw grow large as he clenched his teeth. I was reminded of that morning so long ago, Daisy's birthday, and my heart twisted in my chest. There would be no wonder today, no shouts of joy. Still I looked at Dr. Alyce. His eyes seemed even more lined than usual. *"Klaŭnoj denove?"* I asked. He nodded, and I saw the faintest of smiles flicker across his face.

"Clowns again, Charlotte," he agreed. I tried to speak around the lump in my throat, the quiver in my lips, but the corners of my mouth kept jerking repeatedly downward as if on strings.

"Looks like the joke is on me," I forced out. That stopped them cold. Basanti turned away, curling her jeweled hand in front of her mouth. Even Nu flinched.

"No, dear," Dr. Alyce said. "It's on all of us."

It seems they've been working around the clock, these four plus a score of others, holo'd or flown in. They've been writing programs, cutting cadavers, playing out a hundred different simulations. And the answer is that there is no answer. No cure. No fix. There is a way to slow the descent. The descent into what? The *freneza* thing is they don't know. They don't know for sure what this "abnormality" will do to me, only that it is growing exponentially, half again as big as it was only a week ago. They don't know, but they have expectations. Then again, haven't they always? There's a dark irony in the thought that I might be able to live up to these. Seizures. Depression. Lethargy. I could lose the ability to move, to speak. I could forget, well, everything I guess. Except of course the horrors, those I'd be willing to be will be with me until I die. Suddenly, in the space it takes for a pulse to run down a wire, the improbable has become the inevitable.

They don't know what will happen, but I can tell you what they think. They think that, somehow, my own brain will kill me. Oddly enough, they're the ones who told me. In their defense, I don't think they anticipated me to make the connections that I did, but it was so *fekanta* obvious. I told Basanti that, and she started fighting tears again, and I found myself comforting her. They left her behind, the cowardly *anusuloj*; left her behind to do her dirty work. She had a comp in her hand, with a score of forms already loaded. Release of Responsibility, Power of Attorney, Accommodation for Care. God, they want to send me back to East. There is no room for their failure in these hallowed halls. No. They want to send me back to the vomit green walls and hatchet-faced nurses. To be raped by orderlies and die in my own piss. I wouldn't sign it, not that one. I will not go there, while I'm aware. When –IF– I'm completely gone. Once I'm just a shell they can put me wherever they want. Until then, they will just have to look at their mistake, to pay the price for them. Basanti nodded and said that she would try. That she would write something up and see if they would go along with it. I believe that. She has become, unexpectedly, very dear to me. So far from the vapid child I was her to be on our first meeting. She also brought a Last Will and Testament. That one wasn't' a required Facility form. She just – she thought it would make me feel better to have anything in place. Maybe it will be a comfort. I'm sure I will need that comfort soon, once this bell jar shatters, much as I don't' want to think about i9t. The thing is, most of the decisions I had to make weren't mine to make along. Legally, maybe, but practically, not. I cried out to Aidian. He'd walked to the window once Basanti entered, and I had started talking to her. He wanted to give me some privacy I imagine. "Love," I called, "will you take care of Daisy?" He didn't answer and I thought he hadn't heard, hadn't realized that I was speaking to him. Then I turned a bit and saw his shoulder shaking, and heard the muffled sounds of his sobs. "I' sorry," he choked, "I'm sorry." I held out my arms, and he came to me, holding me tightly and burying his face in my hair.

"I'll fix it if I can, Bird", he whispered fiercely. If there's any way I promise I'll find it."

"I know" I said over and over but my eyes locked with Basanti's. I think that's when it hit me, really hit me. I'm going to die. Badly. I will walk into that dark night. The only question is how long I can cling to the light.

MAY 11

There is so much that I want to do. So much that I want to live. I want to bake and laugh and cry. I want to dance. But it's like most of me is still sitting in the *fikfek* hospital bed, hearing the news for the first time. Numb, yeah? I think if I could cry then I could break free of this. If I could grieve then I could feel the rest, the joy and the wonder and the love. But it's so big. It is so big and I'm afraid that if I let go it will overtake me. That I will be consumed by that I'm trying to comprehend. So, I'm stuck in this fog. Dr. Alyce says that it is shock, just shock, but what it really is this giant clock ticking away the minutes of my life and worming its way into my brain. I tried going to work, buying myself in the dough and the batter and my friends. They are trying really hard. They covered the concrete walls of the café with micronotes, all of them wishing me well. The whole place is lit up like a Christmas tree. I have no idea where they got the damned things. How they could afford a piece of tech that they are just going to use once and give away, and so I know that it should mean something and it does but it is so, so far away.

I sat for an hour in front of mom's shrine. I sat there forcing myself to remember all of the things she had done to me. All of the beatings, all of the hours sitting on the sets waiting for her to come home, all of the men. I thought that bringing all of that up would crack this shell. Buy my eyes got hot a couple of times and my shoulders got tense and I walked away feeling just as numb but with a headache in the bargain. At some point, I thought about the other candidate; the one who was supposed to have my surgery. How his hope has been delayed, if not deleted entirely. How he must be feeling. I suppose that lays at my feet, too. Even that, though, even that wasn't enough.

By the time Aidian came home I was desperate. I'd had to push him out the door and had regretted it ever since. I ran across the room and kissed him. He shied away at first, but I kept kissing him harder and harder, biting his lips until I drew blood. He backed away but I followed. This had to work. Kissing, pressing, ripping off his shirt and clawing at his back. I took his hands and buried them in my hair. "Pull," I hissed. He removed his hands. Gently, so *diable* gently, and so I did it again. "Pull" I demanded. He wouldn't. He just held his hands up by his shoulders, like he was *fekanta* surrendering. Like I was some *krima* holding him at gunpoint, and saying my name over and over. I didn't care. I reached for him, reached for his sex. He was still flaccid, still soft and suddenly I could feel. I could feel the rage. Damn it, I needed him. Who was he to deny me this? I scrabbled and tore at his belt and he grabbed my wrists. "No, Bird," he said, and I jerked hard against his hands, hoping he'd keep his grip, hoping I could feel the vise, but he just let me go. I grabbed at his arm. "Come on," I insisted, yanking him towards the couch. "I need you. Come on." I took his hands tried to make him squeeze my flesh, but he pulled away again. *Diable infero*. Why didn't he get it? Maybe if I had him hard enough, maybe if it hurt enough it would wake me up, it would break through. Anything to break through, but he pulled away again. "Not like this, Bird," he said softly, "not like this." Andy didn't know which was worse, that I was willing or that he was refusing, but I needed him. He could help me and he wouldn't and I couldn't take that. He had to, eh just had to and so I hit him. I pushed him and hit him as hard as I could, over and over. The pale skin of his chest turned red immediately and for the first time that night he stopped backing away. "It's okay," he said. I did it again. And again. He just sat there *fikfek* helpless while I pounded on his chest over and over and over until finally I collapsed, sobbing in his arms. He held me then. Finally. Wrapped me in his cars and took me to the couch, murmuring softly while I sobbed, "I hate you right now" I said, and "why won't you help me" and "I don't want to leave you." "I love you." He said to everything just that. And I hate myself for it. Mostly because I'm not sorry because it did it, it broke the barrier. And now I can still hear the clock but I can feel. I can feel again and I would do the same thing again if I had to. To have the time that I have left back to be able to love him, that's worth anything. God, what's happening to me? This will take me. Unless there is a miracle this will transform me into a monster, but I will not help it by doing its dirty work. I have to fight. Somehow I have to fight.

MAY 30

These are the things I want to remember. No matter what the corrosion takes from me, there are things that I must not forget. I cannot. So, I'm writing them here. That way, I can use this to remember.

- Aidian is a good man. I have a fiancé who loves me. I am not untouchable. I can love and be loved.

- Aidian isn't the only one. There are many people in my life who genuinely care about me and who I love: Suri, Basanti, Akhiro, Tom, just to name a few.

- Basanti is my friends and she wants the best for me.

- De. Stevens is not my friend and never will be.

- I have been running a successful business. I took what was left for me and made it something greater.

- There are so many things that make me happy. The smell of bread, the feel of my orange dress, the whoosh of the windmills overhead, the smell of fish and salt.

- Daisy is my little love. She depends on me and she makes me so proud and makes me smile so much. She is an inspiration. She needs me.

- I have made a difference in the world. I saw how people listened at the conference, how they really cared about what I had to say. Even though the procedure still needs work, I made an impact.

There they are. Most of them, anyway. There is joy in this world and I have to remember that. I think, I think if I can remember that I will be okay.

JUNE 9

I went back to East today for the first time since well before my surgery. How long has it been? Years? I never wanted to go back ever, never thought I'd have to, but if they're right I'm going to be going there sooner rather than later. I don't believe it; I still think that they're going to figure out something somehow. Nu, Aidian. Someone. God, please someone.

But I felt like this visit was something I needed to do while I'm still wholly me. I had this vague hope that it wasn't as bad as I remembered. *Ai aya* It was worse. It was so much worse. The sounds. The smells. The *fikfek* bars on the windows. I wished that I had let Aidian accompany us. I couldn't though. I didn't want him to equate me with this. Still, even with Dr. Alyce there with me, I felt like I was walking into a minefield. Danger. Danger and death everywhere. "How can you treat them like this? I whispered. "How can you keep them here like they're some kind of animals. " Dr. Alyce looked pained at this. His eyes drooped even more than usual and he signed deeply.

"We do our best, Charlotte. There are matters at work that I don't think you understand. Funding and perception. . . That's why our experiment was. . is. "He stopped, realizing his slip. He looked so weary, drawn, and I saw that I wasn't the only one feeling the strain. The boy! That poor boy from somewhere along the Rim. He's here with me. And Basanti. And Suri. And Aidian. *Inferi* , even Stevens must be feeling something. The loss. God, it's so big when I let it in. Which is why I can't. No, not yet. Not while there's hope.

"Laws are presented for vote almost every year, Charlotte," he said. "Non –contributing citizen laws. Trying to determine what to do with patients like ours."

"Do?" I whispered. "What are the options?" I knew though. You can't live your life on the rim and not know.

"Colonies in the outers." He swallowed and his tongue clicked.

"Euthanasia." He continued in spite of my gasp," they are considered a drain on already limited resources. I fight them. I'm always in the Capital arguing, but some days. .. "

I clenched his hand. Hard enough that his eyes widened. "Don't stop," I pleaded "Promise me you won't stop. There is hope out there. Maybe it wasn't it, but it exists. Don't stop." He hugged me then, the first time he'd even done that. He smelled on antiseptic and tobacco smoke, and then we went to the floor that is – was – mine. We were met with an ear-splitting scream and two cyber orderlies came charging out of their stands so fast that they almost knocked me over. We walked down the hall and I peered in the rooms, remembering the bolted down beds, temperature regulators so that there was no need for sheet or blankets. Hanging risks, ken? Not that the regs worked. Most of the time we just shivered in the winter and sweat in the summer. I saw the patients bolted down too, restrained anyway. One rail-thin girl sat next to a plate of cold, congealed SynthSoy, a nurse stationed next to her. The nurse commanded and cajoled in turns while the girl just stared out the window. In another room a young man was scribbling intensely with a box of crayons. I wanted to see what he was drawing, but he noticed me staring and slammed the door in my face. I couldn't blame him. Most of the rooms were empty, though. The occupants at appointments or down in the common rooms. We came to one of those soon enough.

"Well, look what the cat dragged in," a voice yelled. There were a couple of other greetings as well, "Hey Charlottes" and "You backs?" I searched the room and saw her. Denae. The one person I wanted to see. Eventually I made my way to her. She stood and I hugged her, tight. She hugged me back but it was different. Hard, somehow. I looked in her face and that was hard, too.

"What's wrong, Mama," I asked.

She didn't answer, just turned and sat on the sofa, staring at the flickering, blurry, SimCenter in the wall. I joined her but it was just silence, spinning out and out.

"It's been a long time," she said, finally. So that was it.

"I've been busy," I said. God, it sounded lame even to me, and I started babbling, I told her about Aidian and the café about Daisy and the apartment. I kept talking and talking, trying to find something, anything that would get rid of the stony expression.

"You should come with me," I nearly shouted in desperation. It was all that I had to five, ken? "They'd let you out. You know they would. You should tell them you want out and you could some work at the café. With me. You can live there and we can"

"*Fek de*," she exploded "Why would I want to go out there? So I can be some *franzia inaco* who forgets her friends? So I can work in your shot, live in your house, be your slave? So I can get beat again, laughed at, outcast. It's not safe out there, Lotta. You used to know that. Now you in here talking like your better than me. You're not better. You hear me?" She stood up, towering over, "You ain't better than me. At least I remember' and she strode out. I could hear her yelling, "You isn't better than me," and "I'm staying here" all the way to her room. I put my head in my hands and started to cry. Not

Denae, She was the only thing that made the thought of East bearable. God, not her. I can't take this. Dr. Alyce took me back to his office and we talked a little while I got myself together. Finally, he led me outside. I started taking huge gulps of air as soon as we got there. I flashed back to being a child, the time that I'd gotten knocked off of one of the piers at the harbor. I didn't know how to swim yet, a surprising number of us don't, and no matter how much I flailed and kicked and panicked I just kept sinking farther and farther down. My lungs ached and I started to see dark roses bloom on the edge of my vision, when suddenly strong hands yanked me up. I remember, once I'd gotten my breath, asking what took so long. The sailors laughed, "It was less than a minute, Love," one of them replied. I didn't believe him. For years I didn't believe him. After today I do.

JUNE 17

Dr. Stevens told me to expect the nightmares, so I guess that I shouldn't have been surprised. Still there's no way that you can prepare yourself for them, really. Treacherous *bastardos*. Attacking you when you sleep That's when you're supposed to be able to escape from the shit that is your life, not to have some sort of reverse *fikfek* highlights reel shoved in your face.

Last night it was every *diable* minute, too, from the second I closed my eyes. First Mother was there, burned and blackened, her blistered skull painted with bright colors and swirls. She stood beside my bed, pointing and laughing. Then Aidian and I were on a boat when this storm came out of nowhere and we capsized and we were screaming and swimming for each other, but we couldn't make it. We just kept getting swept further and further away. Then I was in a box. It was cold. Cold and dark and cramped. The box kept shrinking and everywhere it touched me the cold burned and so I kept curling up smaller and smaller but after a while it didn't help. There were more. Endless, and I could have told you about each of them when I first work up, but I can't remember them now. Vivid. They were all so *diable* vivid. Aidian tried to help, but even in his arms they didn't stop. Besides it hurts sometimes when he touches me because all I can think of is that I'm going to lose him, and so finally I told him just to leave me alone. So now its morning and I'm even more tired than I was when I went to bed. Now I'm more tired than ever. I have an appointment in a few hours, but I think I'll call them and cancel. Just this once. Just to get some rest. The rest will do more than the doctors anyway; I just need to get some rest, that's all.

JUNE 20

Headachy. Tired. I can't seem to focus on anything. It's like I'm walking through fog at the harbor. Everything seems fuzzy, distant, and I'm moving in slow motion now matter how hard I try. I ruined an entire batch of cupcake batter the other day because I put salt in the place of sugar. I can't use the compounder for anything new; I just have to use the formulas I've already programmed. I just keep fading out, yeah? I'm snarly, too. Short-tempered. I don't realize how angry I sound or how hurtful I'm being until I see the look on someone's face. Aidian. Suri. Even some of the customers. I don't mean to be an *inačo*, and I feel genuinely awful. I just spend all of my time angry and lost. I think I'm just overwhelmed. Even reading the list several times I day the hurt and the fear, I can feel them pressing in. I close my eyes and I see Denae, my sister, Don, all of the people that I've let down. I can't eat. Food smells good but it all turns to ashes, to paste, in my mouth and makes me gag. Even when I'm in Aidian's arms I feel disconnected, distant, like he's not even there.

I just need a rest, that's all. A little rest. If I could relax, sleep, I'm sure I'd be okay. I can't go to bed, though. It's too quiet and as soon as I lay down my brain starts to spin and I can't breathe. I just know the nightmares are waiting. The sharks circle, neh? So I'm just going to lay here on the couch for a little while. I'm going to lay here and put Daisy on my chest and turn the SimCenter on low. Then, maybe I can rest. I'm sure when I wake up it will be better. Just a little nap.

JUNE 25

It's over. It's over and I'm the only one who sees it. There was a message on my micro from Dr. Stevens. The surgeon, I don't remember his name, some *franzio* from a Northeast circle who has been performing surgeries a lot like mine, he finally got back with us. He doesn't think that a surgery would be beneficial, doesn't think it would be a success. This means of course, that he doesn't want to try. Figures. Doctors don't like doing things that are risks for them. Risks for us, that's okay thought. We're just poor gutter rats anyway, neh? Nu isn't willing to do anything either. He says there is a "significant chance that the reprogramming would result in catatonia." I don't' care! I'm probably going to end up there anyway, and catatonic would be the best case. There's so much that's worse. Apathy. The kind where you want so desperately to care, where you feel the absence of emotion stronger than you ever felt anything real. The suffocation panic, the kind that makes you feeling like it's going to drag you down any minute and that you can't do anything to stop it and part of you just wishes that it would. Still, I can't convince them. Aidian gets it, he's been trying, but he says that the problem is in the hardware not the software. He thinks that there are a few tweaks that he could make to help me function better longer, but he says the firewalls are impenetrable, like nothing he's seen before. He called the Facility, begged for access but they won't let him. They've just given up on me, moved on to something else.

So, it's over, but I'm the only one who sees it. The facility, they want me to keep going to appointments, to keep checking in, but if there is nothing to do what does it matter? And Suri. Suri came up to check on me. She said it's been a week since I've been down to the café. That can't be true, though. She's exaggerating, but I know what she really wanted. I cut to the chase and handed her the ownership papers that I signed while ago. She cried and tried to hand them back. "Not yet, not yet" she kept saying and forcing the papers in my hand. I don't understand the charade. Coming up here, *fek* with my mind by telling me it's a week, then not even having the courage to admit what you really wanted. Besides, I'm as useless down there as I am anywhere else, might as well get it over with.

And Aidian is no better. You'd think he would be, but neh. He keeps begging me to marry him right now, to go down to the GovCenter. It's a farce though. A fake marriage. He just wants to feel better, like he's done something for me. Something in exchange for living in my house. For my shop making him a real artist. That or it's not enough that he *ŝraŭbita* the girl with the computer brain; he wants to be known as the *kovr* who married her, too. I told him that, told him that if all he wanted was a fake marriage he could just fake the records. I don't care. He swears that's not it, even managed some tears, but we both know it is.

Daisy understands me at least. How could she not. We are two of a kind. Half-breeds. Man-made. Fake.

JUNE 27

I tried. I tried and I failed. That's what I do. The story of my *fekanta* life. I failed at being a sister. I failed at being a friend. A daughter. A business owner. A lover. An experiment. Why did I think that today would be any different?

You know I thought, I really thought about what people had been saying. After a while I began to believe that maybe they were right. That's part of the disease, ken? To think you're the only one who understands. So, I got up, got dressed and went downstairs. I knew as soon as I did that it was a mistake. Everyone was staring and I knew that they were whispering about me. I just knew that they were talking about how crazy I was or how bad I looked, how lazy I've gotten or worse, pitying me. "That poor thing" and I knew and I could feel it, so I turned away and closed my eyes and covered my ears just to take a break for a minute. Just a second. It was only for a little but they were looking for a reason to get rid of me. They don't want to have to look at the broken ones, even if they're just as broken. They have no problem looking at me when they need something, though. Neh. "Charlotte I need you. Open no matter what. Charlotte I need a job, Charlotte I'm hungry and busted. But when I got nothing to give they stare and they whisper.

Even Suri was part of it. She came up to me and told me that I might be more comfortable working in the back. She's embarrassed of me, that's what it is, and I don't blame her but damn it, it's my shop. Still, I went. I went and I frosted cookies and I felt okay. Felt something like the old me for a while.

Then it happened. I was getting some cookies out of the oven and I bumped my hand on the rack. It hurt. Hurt like hell but in a way it felt good, too. To feel something. To really feel it, not this disjointed fractured fog, but something real. Something I could put my finger to and say THIS, this is why I'm in pain. And that break in the skin, it was like a barrier opened and I could feel all of the apathy and the anger just rushing out. It was leaving me getting out and I could feel it all again. Love and joy and hope. I could breathe again. So I lay my land on the rack and I just left it there. It was amazing. Bliss. Then Suri came in and he pulled my hand off and sat me down and I just stared at my hands in amazement. I could feel. I wondered where else the pain was hiding. In my ankle, maybe, or behind my ear and I was trying to explain but she was screaming, rushing around, shoving ice at me.

By the time that Aidian got there I was tired again. Tired and shaking and cold and I just wanted to go home. I wanted to go home but he stairs seemed so far away and besides it wasn't safe. The café, my café wasn't safe anymore and the apartment wasn't safe. The only thing that I knew was safe was the chair that she'd put me in. I could do okay there so I just stayed there, looking at the Formica that had been my friend for over half of my life. He wanted to take me to the hospital, Aidian did, but I wouldn't go. They'd keep me there. And they'd look at me the way they do. Like I'm trash. Nothing. I begged and pleaded and finally he carried me upstairs and to the bathroom.

We got there and he tried to take my clothes off. He was gentle, so gentle but I just- I couldn't. I need my clothes. I need my clothes to protect me from the world around me. My skin. I can't have the world touch my skin. It will hurt too much. So I, I hit him and I screamed and so he put me in the bathtub clothes and all so I just sat there. I sat in the water with ice on my hand and I knew that I should have been doing something but it just seemed so hard. The steam was pretty. Dancing on the water and it was beautiful and that wasn't hard so I just watched it. After a while Aidian washed me, the parts that he could reach, and poured water over my hair until I stopped shaking. Someone knocked on the door and then Aidian came back with a small jar of something and fixed up my hand. He put some sort of cream on it so it doesn't even hurt and he carried me to the couch. I wish he hadn't. I liked the hurt, but he just didn't understand. So, I was right in the start, yeah. In a minute I'm going to put some dry clothes on. In just a minute.

JULY 3

God, I hurt. My body aches all over and I'm more scared than I can ever remember having been. I jump every time I hear a hovercab go by, flinch every time a customer comes in downstairs. Aidian is doing better than I, but not by much. I can see the stress in the way he holds his shoulders, the extra white in his eyes, and I put it there. The fear, the distance that was me but *diable* how can he blame me? Who is he to point a finger at me? Him or his *kunularo* or the *oficiales* or the Facility. Anyone for that matter. They don't understand what I'm going through. They don't know how it feels to be trapped inside this prison, one that's a million times more painful, more devastating than the open they were threatening last night. How dare they? How dare they blame me for trying to break free. They don't need to worry. It won't happen again. That hope can join all of the others in the stinking mess that torments me every minute of every day. I hear them even when I sleep.

I'd been asking Aidian for a while, begging really, to try something, anything. To help me. To help us. I don't know why I should have had to do that. He should have been trying everything on his own. Eventually, though, he decided to try and last night was the night.

I waited upstairs for hours. It took forever and I kept flashing him, every fifteen minutes gut he never replied and they just kept not showing up. I was a wreck, they made a wreck, pacing back and forth and I couldn't believe that he'd just disappear like that. How could he just leave me there, waiting? I thought he'd left me for good. That he was never coming back. I'd rubbed my wrists raw by the time he got there, followed by three men that I hadn't met before and they scared me. They where horrible,. Pale, hard-looking, even though they were almost skeletal in their thinness. "Where have you been? Who are they?" I demanded as soon as they were through the door. Aidian's hug was brief, perfunctory and suddenly I was so scared I was nauseous. I ran to the bathroom and vomited until my stomach hurt, sobbing. Finally, I came out. "It took longer than I expected to get things together," Aidian said after looking me over. He'd given up on me already, I was sure of it. I didn't blame him. "they're here to help." He nodded at the others. The other men never said a word, lit was like I was nothing. Fine. I'm used to that. They just started unlatching the locks on these giant, hard black cases. I followed Aidian around, so close that I was almost stepping on his heels. Everything gets quieter when I'm in his arms and I had to have a little quiet. Had to have a little bit before I chickened out, before the panic took told. I needed need brief and perfunctory. I needed a little bit of *fekanta* comfort, is that too *diable* much to ask? Apparently it was. He stopped and folded me in his arms but there was no warmth in it. It was like I'm gone already. Maybe he wants it that way. He tilted my chin up and looked in my eyes and his were so intense, the green brilliant but he wasn't there. He brain was somewhere else and I was terrified. "I love you, Bird," he said, "more than anything, but I have to focus right now. Do you understand?" I didn't. I couldn't comprehend why he couldn't do both. I do, all the time but I couldn't take the distance I just couldn't so I just nodded and went and collected Daisy. We sat together on the couch, she and I, while a series of holos started to shine up from the machines and the men settled back, arranging screens and putting on their interactive specs. Aidian set up the biggest computer of all, it had five screen and a keyboard twice as wide as usual. When this was done, the men looked at Aidian and nodded wordlessly. Aidian came and knelt in front of me and for the first time he was there. Distracted, but there. "You're sure you want this, then?" he asked. "I can't guarantee anything. There may be nothing or. . " his throat worked as he swallowed. "worse." I clutched his hands in mine. They were cold. Colder than my own. I took them and put them on my face. For a minute, it was like it used to be. For a minute I forgot about everything I have lost, was losing with every second. "It's our best shot," I said. He nodded, but didn't look convinced. "Right then," he said, "let's go."

I took Daisy to the bedroom and put her in her cage. Aidian assured me that nothing was going to affect her programming, but I wanted to be sure. I took a moment to reset her, just in case I didn't wake up they'd have some time, some time to make sure she was taken care of. Then I sat on the couch and suddenly there was nothing to do but wait. The screens jumped to life and I was the stillness in a hive of activity. The eye of the hurricane, neh?

For the longest time there was nothing. The men were looking at each other, their fingers flying on the keyboards as they tossed screens back and forth, and I felt nothing. Suddenly, a brief bark from one of them and there it was, a tugging like a fishhook in my brain. Aidian moved even faster, her brow furrowed in concentration. The feeling got stronger. "You have to increase voltage," one of them said. Aidian blanched. "I can't," he said, "we could kill her." "Why we here then, you gonna flinch?" the other cried. Aidian took a deep breath and then tapped again. The pain was instant, excruciating. I screamed as my body was thrown backwards, my back arched unnaturally, my legs pistoning up and down by still my mind was there. I knew everything and God I wished I hadn't. I begged and pleased through a locked jaw for them to stop please stop, please release me, but still I was there, there in as some mechanical monster gnawed its way through my brain. Aidian cried out, it was terrified, guttural, and he jumped to his feet. "Neh" one of the men cried. Aidian sat back down. "More." I won't" Aidian panted, "just a little longer here." I wanted to say something. Anything. "No more" I tried to yell, but I couldn't make words. That's when I heard it; the official sounding pounding down in the café, the deep authoritative voices. Aidian's friends jumped to their feet, started grabbing their gear. "No!" Aidian shrieked. There were tears on his cheeks. "It's time to go, man" the largest said. "You didn't pay us enough for this." "We ain't doing anything anyway," another said. "If you stop now, she could die," Aidian said. "Sorry man." A couple of clicks and the computers just, I don't know, imploded. There was nothing left but black dust. The men ran out, through my room and I could hear their feet flying down the fire escape. Suddenly I went limp, paralyzed. My body felt heavy, so heavy. My thoughts were thick. I tried to remember to breathe but I couldn't. Aidian clicked on his computer for a little while, and then his lips were on me, forcing air into my lungs, when they burst in. "Stand back" the oficiales growled, they hands on their destablilizers. "I can't" Aidian choked. He breathed into me again. There was a noise and Aidian was torn off of me, screaming, and then suddenly frozen. I saw black roses start to bloom and then, with no warning, my body started to work again. I was breathing. I didn't know how or why, still don't, but I've never been so grateful for that Rim air before in my life. "Leave him alone," I shrieked with my first real breath. I was sobbing. "Just leave him alone." A medic rushed I then, started poking and prodding anywhere as they bound Aidian for transport. I was fighting as hard as I could, but it was no good. Weak. I was so weak. Then, there was a chirp form one of the ear communicators. A few brief words and then he turned. "Let him go," he said. The other oficiales were obviously confused. "Let him go," the officer repeated, and they complied, though I could tell they hated it. "It's from Sector 6," The Facility must have called. My head was pounding and my throat was raw. They released Aidian and he slumped, exhausted. "Let her go, too," he said to the medic. The men looked disgusted but stepped away. Shortly after that, they left. "You'd better tread carefully, boy," one said to Aidian. Aidian nodded, defeated. And then they were gone. I crawled over to Aidian and climbed in his lap. "I'm sorry," I said, as my microcomp chirped. A cab was coming. Sent by the Facility as well. "I'm sorry," I said over and over, "I'm sorry."

JULY 11

He said that he loved me. He told me forever. He told me that being in my arms was like coming home. And me, *tromp* that I am, I believed him. I know better now, can't believe I didn't see it before. It's so *fikfek* obvious, yeah? If he loved me he would have married me whether or not I was sick. Sickness and health, that's how it goes neh? If he really loved me I wouldn't be sick in the first place either. He could have stopped it. If he really tried he could have. I know it. He knows it too, the *malkuraĝulo*. He can do anything with computers. I've seen him. *Li povas iru la diablon!* I've seen him change laws. I've seen him erase entire *fekanta* identities. Now you see him now you don't, and build new ones. This? This just electrical, a little tweak and he could fix me. Or maybe he couldn't fix me but I bet he could override it. He could just reboot everything and install some good memories and program me how to act and it wouldn't be me, not really, but it would be close enough and we would be happy. But he won't even try, that *bastardo*, he won't even try. He cries his *sufiĉe knabo*, oh-so-manly tears and he strokes my hair and tells me that he wishes that he could as if I believe that. Like that mess of an evening counts as anything. Neh. Oh well, least he gets out of having to be seen with me. I know. I know what I been to him. An embarrassment. A strain. Unreached potential. A giant *fikfek* albatross hanging around his neck. Did he think I didn't know what his franzia friends said about me? He thinks I didn't know how I hold him back, hold him down. I tried, I tried to make his live better but it's me. Even when I was whole I was too broke. He won't have to worry about that no more, but I wish he'd have waited until I was gone to do me like this.

And that's what I told him when he came home tonight, late. *ŝraŭbanto iuj prostitutitino*, probably. Can't even wait until I'm gone. He said he was showing someone his art. Thought maybe it would make me happy. Bring me a little joy. His art, that what he calling it now, yeah? Why did he have to do it tonight? He has all day, doesn't need to be out. It's someone else. He tried to explain, some lie, probably, but I don't' want to hear it. I couldn't. He says he got nothing left. That he used every favor, all his money, on that last try. That he hasn't been working .Right. What does he need money for anyway? I've got plenty. "For how long?" he said. "What about my family, they still need me." *Absurda*. I need him. Me. It's all excuses. Lies. He's always had money, why suddenly he doesn't? So he can get away from me, have a reason to go away. That's why.

He tried to touch me, tried to hug me but I swear I could smell her and he wasn't going to touch me. That's how he treats me. He hugs me and tells me everything's okay but it's not. It's not and it never has been and it never ever will be. I should have never believed him, 'because he never loved me, not really. I threw the sculpture at him. The one from the carnival. And it hit the ground and broke and I don't' care. He's sitting there chanting my name Charlottecharlottecharlotte over and over again and he's on his knees but I just told him to go on. Go show his art to someone else.

JULY 18

You would think, all things considered, that people would just let me the *fek* alone. Would stop bothering me with their selfish requests and just let me rest, yeah? Neh, they're constantly barging in here. "You have to take a shower." "You have to come to your appointments." "You have to let me take care of you." Why? Why do I have to do any of those things? "For your own good," they say. *Absurda*! Thos things don't make me feel better. Neh. They make them feel better. And I wish they'd get out of their own *fikfek* me-me heads enough to see that they're just making things worse. But they won't.

And I can't. I can't deal with the pressure of their need. I feel like I don't have any skin anymore, that he corrosion isn't on my brain but on my flesh and I just feel the pressure and their disappointment and their expectations and their hurts and it hurts me so bad and I don't want to hurt anymore. I want to run away. I want to run from it but I'm so tired and I can't take it. I just. . I can't. And the couch was safe. It was a place where I could cope with what was going on. As long as I was on the couch the hurt couldn't touch me as much. God, going to the bathroom, even going to the bathroom was more than I could handle. I'd wait until I throbbed and was rocking because I'd have to go where it wasn't safe but I wouldn't when I would come back to my spot. The clock. The clock was safe and I would breathe with it. Three ticks in, three ticks out. One breath. I could hang on for one breath. So I did, over and over. And I tried to tell them this, tried to reason with them but I don't think they were even speaking English. Spanish neither. I don't know but I would watch their mouths move but nothing made sense and then I would just get so tired. So I would look at the clock again. It was my safe place, it was safe and then they came in with their need and their judgment and they took it away. Why couldn't they just love me? No, I know that. Why would anyone love something like me? So, why couldn't they just leave me alone?

So I locked the door today. I went into my room and locked the door. I took the. .thing, the bokt the, magnalock. Yeah. We kept it under the bed in case of emergency and so I locked it and they couldn't get in. They've been knocking, they've been knocking and yelling and saying something, but if I put my head under the covers, if I hit my head I didn't have to hear. Daisy came up to me, thinking we were playing, but I pushed her away. She's been sulking ever since. Lethargic. Pouting. I can't deal with her need right now either. Maybe after I've had a break from the others I'll have something from her. But I need a break. And now I can get it. Whether they want me to or not.

JULY 27

No! Nonononono. Not my Daisy. This can't be real. She can't be dead. Nightmares. I have horrible nightmares all of the time and that has to be what this is. It has to be because a world that doesn't have Daisy, her love and her joy, is not a world that I want to live in. That I can lie in. Not even for a minute. Because she was mine. She was my responsibility and so if she is dead it was me. I took her. I killed her. I took her out of this world and I can' bear that. So it can't be true. It' just too big it's too much and it can't be true.

The thing is, I've screamed until I coughed up blood. I've pinched myself over and over and the nightmare just goes on. So maybe they can bring her back. They can take me instead. Her skin, her soft skin oh God it's started to rot but what is skin anyway. It's just a covering. It' just for show. It's now who she was so they can fix that. They can regrow her skin or they can put her in me. Yes. Take me. Take me in her place. My brain is broken but my body is fine and she can have it. She can have it if she would just come back. Take me! Take my life instead of hers. It isn't worth anything anyway. Never was. They back up everything now. They back it up and they have records and they've been collecting data so it has to be somewhere. And they can just upload it into me. Fuck. She has to be alive somewhere. They have to fix this. But no, I know that' not how life works. Not my life, anyway. Fine. I'm dead anyway. IF I can't take her place I can at least join her. I don't know if there's a heaven for creatures like us. For half-breeds, for created things. I don't know if they'd let me in even if there was, but I can try. If there is I know she'll be there and if she's not we can go into the dark together. I won't let her go alone. So that's it, then, I'll go with her. I'll make this right. I'll pay the price for what I did. I'm coming, Daisy. Mommy's coming.

JULY 28

Charlotte? Charlotte, I don't know if you'll get this, but I had to try. Charlotte, its Aidian. Your microcomp is home but I thought maybe, I mean they're going to want their damned journal entries, so I thought there's at least a chance. Charlotte I didn't leave you. I tried to get in the ambulance and they wouldn't let me. They said that you weren't stable enough and that I had to follow behind, so I did, but when I got to the hospital they barred me at the door. They said, Charlotte they said that since I'm not family I can't see you without permission. I talked to Dr. Alyce and Dr. Stevens and they told me that you are still alive, but there's nothing they can do because of the floor that you're on. You have to tell them that you want me there. I've tried to hack the records, but they have them locked up tight. Please, love. Please give let me come and be with you. I want to take care of you. I love you, Bird. I couldn't love you more if you were my wife. Please know that. Please let me in. I hope that you will; it's all that I can think about, but Love, if you don't there's something I want you to know. I want you to know that I will love you for the rest of my life. Not yours, mine. And you have touched the world around you more than you know. Not because of your surgery, but because of who you are, and there are so many people who love you. You are loved, Charlotte. Not your brain, not your advancements, you. And nobody can take that, Bird. You told me once that if you died, it wouldn't even cause a ripple in the water. I want you to know that you are a tsunami. You have changed the face of the world, carved a place in it, and we none of us will ever be the same. I love you. Please, let me come and hold you. Please.

August 4

Back at the Facility. Don't think I'll be checking myself out this time. I don't believe I'll be going from here to a little place by the sea. Not that they've said. Don't say anything at all. Diamonds in the windows so I can't jump, though, No wires. Must be keeping me on some high powered meds because I can't stay awake. I miss Aidian. I miss Daisy. So much. My baby. I miss me most of all. They should be happy. They got what they wanted. I'm finally under their control. Too tired to fight. Whatever they want. No one here to stick up for me. It's better this way. All I do is hurt people. That's really how I'm programmed. I was a damned fool to think I could be more.

AUGUST 12

Day. Night. Don't even know. It doesn't matter. *Anusuloj* coming all the time, waking me up. I don't want to be awake. I just want to sleep. When I sleep I don't know. I know remember what I've lost. Don't see Daisy's rotting corpse. Don't see Aidian's face. I don't see what I've become, but they keep dragging me back, telling me what I have to do. Like broken Cybers. Repeat. Repeat. You have to eat. You have to take your medication. You have to leave the IVs in. Why? Will it make me better? Will it get me my life back? Neh. So what's it matter? What, do you think you can learn from me still. *Fek de!* You've learned enough. Drained me dry. I have nothing. I am nothing. And I need nothing. No food. No meds. Not your orders. Just leave me alone. Let me die. Let me be nothing all the way. Let me go, please, please just let me go. Death comes for us all. I'm just meeting him halfway.

AUGUST 22

This will be last entry. Too hard to type. Focus. Got mad feeding tube. Didn't want. Chewed off tongue. Though I was going to drown. Hoped. Still no *fekanta* luck. Why? Why me? They say leaving for East tomorrow. Back to beginning. Wouldn't be so bad if I could remember the middle. Can't. Not much. All behind a door. Knock knock. No answer. Only respite dreams. Dream Aidian, Suri. Café. Mother.

Can't blame them. I'd get rid me, too, could ken? Wash hands of me. Get clean. Wash hands of what they did. Wash clean. Wash.

Tell Aidian I love him.

Tell Basanti not her fault.

Tell Daisy I'm sorry.

Sorry Daisy. Sorry Aidian. Sorry everyone. I'm sorry. Sorry.

EPILOGUE

"All these people came all this way
Faces stained with loss but smiling as they're crying
I would rather see you laugh at my tragedy
Then choke on these tears while I'm curtsying."

Unwoman "Herione"

The hallways of Eastern Psychiatric Facility were never pleasant, even in the best of circumstances. The concrete walls were painted a virile green that had flaked and been repainted so often that they resembled walls not so much as rotting flesh. There was no cloth to speak of. Cloth could be used to conceal participants or, in one unfortunate incident, strategically knotted around one's neck. It was much safer this way, everyone agreed, but practically it resulted in the everyday noises, the laughter, the screams, the tears, the brainless droning of a dozen SimCenters echoed and melted together into a cacophony that inevitably causes headaches to newcomers. This day was no different. Even so the small entourage gathered around the narrow window comprised of Dr's Kevin Alyce and Lavinia Stevens, as well as former Rehabilitation Therapist Basanti Patil didn't seem to notice. They were starting, grim-faced through the glass. Basanti wept openly. "We discontinued medication and nourishment three days ago. It's getting close," Dr. Alyce murmured. "I thought you'd want to be here. Dr. Stevens pursed her lips, nodded briefly, and went back to staring. On the other side of the glass, two nurses, Cybers, waited motionlessly, serene smiles programmed onto their faces while vital statistics flashed on panels on their chests. In the center of the room sat a bed. The rails on the bed were down and a large woman with a wig sitting slightly askew sat rocking and holding another woman in her arms, cradling her as if she were a small child.

It was the second woman who everyone watched. Her head and been shaved and so there was nothing to hide her savaged face, with her slack mouth and the scars running down her cheeks, put there by her own nails. She stared, unblinking, at the only ornament in the room, a small abstract painting of a mouse, done in bright, childish color.

She was thin to the point of emaciation, and bedsores showed under the hem of the hospital gown, almost cartoonishly bright against her ashy skin. Bruises and punctures form IVs still showed on her hand and arms. Every now and then she would exhale a shallow, shuddering gasp and then stop. Everyone would lean forward expectantly until she would draw a deep ragged breath and begin again.

"Who is that with her?" Basanti asked.

"A friend, I think probably her oldest."

"Good," Basanti said, a whisper, "that's good" and then the sobs that she'd been chocking back broke through and she left, her footsteps clicking into the distance. A moment later the buzzing of the door opening echoes through the halls.

Back in the room, Denae continued to sit vigil. Every now and then a single large tear slid down her cheek, but mo of the time her face was serene. She hummed as the rocked, old ballads and hymns, and she murmured endearments. Once in a while, she would shake her head sorrowfully. "Oh baby, you shouldn't' have let them do this. Why couldn't you stay where it's safe? Why didn't you just listen to Denae? Folks like us, we ain't meant for the light. Some people it just burns. You poor baby. Poor baby. . . "

AUTHOR'S NOTE

I have ever been a voracious reader. It didn't take me long to consume our school's library, and because I was notorious for forgetfulness, my father was hesitant to allow me access to the public library. The fees would have been astronomical! Eventually, my personal library was decimated, the books loved to dog-eared ruin. At that point, I started searching my step-mother's shelves. The books she had were inappropriate to say the least, but I was desperate for a new story, and so I read in wide-eyed horror some of the tomes she owned. One of these, I took to my mother's house for the weekend. When she caught me, she was furious, but kind enough to listen to my explanation. While I never saw that particular book again, she took me downstairs and rummaged through her boxes of high-school remnants until she found four books. Three of those have gone on to influence me immensely. The first two were "Watership Down" by Richard Adams and "Jonathan Livingston Seagull" by Richard Bach, and I cannot recommend either of them enough. The third was "Flowers for Algernon" by Daniel Keyes. That book is truly the work of a master. I have read it scores of times since then, and each time it leaves me emotionally raw, lost in thought, and reveals another layer of itself to me.

That book is also what inspired and greatly influenced the book that you have in your hands. In many ways, Charlotte's journey reflects Charlie's every bit as much as it does my own battles with anxiety and despression. I think, looking at those whom society often values as "less than human" often reveals the humanity (or, sadly, lack thereof) in ourselves and society as a whole. So, to my mother and to Mr. Keyes, and to Charlie himself, I give my heartfelt thanks.

ACKNOWLEDEMENTS

First and foremost I give thanks to God, who has proven ever faithful as I pursue this dream.

To my family, my amazing, quirky, and supportive family, who are courageous and patient enough to join me on this adventure.

To Brick Marlin, an amazing author in his own right, a conversation with whom planted the seed that became this novel.

To Unwoman, whose music inspired me in this process and who graciously allowed me to use her lyrics.

To Bekah Lynn, for being my willing cover model and inspiration.

To Stacy Garrett and Christine Scanlon, Rachel my beta readers whose wisdom helped elevate the final product.

And, finally, to Thomas Lamkin, Jr., my wondertwin, who has been involved in every step of this novel, and without whose encouragement, art, and editing, it would not have come to be.

Thank you all so much.

ABOUT THE AUTHOR

Amanda Rotach Huntley can be found. Where is anyone's guess. She travels the country 46 weeks out of the year, promoting not only her personal novels, but also the pieces publishing through her publishing house, Line By Lion Publications, LLC (www.linebylion.com). She is accompanied on her travels by, a dog named Shadowfax, and lizard named McIntyre. For information on upcoming events or to contact Ms. Huntley, please visit her website.

ABOUT THE ARTIST

Thomas Lamkin Jr. is a photographer and artist hailing from Louisville, Kentucky. He specializes in surrealism and fantasy and especially enjoys manipulating images he has taken into works of art. He can often be found wandering around his city, camera in hand, or performing at local events. Thomas graduated from University of North Carolina. You can find more of his work at www.tljonline.com